I0760445

EILEAN IN THE OTHERWORLD

FRANCESCA MCMAHON

EDITED BY
ANTOINE BANDELE
CALLAN BROWN
EMILY DRAGON

ILLUSTRATED BY
MARCI KLUGIEWICZ

BANDELE
BOOKS

Publisher: Bandele Books
Interior Design: Vellum
Editors: Antoine Bandele, Callan Brown, Emily Dragon
Illustrators: Marci Klugiewicz, Randal PC
Cover Design: Mibl Art

ISBN: 978-1-951905-41-5 (Ebook edition)

ISBN: 978-1-951905-42-2 (Paperback edition)

ISBN: 978-1-951905-43-9 (Hardback edition)

First Edition | September 5, 2024

CONTENTS

A series of young adult novels and short stories that follow the journey of Eilean MacAlistair, a girl with a complicated past and an even more complicated future.

Percy Jackson meets *Merlin* in this otherworldly series of stories based on Celtic mythology. Join Eilean on her thrilling journey, where she will find adventure, friendship, and the strength to believe in herself.

If you enjoy this story and are interested in the rest of Eilean's adventures, you can join Bandele Books' e-mail alerts list. We'll send you notifications for new book releases, exclusive updates, and behind-the-page content.

Visit this link:
antoinebandele.com/stay-in-touch

What happens when a God grows ill?
He goes in search of a cure.

Cernunnos, Lord of All Wild Things, has lived in joy with his wife, Danu, for centuries in their world. But all of that changed on the day of the Spring Equinox.

The creatures of his world, from the ants in the grass to the birds in the sky, have disappeared. What's more, Cernunnos himself feels as if he is too. Something is draining him and the land of Ar Dachaidh, and he doesn't know what.

Will Cernunnos be able to save his creatures and cure himself of this ail? Or will whatever has taken root in the world tear him down too?

Find out in this prequel short story to The Spiral of Life, a young adult fantasy based on the Celtic figures of Irish and Scottish folklore.

Visit this link to read the prequel story:
https://www.antoinebandele.com/book-page-the-green-man-falls

PRONUNCIATION GUIDE

Characters

Ba·lor – bah'lore
Bhra·dain - brah'dane
Brig·id - bridge'id
Cer·nun·nos - cur'nun'us
Cú·chu·lainn - koo'kul'in
Da·nu - dah'noo
Di·an C·echt - gee'an ke'kt
Ei·lean Mac·Al·i·stair - eye'lean mack'al'ih'ster
Fey – fae
Fi·onn Mac Cum·haill - finn maa'kool
Fre·ya In·nes - frae'yah ih'ness
Gai·an - guy'uhn
Li·a·na Shade - lee'ah'nah shayde
Ma·mó – ma'moh
Mor·ri·gan - more'ee'gun
Ruth Mac·Al·i·stair - rooth mack'al'ih'ster

Locations

Ar Dach·aidh - ar dah'he
An·nw·fn - ah'noo'vun
Av·a·lon - av'uh'lon
Bal·loch - bah'lock
Loch Lo·mond - lock loh'mond
Tír nan Óg - tear'na'nog

Terms

Dru·id - drew'id
Scot·tish Gae·lic – scott-ish gah-lick

Creatures

Ban·shee - ban'she

Kel·pie - kel-pee
Le·an·nan Sìth - lee'ah'nan she
The Fae - the fay

Items & Symbols

Ai·lm - al'im
Ca·led·fwlch - cah'led'voulk
Ex·cal·i·bur - exs'cal'ih'ber
Tris·kel·ion - tris'kel'leun

To my Celtic ancestors, may you find peace in the Otherworld.

This story is a work of fiction and not an accurate depiction of the modern and historic practice of Paganism and its many branches.

1

MEMORIES CAN HURT

THE HAMMER CAME DOWN ONCE, TWICE, THRICE AGAIN TO flatten the smoldering metal. Eilean smiled as she pulled out the piece with her tongs and twisted it this way and that, checking for inconsistencies in the shape. She frowned when she found an imperfect line and shoved it back into the flames.

When the metal turned a bright orange, she pulled it from the fire and took it to the anvil. She grabbed her hammer and slammed it into the sweltering metal in a precise rhythm.

"Ease up a bit, lass," Mr. Lawton's gruff voice called from beside her. "It's a belt clasp, not your ex."

Her teacher laughed as he walked away, ready to comment on another student. Eilean buried her grimace. *He wouldn't say that if he knew.*

Eilean continued to pound her hammer into the metal until her muscles ached. More carefully this time, like Lawton said. She relished the workout. Smithing beat the gym any day of the week. Not only did it feel great, the precision of the skill helped her focus. And Eilean needed focus.

She had taken up the art nearly two years ago when her therapist had recommended finding an activity that required concentrating the mind and draining the body of energy. Best way to stop the fits of rage. Of course, that part went unsaid.

She had stumbled on blacksmithing purely by accident. On her social media feed, she'd found an edit of the character Kate from the movie *A Knight's Tale* blacksmithing. Beyond finding her beautiful, Eilean found herself fascinated with the art after that.

Two years later, and here she was, an apprentice blacksmith at Lawton Forge, working toward her apprenticeship qualification. She had a long way to go, but one day she would be out in the world as a real modern-day blacksmith. Hopefully.

The sounds of banging, sizzling, and quenching from her classmates' work benches calmed her. She wasn't fond of being around so many people but, as she glanced around at their class of eight, working at their forges or shaping their tools on their anvils, she knew that these were her exceptions. Even if she never talked to any of them. Blacksmithing, after all, was a rather solitary experience. Your work needed your full concentration, no time to chit-chat unless you were asking to borrow some tongs or the one hot-cutter Lawton had. It was because of this that the forge had become the one place where, despite everything, she could forget her past and focus on the present. Most of the time, at least.

As her hammer hit against another section of metal, she could feel the intrusive memories slipping through. She brought her hammer down again and the image of a fist against a nose flashed in her mind. Eilean tried to distract herself. She pushed the metal back into the flames. A familiar spark tickled at her fingertips. Shaking her hands, Eilean took in deep breaths. She just needed to concentrate on what she was doing, and it'd be okay.

After taking out the piece, Eilean hit the smoldering metal and tried to picture anything but that image. As she twisted the piece, bending it into shape, all she could hear was—

CRUNCH.

Her fist breaking David's nose.

SMACK.

A fist connecting with his jaw.

Eilean shook her head and stepped away from her workstation, back to the fire pit. She pushed the metal into the flame and took a breath. Turning from the fire, she wiped a hand against her sweaty forehead. She couldn't let her mind slip back there. Eilean needed to focus on the belt clasp she was making.

It was as she tried to clear her mind that she noticed the bright white sparks coming from the fire.

"Crap," she spat out.

She pulled the sparking metal from the flames, only to find that half of the material had burned off, melting away while she was distracted. She could just about make out the lost material among the coke. There was no saving it now. Dumping the mess on her worktable, Eilean tugged off her gloves and threw them down.

"That didna go well, did it?" Mr. Lawton and his thick lilt of a Geordie accent said, making Eilean jump.

Mr. Lawton stood in front of her, eyes solely focused on her destroyed piece. She hadn't expected him to engage with her again after his last comment. He was very much a hands-off teacher.

"Sir, I—" Eilean started, only stopping when he raised his hand for silence.

She gulped as the scruffy man examined her piece. Mr. Lawton was a large man, a benefit of working his trade for three decades. He could scare anyone trying to start trouble with one look, but that gentle smile he would give his students when they did a good job made his intensity easier to be around. When he reached out and tenderly lifted her piece into the air, Eilean caught the fascination in his gaze as he focused on each part of her creation.

"It's crap now, but ya can fix it." Lawton carefully lowered the half-constructed buckle back onto the anvil's surface. "Just gotta concentrate, aye?"

"Aye—I mean, yeah."

Mr. Lawton chuckled in his deep and gruff way. "Keep that fire an' all, Red, you need it."

She nodded. "Will do, Mr. Lawton."

He smacked a hand on her back, and she braced herself to avoid flying into her workstation. Eilean expected him to leave after that but he didn't. She pretended he had and went back to work on her buckle.

"Can I ask you something?" he asked, his voice low as if he didn't want the others to hear.

Eilean put the hammer down. "Uh, sure."

His gaze stayed on the buckle as he tilted his head. "Why have you never made a weapon? Don't get me wrong, lass, it's a refreshing change o' pace from all the swords and shields new students are always clamoring to make. I'm just curious."

Eilean rubbed the back of her neck. "Someone needs to make a belt buckle to stop the sword wearers from losing their trousers." She went back to her table of materials to avoid meeting his eyes. "I'll make a fortune with buckles, just you wait."

Lawton hummed in response. Thankfully for Eilean, he didn't push it any further and took his leave. She let out a sigh of relief.

Focusing on the buckle in front of her, she collected more metal to put into the flame for shaping. As she pulled the metal slab from the fire and used her hammer to flatten its edges to the shape she needed—a spiral frame—Eilean found her mind drifting back to her professor's question.

How do you explain that you're afraid of hurting people so much that the idea of even making weapons terrifies you?

Eilean shook her head. It was the last day at the smith's before their time off for the weekend. At least, in theory. Mr.

Lawton would often open up the shop on weekends for the students, so Eilean would be back tomorrow. Especially considering the upcoming break.

A week from now it would be half-term and—unlike her usual term breaks—Eilean wouldn't be able to spend it at the forge. She'd be heading home to Balloch, Scotland. Eilean wanted to finish the buckle before she left.

Thinking of Balloch made Eilean nervous. She hadn't been back in five years. Not since… The idea of seeing anyone she knew there made her feel sick. In the end, though, it would be worth it, as she'd be seeing her nana again. Or as she called her, *Mamó*.

Eilean was making this buckle for her. The special touch, as she marked on all her creations, was the image of a spiral: An intricate curl starting from the center of the circle that swirled until it reached the edges. Eilean had been obsessed with spirals since childhood, ever since her Mamó told her of their importance.

"A spiral has magical properties, Hen." Mamó would reach up to hold the spiral pendant necklace she always wore. "They can represent many things; from your life cycle, to the passage of time, and even death."

Eilean had taken in every word. She never expected that Mamó would gift her a matching spiral necklace of her own that day.

As she waited for the buckle to cool, Eilean reached up to touch the necklace that still hung around her neck. She'd followed Mamó's instructions and never taken it off.

Touching the carved twirl on the wooden pendant—tracing it with her fingers—always made her feel calmer. Her therapist had told her it was a coping mechanism for when she felt overwhelmed, but in reality, it just reminded her of home. Not Balloch, but the two places that always made her feel safe.

Eilean could picture it easily in her mind whenever she touched the pendant. The color-patched house she decorated with Mamó. The sound of the green-leaf trees that rustled in the gale winds. She could picture the path from Mamó's house to the shores of Loch Lomond. Eilean could even smell the freshwater of the loch, which filled her senses to the point that she felt she was drowning in it.

A clap of hands shocked Eilean back into the present. "All right everyone, let's finish up quickly now." The sound of fires going out, tools slamming up on shelves, surrounded Eilean. "We ran over so dunna worry, I'll clean up for those who gotta run."

Wrapping her belt buckle spiral in a heat-resistant wrap, Eilean went to leave her piece on the side alongside the others when Lawton came up to her.

"I'll get that," he told her. "I'll make sure it's kept safe while you're away."

Eilean frowned. "What do you—"

Lawton's cuckoo-clock chimed 5 p.m.

"Bollocks."

She didn't have the time to ask what he meant. With a quick "thanks, bye", Eilean rushed off at top speed.

She was going to be late for therapy.

2

THERAPY SOMETIMES HELPS

EILEAN HATED GROUP SESSIONS. SHE UNDERSTOOD THEIR usefulness—sharing pain, seeing the progress and successes of those in the group—that was all great. That is, if you believed you were capable of that progress yourself. Eilean couldn't stand talking around others.

Her old solo therapist had said she was an anxious introvert who had closed off from others because of past trauma and needed to work through it to address her history. Suffice to say, she thought that her therapist was a moron.

As the girls of the group engaged in conversation, discussing their past and what triggers had occurred that week, Eilean let her mind wander. She knew it was rude, but sometimes her mind just did that. A lot of emotion in one room could be overwhelming sometimes. And that feeling wasn't helped by the fact they were sitting in a close-knit circle on the cold, hard floor in the middle of a Catholic church.

The group took place at the front, near the altar. Lines of wooden pews stretched out beside them, giving an eerie feeling that, though empty, something still sat watching them. Stained glass windows left reflections of light on the floor, illuminating them in whatever colors the sun had caught.

It had always been unnerving for Eilean to have the images of saints staring down at her in session. It felt like they were listening in and passing judgment on everything she said. The echo that many old buildings had only worsened that feeling of unease. Everything they said and did bounced off the walls and was thrown back, as if the church were communicating its disapproval.

"Eilean." Mrs. Desai's voice brought Eilean back from her stupor. "Do you have anything you'd like to share today?"

All eyes turned to Eilean, and she wished the ground would swallow her whole. This was the other part of group therapy that she hated: being the center of everyone's attention. She hated being watched.

"Uh, well... I made something cool at the shop today. This nice belt buckle that I'm giving my Mamó when I see her during my term break." Eilean stared at her fiddling fingers. "It'll be nice to see her. It's been a long time."

"Are you nervous about going back home?"

Her hands closed into fists as her heart beat faster. "Nope."

The girl nearest to her—Emily, she thought it was—rolled her eyes at that answer. Eilean's nails dug into the skin of her palms as she tried to focus on controlling her breathing.

"You can speak about how you're feeling here, Eilean," Mrs. Desai continued. "Have you felt anxious about returning?"

Eilean turned away from the therapist's prying gaze to the window nearby. She couldn't see out of it, having to look at an image of Jesus and Mary instead. At least they'd only judge her silently.

"A little, I guess." Eilean stared down at her closed, trembling fists.

"What do you feel worried about?" Mrs. Desai asked.

Eilean's knuckles were white from how hard she was clenching them. Worried about how that would be perceived, she quickly unfurled them and reached up to grab hold of her pendant.

An instant sense of calm washed over her then. Her chest, which had felt tight, loosened, allowing her to breathe. The window didn't show the outside world easily, but as she stared harder, she glimpsed the trees of the nearby park. When she breathed in again, she could almost smell the spring air of newly blossoming nature rather than the musty smell of the old church.

What *was* she worried about?

"That I'll see David." Eilean didn't let go of her necklace. "I-I don't have anything else I want to say."

Mrs. Desai nodded, clearly recognizing the signs not to push her any farther. Eilean was grateful. She'd never been a big sharer, even before her issues manifested.

The other girls looked away, disappointed. Working with a group, to them, meant that everyone should engage and contribute. "It's the only way to heal," they would say. Eilean would hold back a scoff whenever they mentioned it. Talking about your feelings did nothing. All it meant was that they could act like what they did was okay, because they felt bad.

They don't understand, her mind told her. *They don't know what you are. If they did, they'd wish you weren't here, too.*

"All right, team," Mrs. Desai said, standing. "Great session today, and I'll see most of you next week at the same time. Grab your forms from me at the door on your way out."

Eilean slowly collected her things. She liked to wait until everyone else had left before she did. The other girls liked to chat as they left or organize going out for tea to relax after. Eilean, on the other hand, preferred a solitary walk through the nature reserve nearby.

After everyone was gone, Eilean headed for the door where Mrs. Desai stood with questionnaires. She expected two, but was given six.

"I think you gave me too many, Miss."

Mrs. Desai frowned. "These are for when you're away so we can track your mood, enough for two weeks."

"Uh, no, I'm only away for one week a week from now."

Has she gotten confused? Eilean wondered.

"I received a call from your mother earlier today explaining the situation," Mrs. Desai said. "Has she not spoken with you?"

Eilean reached for her pocket before remembering she'd left her phone at home. She often did on days when she was doing intricate design work for class. Technology easily distracted her. Playing music or having access to the internet just kept her mind off what she was meant to be doing. Once she'd tried searching for a match image for the design she was working toward and then, four hours later, she'd somehow ended up watching a two-hour YouTube video examining the *Andor* TV show. Eilean would have to remind her mum about getting that ADHD diagnosis. And try to cut back on her media consumption in general.

"I'll see you…" Eilean didn't know how to finish that sentence. "Bye, Mrs. Desai."

She rushed away from the church. It seemed today she would have to miss out on her walk. She had some questions for her parents.

3

PUNCH IT OUT

Eilean's house wasn't far from the church. It took less than twenty minutes for her to get back most days. Fewer today, considering she was running full tilt across the open field toward her house.

Usually, Eilean was grateful that the house her parents had bought when they moved here had the field. The city of Carlisle wasn't as green as Balloch—the loch making the vegetation grow stronger and more vibrant—but the natural land was still a place of peace. Except for today. Today she didn't soak in the unexpectedly warm sun above or the chirp of the birds in the trees. Today she stormed right across the field, leaped over the fence, and made her way toward the house.

Compared to their house back home, on paper, the one here in Carlisle was far superior. It was a large, modern-day, red-bricked terrace with a humongous garden, an insanely big garage, and three huge bedrooms, the third of which was used as an office. Everything about the house was perfect, but it still wasn't home. Home was a cramped two-bed house with a tiny kitchen and a well-loved living room. Home was Eilean's height marked on the doorframe and the forts they'd made with the sofa cushions and blankets. But Balloch wasn't home anymore.

And that was her fault.

Eilean opened the door harder than she intended and cringed at the slam of the handle against the nearby wall. She expected her dad to yell at her from wherever he was in the house, but nothing followed. That was when she noticed the suitcases by the kitchen's entrance.

"Ma?" Eilean called out as she stepped toward the kitchen. That's where her mum would usually be found after work. "Ma, where are you?"

"Upstairs!" a distant voice yelled.

Eilean was almost to her parents' bedroom when her mum's strawberry blonde head popped out from hers.

"In here, sweetie," her mum said with a smile.

Eilean followed but clenched her jaw. She hated when her parents went into her room without her permission. There was a lot of private stuff in there and she dreaded the day they'd find something by accident while snooping.

"What are you—" Her question dropped off as she took in the mess her mum had made of her room.

Eilean prided herself on being organized, with her bedroom especially. It was her sanctuary, her space. It was only fair that Eilean respected the one place that offered her the peace and quiet she needed. But now all that calming energy she'd made for herself was… whatever *this* was supposed to be.

"Ma! What are you doing?" Eilean yelled. "You're going to ruin my clothes!"

"It's fine," her mum said with a wave of a hand toward the bed. "I'll fold them as they go in the suitcase."

Eilean glanced toward her ever-made bed and saw her large suitcase and a pile of clothes atop it. On the wall by her bed was her blacksmithing shelf which, thankfully, had not been harmed by the careless tossing of outfits. That shelf was Eilean's pride and joy, holding an array of creations she'd made throughout the years. From the terrible unusable trowel she'd made in first year to the handmade dice and keychain. She'd even made the hooks and shelf itself by hand. Seeing that it was unharmed, as well as most of her room beyond the disaster of her wardrobe and bed, Eilean took a breath and turned back to her mum.

"Why are you packing today? We don't leave for another week, right?"

Her mum didn't answer. She just grabbed another pile of clothes and, thankfully, carried them to the bed this time. Eilean watched as her mum slowly began to fold and pack the items into the case. Eilean bit her tongue over the way she was folding. Now wasn't the time to be picky. She needed answers.

"Why does Mrs. Desai think I won't be here next week?" Eilean asked.

Once again, she was met with silence.

"Ma?" Eilean stepped toward her mum. She tried not to let the hurt show when her mum flinched away from her; it's not like she could blame her. "What's going on?"

"We're leaving for Balloch tomorrow," a deep voice said from behind.

Eilean stuffed her hands in her pockets as they tightened into familiar fists. She faced the newcomer in her bedroom doorway.

She loved her dad; she did. She'd been a daddy's girl when she was young. But that was before Eilean ruined everything and made her dad give up the job he loved in Glasgow to become the local doctor in Carlisle, Cumbria. They'd only been here five years and his once fair blond hair had already dulled to gray. Since moving, their relationship hadn't ever been the same. And that was Eilean's fault too.

"What?" she asked in surprise.

"You heard me." Her dad's voice held no room for argument.

"I just—" Eilean started, confused as to what was happening. Why were they leaving tomorrow? Her half-term break wasn't for another week. That's when it hit her. "What happened?"

The brief silence that followed was enough of a clue. When her mum moved around her to stand beside her dad in the doorway, a united front, Eilean knew.

"Your Mamó's taken a turn, Lean," her mum whispered.

Her heart leaped into her throat. She knew her Mamó had been sick; their phone conversations and video calls were enough of a sign to show how quickly she was deteriorating. It felt like only yesterday they'd received the dementia diagnosis, but it had been six months at least.

"Your Pa called us this afternoon," her mum continued. "I tried to call you but..." she gestured toward Eilean's bedside table where her phone lay. "So, I called your teacher and Mrs. Desai to let them know."

"I'm okay with us going earlier. I want to see Mamó and help Pa," Eilean said, clenching and unclenching her hands to fight back the electric feeling that tingled at her knuckles. "But why didn't you have them tell me? I could have left class early." She gestured to the state of her room. "I could have packed my own bags. We could have even left tonight!"

"We did what we thought was best," her dad said in a tight voice. "Your routine helps you. We didn't want to disturb that."

"But this is Mamó!" Eilean snapped, unconsciously taking a step forward.

Her mum half-stepped back, away from her. Eilean stopped in place. The glance between her parents was enough for the growing frustration, fear, and grief to fall away in that instant.

"Sorry," Eilean moved back. "Sorry, I'm just—I'm tired and, I like my things in a—it's fine, I'm fine. I'm sorry."

"No, Eilean, it's not your fault—"

"I'll check my bags later. I—" She cleared her throat, trying to dislodge the pain she felt at seeing the distrust in her parents' gaze. "I'm just going to go work out for a bit."

Wordlessly, Eilean picked up her phone and slipped past her dad, rushing quickly downstairs to the garage. The garage had been converted into an exercise room a year after they'd moved here. It was a sparse area, filled up by a few different machines and stations, but only two of them were used regularly. Only by Eilean. Her eyes focused on the black cylinder bag hanging from the roof. It was time to work out some stress.

She stripped off her clothes from the day and dropped them into the laundry basket they kept by the stairs. She opened the top cabinet drawer, chose a loose threaded tank top and a pair of lycra shorts, and put them on. She then grabbed up her favorite pair of gloves and opened her phone.

"Bluetooth connected," the robotic voice of the music speaker said, echoing around the room.

Eilean focused on the bag in front of her. "Play 'Punch It Out' playlist."

"Playing 'Punch It Out' playlist."

The beat of the first song had Eilean bouncing. She warmed up her muscles with some quick steps around the bag as the music built up its pace. As the first song kicked fully into high gear, Eilean pushed forward, almost propelling herself toward the bag. Her gloved fist hit the soft synthetic leather with a *SMACK*. The frustrations of the week, the months, the *years* flowed through her. It was as if her mind was slipping away from her body as her fists smacked against the bag, once, twice, thrice in quick succession.

"Never hit angry," the voice of her old coach echoed in her mind, grounding her. "That's how you get hurt."

Eilean had taken up kickboxing when she was fourteen. Her parents had hated the idea, which made sense after everything that had happened, but Eilean had loved it. Just like blacksmithing, it gave her a constructive way to channel her frustration, but in a way that hurt. Eventually, her parents understood after they'd seen how much calmer she would be after a session. They even bought her her first bag for the garage.

Her fist slammed into the bag, hard. Too hard. Too angry. Pain reverberated up her arm and made her wince. Pulling away, she shrugged her shoulders and went again, landing the blow perfectly, this time in the center of the bag. Energy surged within Eilean. Like an adrenaline rush that she couldn't get enough of.

That's when she knew she had to stop. Or at least, when she should have stopped.

Electricity sparked all up her arms, making her feel stronger than she ever had. And that was terrifying. The first time she'd felt that spark, she'd broken David's jaw. And then his ribs. That feeling was the sign that her anger was taking over. That feeling meant she was dangerous. Eilean didn't even know why she was so angry.

She just always was.

Throwing another punch, unfocused, she missed the bag and slipped, colliding with the heavy object face first. She heaved great, panting breaths as she wrapped her arms around the bag, hanging onto it for support.

As she clung there, the beat of her music pounded in the background and under her feet. She could barely feel it now, the voices in her mind so much louder than the lyrics as the worst-case scenarios of returning home played in her mind over and over again.

She sniffled, her eyes watering suddenly. She wiped tears away in frustrated surprise as she slumped to her knees against the bag.

I don't want to go back.

4

FAMILY IS EVERYTHING

THEY LEFT FOR BALLOCH AT 8 A.M. THE NEXT MORNING with a car full of bags and an engine full of gas. Eilean's family weren't chatty travelers; she was, thankfully, able to slip on her music and tune out everything as the world passed her by.

Outside her window, the land changed around her: from the sloped green pastures of England to the stony remains of Hadrian's Wall and, eventually, the expansive fields and hills of green that spread farther than the eye could see. Even when they passed by the city, the land never really disappeared, it only receded a little. As the world around them became more familiar, the anxiety in Eilean's stomach grew.

Reaching up for her necklace, Eilean closed her eyes and took a breath. She'd be with Mamó soon; that's all that mattered.

Then they pulled into the town.

Balloch had changed little in the five years since she'd been gone. Her part of town had always looked old, but in a way that felt more homely than dated. Its white-painted, red brick houses with tile roofs stood out compared to the orange brick of Carlisle. Add in that none of them lined up symmetrically—

the tall and thin right next to the stout—and it made for an interesting sight. The streets began to blend with more vegetation the closer to Loch Lomond they drove. She'd been gone so long and yet it felt like no time had passed at all. Unfortunately, that last part couldn't have felt more real as their car slowed down to a crawl, matching the busy street speed limit. Eilean knew it wasn't possible, but she was sure the people on the street were glancing her way. Her actions had made her the talk of the town all those years ago; she'd half hoped they'd have forgotten her face by now. She realized she'd been naïve to think that.

Eilean slid down in her seat, hiding herself from view.

She stayed hidden like that until the moment they stopped. When her mum glanced at her for the first time since they left Carlisle, Eilean caught her confused expression at Eilean's scrunched position.

"Fell asleep," Eilean mumbled, rubbing her eyes for added effect.

Eilean's mum nodded in response, though the frown on her face told Eilean that her acting skills were lacking.

As they all exited the car, stretching their aching limbs, they collected their bags from the trunk and headed toward the door of the house. Despite it all, Eilean couldn't help but smile as she saw it.

Unlike Balloch, her grandparents' house had changed a lot. That didn't surprise her much. It changed every year, as per Mamó's command. Last time she'd been here, the door and window panes had been painted yellow to match the summer sun. The window boxes were an array of sunset colors. Orange Mexican sunflowers and yellow bulb-like berberis darwinii were mixed with the purples of lavender and the reds of liliums. The aromas reminded Eilean of hot, sticky nights in this bungalow house during the height of the summer holidays.

Eilean smiled to herself at how easily she remembered the

flowers. Mamó had made it her mission to teach Eilean everything she knew about plants and had gifted her herbology and botanist books for every birthday and Christmas.

The house plants were different this time. The colors were slightly more muted, though from the empty paint pot Eilean saw tucked away behind the garden wall, it was clear it had been done recently. The door and window panes had been painted a dark, almost black-green that glowed in the sunlight. In the plant pots and window fillers, there were more green: some Bells-of-Ireland, green dahlias, and a few lady's mantle flowers.

It was odd to only see plants of the same color. Mamó couldn't stand uniformity. Everything needed its own signature and to have a role in the image of the house. To have anything be one uniform color, green, just didn't feel like something Mamó would like.

She then remembered what her parents had been telling her. Mamó wasn't the same person anymore. Before her mind could run off with the thought, the front door was thrown open and the sudden image of her Pa was running to greet her.

Pa had aged a lot in five years. She may have seen him in video calls but, in person, the grays were more prominent and the wrinkles deeper. Though that shouldn't have really surprised her—he was eighty after all—it still hurt to think about. He may have looked older, but he was still sprightly for his age, jogging quickly to Eilean's side and pulling her in for a bear hug.

"Here's my girl," he whispered and held her tight.

Tears pricked Eilean's eyes as she gently reciprocated the hug. It'd been a long time since someone had been this unconditionally happy to see her.

Pulling back, Pa smiled warmly at her, his wrinkles disappearing with it, and he suddenly seemed many years younger.

"It's been too long." Pa took her suitcase from her and led

her to the house. "You should come back more often than you do. Your Mamó and I have missed your visits."

She knew he wasn't saying it to make her feel bad. It was just what grandparents do. That didn't stop her from feeling guilty about it as she followed Pa inside. The moment she stepped in through the door, the smell of freshly bloomed lilies and lavender filled her nose.

Taking a deep breath, she inhaled the aromas of home before searching for Mamó. Her Pa caught her attention with a pat to her shoulder. He nodded toward the study.

"Tea? Coffee?" he asked, guiding mum and dad to the kitchen with one hand and ushering Eilean away with the other.

With her parents easily distracted by the promise of caffeine, Eilean snuck away to finally reconnect with her Mamó. Her steps were initially quick, until she got closer to the white flaky door that led to the study.

What if she doesn't remember me? Eilean wondered, coming to a stop. *They said it was bad, but what does that mean? Who will I see when I go in there?*

Shaking her head to clear those thoughts, Eilean took a breath and reached for the door. She pushed it open, only to hear voices inside.

"Are you sure I can't change your mind on this?" said one that Eilean didn't recognize. It sounded distinctly female—though there was a gruffness to it that reminded Eilean of the voices from her dad's old war movies. She hated those films.

"It is not her burden to bear," an older voice responded, this one softer than the other, though still croaky in the way age sounds. It was Mamó. "*Tha beatha ro goirid,* Morgan. I won't make it shorter."

"You can't protect her forever."

Eilean frowned and leaned forward, trying to see through the small open gap of the doorway, but whoever was in there wasn't in view. She could only just see Mamó sat in her armchair, staring directly at whoever she was talking to.

"No," Mamó glanced away from her companion, "but I can try."

Silence fell in the room and, not wanting to disturb just yet, Eilean waited a breath before she opened the door.

Mamó, who had been staring in the direction of the bookshelf, turned toward Eilean, her green eyes locked with Eilean's own. They were duller than their usual brightness. She appeared lost somehow.

"Hi, Mamó," Eilean smiled as she entered the room fully. She then went to speak to Mamó's guest only to find that no one was there. Frowning, she looked behind the door in case they were hiding for some strange reason. "Uh, where did your friend go?"

Eilean scanned the room and found no sign that anyone had been here, and there was no chance they could have slipped past Eilean. Even the window behind Mamó was closed. There was no way anyone could've left between her eavesdropping and her entering. She stepped closer to Mamó to check to see if she'd managed to get hold of a phone but saw nothing in her possession beyond a cooled cup of tea on the chair side table.

Shaking her head, she turned back to Mamó, who hadn't answered yet. When Eilean saw her, she felt her heart break. Mamó was looking around frantically as if she were afraid.

"Morgan, you shouldn't be here."

Eilean frowned. "It's… It's Eilean, Mamó. Not Morgan."

Who the hell is Morgan?

A hand tugged her forward with a jerk, bringing her close to Mamó's side. She stared at the face she knew so well and saw no recognition. Even worse, she thought Eilean was someone else entirely.

Someone she didn't want here.

"You'll get in trouble for being here again," Mamó said, frantic. "You shouldn't have come."

"Uh... I'm sorry, um..." She had to wrack her brain for Mamó's real name. "Ruth. I'm sorry I came. I'll go if that's what you want."

Mamó didn't respond. Instead, she stared at her plant pots that rested on the windowsill. She appeared almost lost in thought. Eilean wondered if she often looked like this, like someone chasing after a memory that wouldn't come to them.

Her hand came to rest up on her chest, reaching for something that was no longer there.

"Mamó," Eilean spoke, trying to draw attention back to her. All she received in response was a heavy sigh. "Mamó, where's your necklace?"

That gained Mamó's attention. She peered down, confused, as if she was just noticing the empty space. Then her expression became serious and intense as those familiar sharp green eyes fell on her. She laid a hand atop Eilean's. "Where it needs to be."

"What does that—"

"Are you sure she'll be the one, Morgan?" Mamó interrupted, her voice urgent. She shifted anxiously in her seat, as if she were afraid something terrible was about to happen.

Eilean frowned. *What does that mean?*

"Um, yes?" Eilean responded, though from the way her Mamó seemed ready to burst into tears, she wished she hadn't. "But... but she'll be fine. I'm sure of it."

Mamó's other hand reached out and, for a moment, Eilean thought she was about to be slapped. Instead, Mamó's coarse, garden-worked hands pressed gently against her cheeks.

"Don't make empty promises to me, Morgan. I've always seen right through you. Walter as well." Her thumb stroked Eilean's cheek. "You don't need to promise me anything."

She removed her hands then and leaned away from Eilean

entirely. Folding back into her armchair, she stared out the window once more.

"I'll protect her," Mamó said, resting a hand beneath her chin to hold her head in place as she stared out into the garden. "I always will."

Eilean ran a hand through her hair. She did not know how to deal with people who weren't well. Mamó was no exception. All Eilean could think was about who she was protecting.

Did she mean me? she wondered, though she couldn't remotely understand why that would be the case. She didn't know any Morgan. And she wasn't exactly in danger of anything and in need of protection. Except maybe from herself.

"Mamó, what did you mean about being the one?" Eilean rested a hand on Mamó's knee, trying to regain her attention. She had no idea what was happening or what she was even talking about but, maybe she could help somehow. "Mamó, who's Morgan? Could I find her for you?"

Still nothing. Mamó seemed completely unaware of her presence now. She sat staring out the window in silence. If not for the signs of her breathing, she'd have looked as still as a painting. Eilean felt helpless seeing her this way.

"Mamó," Eilean whispered, trying again, desperate this time. "Mamó, I came home. I came home for you."

Nothing.

That moment of clarity was all Eilean would have. Her parents had warned her about how bad the dementia was but Eilean hadn't believed them. Sure, she'd seen adverts for the foundations and heard their stories, but surely that couldn't happen to her Mamó. The Mamó who always had a story to tell and a sweet to give. The Mamó who would let her help with the garden and, frequently, let her choose what color it would be that year. Her Mamó had to be in there somewhere.

A sigh escaped Mamó's lips.

Eilean waited for something more to follow, but nothing did.

Fixing her gaze to the ceiling, Eilean blinked back tears before squeezing Mamó's hand in reassurance.

"Why don't I get you some of your favorite sweets?" Eilean said, standing from her crouched position on the floor. "How does that sound?" She didn't expect an answer, but it hurt all the same not to have one.

As she headed for the door, she glanced over her shoulder to her distant, dormant Mamó.

"Don't worry," she whispered. "I won't leave you again."

5

THE PAST IS A B—

Eilean slipped out of the house without letting her parents know where she was going. She didn't want to deal with anyone right now. She made it to the shop with relative ease, using her hoodie to hide her face from the shopkeeper just in case.

"You know you look like you're going to rob the place, right?" a voice said from beside her.

Jumping in surprise and knocking a line of sweets to the ground, Eilean met the gaze of a brown-eyed girl holding back a laugh behind her hand. She was dressed in a simple t-shirt and ripped denim jeans, and yet, she still made it seem like she'd just walked off a photo shoot. Her Afro curls framed her face beautifully, showing off her soft and kind smile.

The girl bent down and started picking up the sweets. "Sorry, I didn't mean to scare you."

Eilean started picking, too. "It's okay. I was in my own world."

"Sounds fun."

"Oh yeah, I'm King of Camelot there, wizard side-kick and everything."

The girl laughed. "Let me know if you're ever looking for a court jester."

Or a Queen, Eilean thought, but made sure to keep to herself. She wasn't that cringy. Out loud.

"Fox's?" The girl asked, holding the bag in her hands.

Eilean nodded. "They're my Mamó's favorite. She loves the purple ones."

The girl handed the bag over to her with a smile that dazzled Eilean. "Good choice. I love the red ones personally."

Before Eilean could even respond, the girl was out the door with a melodic laugh following her. Eilean hadn't even got her name and yet she was sure that she'd met her future wife.

Collecting the Fox's sweets, and a stick of Pepperoni for herself, she headed up to the counter replaying the mad meet-cute encounter in her head.

"That'll be two-pound fifty. Do you need a bag?" the shop-keeper asked her.

"Nah, I'm good, thanks."

The older man squinted at her. "Do I know you?"

Eilean dropped her chin, not meeting his gaze, and tapped her phone on the card machine. "No, no, you don't."

She rushed out of there as fast as she could. She couldn't risk someone recognizing her on her first day back in town. Most everyone knew what she'd done and, in a town like this, the moment she was spotted, everyone would hear about it.

Munching on her stick of pepperoni, Eilean headed toward the bridge to make her way back home to Mamó. Eilean had barely made it onto the bridge when trouble arrived in the form of Chloe Talbot and her gang of lackeys.

Chloe had been one of the girls she'd gone to school with when the *incident* happened. One of the girls who had always been by David's side back then. They'd never exactly been in each other's good books before the incident. Chloe and her gang were part of the popular crowd. Eilean had been the school loner. They steered clear of each other until that day. Now Eilean was high up on Chloe's shit list.

Pulling her hood lower, she went to cross the road, only to find herself stuck by the number of cars speeding by.

Crap.

"Hey, is that you, Eilean?" Chloe called out in her nasal voice.

Eilean didn't respond, desperately waiting for a break in the passing of cars to make a run for it. If she pretended she couldn't hear them, maybe that would be enough for them to leave her alone.

Eilean took a step to run across the street as the last car sped past, but a tight grip pulled her back. Eilean glanced up to find a lanky teenage boy with slicked-back hair holding her by the arm and realized she was done for.

"I think it is, Clo," the boy sneered. He leaned forward, his breath smelling of cheap cigarettes. "David was one of my best mates, psycho. We don't even see him anymore 'cause of you."

"I-I think you got the wrong person," Eilean stuttered out as she pulled herself out of his grip. "I'm just here visiting my Mamó, that's all."

Eilean moved away from the two of them but found herself stuck when her back hit the wall of the bridge. She could turn and run. The other members of Chloe's gang didn't seem interested in her. She could make it. She just didn't want to risk being wrong.

"Nah," the boy who'd caught her—she was sure his name was Jack—said. "You're definitely her."

Chloe stepped up to her. Her blonde high ponytail gave her a little height, but she was still a few inches shorter. All the same, Eilean still shrunk into herself.

"Can't believe you came back," Chloe bit out. "After all you did."

Eilean glanced around, hoping someone would step in. The five stragglers of the group were standing awkwardly to the side. Two further ahead on the bridge tried to call Chloe away, saying it wasn't worth it. One stood closer to them and was the more vocal one of the group. And Eilean knew this girl.

"Guys, this isn't cool." The girl from the shop said, glancing at Eilean briefly. "Leave her alone and let's just go."

"Jack, mate," another spoke up, an older boy with a barely-there mustache he was clearly trying to grow out. "We only have an hour of free time. I wanna eat before going back to class. Come on, she ain't worth it."

Neither Chloe or Jack reacted to their friends' pleas. The shop-girl didn't seem happy about what was happening, occasionally trying to catch an adult's attention as if she were hoping they would intervene. She seemed to forget that adults wouldn't give a damn about what kids got up to.

Not their kids, not their problem.

Eilean was cornered. She considered pushing Jack out of the way to run but, just as her hand twitched to do it, she tucked them into her pockets, digging the nails into the palm of her hands. She couldn't risk hurting them by accident.

Chloe leaned in close, resting her hand on the bridge wall beside Eilean. She was shorter than Eilean by five inches, but that didn't stop her from shrinking away in response. "What you doin' back here then, hm? We thought you were off at a loony school."

Eilean dropped her gaze. "My Mamó's sick. I'm just getting her something to feel better." She chanced a glance at Chloe. "I'll go and you won't see me again. Please."

"David said please; you remember that?" Chloe snapped; Eilean flinched. "Didn't stop you then, did it? You just kept going." Chloe slapped a hand against the stones beside Eilean's side, making her bite her tongue to stop from reacting. "And going. And—"

"Chloe, that's enough—"

"Shut it, Freya," Chloe snapped at the shop girl.

Freya, the shop-girl, was staring at Eilean, concern in her

gaze. She was clearly uncomfortable, but Eilean doubted she'd be able to take Chloe on. Chloe was the queen bee. And she always got what she wanted. Freya didn't stand a chance against her.

"Did you enjoy it?" Chloe asked, getting in Eilean's face.

A spark of electricity tingled at Eilean's fingertips. *No, please.*

"Do you enjoy hurting people? Hm?"

Eilean's heart raced. Just like it had with David all those years ago. It pulsed so hard and so fast it was almost difficult to breathe. Then her vision would become blurry until all she saw was a threat. *Then* they would back off. *Then* they would leave her alone.

She thinks I enjoy *being like this?*

"Let me go," Eilean whispered, reaching up desperately to grab onto her necklace. "Please."

"You know he had nightmares for months?" Eilean tried not to see Chloe's tears. "I did too. I remember the blood. I remember *four* teachers had to pull you off him. You remember that?"

"I'm sorry..." Taking a breath, she tightened her grip on her pendant. "I never meant—"

Chloe yanked her hand away from the necklace, tugging the chain until it dug into the back of Eilean's neck. A spark shot down Eilean's arms.

Next thing she knew, Chloe was on the floor. Her blonde hair splayed out behind her.

Eilean's hands were out in front of her, shaking wildly. Her hands thrummed with an electric energy. Where they had pushed against Chloe, a warmth now flowed through her veins. Even her fingers thrummed with power, a power that should have terrified her.

Except it felt good.

And that was far more frightening.

"I-I'm sorry," Eilean said, panic making her voice shake.

It was like her words broke them all from a spell. Chloe started crying. Her friends, except Freya, rushed to her side. None of them paid Eilean any mind.

So, like any sane person would do, she ran.

Eilean couldn't hear shouting or pounding feet behind her when she sprinted away. She chanced a glance over her shoulder and found the gang still on the bridge, helping the injured Chloe. All except one.

Freya was still watching her. Eilean couldn't see her expression, but she was just standing there, staring. Even as the rest helped a crying Chloe from the floor. It was unnerving.

Eilean pushed herself faster, the charge of the energy still sparking within her. Ready and waiting for her to do more. She didn't know where she was running to, but wherever it was, it was better than here.

6

DROWNING IS THE NEW THERAPY

A SHOOTING PAIN UP HER LEGS FINALLY SLOWED EILEAN'S pace. She was breathing hard, sweat dripping down her back and dampening her face. She really needed to work on her stamina if she was going to be here for two more weeks. Or maybe become a hermit and never leave the house. Both seemed like good options.

Eilean was walking at her natural pace now, and when she looked up at where her feet had taken her, she still nearly stumbled.

The tree line to Loch Lomond. Eilean breathed in deeply, ready to relax in the surrounding nature. But something was off. The sky above had clouded over. What should be fresh blooming trees surrounding her were wilted, the brown leaves of autumn hanging on as the branches danced in the cool wind. They danced a one-way waltz, almost as if guiding her forward. Even the wild flowers that would grow by the side of the path down to the loch were not in good shape; only a few seemed to have made it to the Spring bloom. Their color dulled as they tangled with the dead beside them. This wasn't the loch Eilean remembered.

It was only when the trees and plants blended together, blurring so much that Eilean could barely see them, that she realized she was crying.

Her body shook with tears as the electricity still fizzled within her. She ran again as she followed the path down to the water. Eilean could only hope that where she was going, there would be no one in sight. She couldn't risk being around people right now. Eilean didn't know what would happen if she was.

She could still feel the weight of Chloe's body against her hands as she pushed her. Her palms felt like they were on fire; a fire that spread up her arms, across her chest, and to her heart. Eilean knew this feeling all too well. And she needed to release it.

She made a turn and headed down a steep pathway to the waterside. Even five years on, the beach of stones and algae was the same as it always was. The powerful scent of water made Eilean feel that, despite the changes further up the shore, she was home. And, thankfully for her, the beach was empty of people. Eilean had never been more grateful for Scotland's poor weather than at this moment. Though the spreading fog across the water was new, for this early in Spring.

Crouching down, groaning at her aching legs, Eilean pulled off her shoes and socks. She placed her phone and the sweets inside her trainers for safety, rolled up her pant legs, and speed-walked toward the water. The stones were painful against her feet, making her wince, but she kept going.

She waded into the water, holding back a series of curses at the freezing temperature, until she was knee-deep and the cuffs of her rolled-up jeans were slowly soaking with water. As she took a breath, Eilean shoved her hands into the water. Her jaw locked at the cold bite at her fingertips, numbing the electric feeling that still buzzed within her veins. She unclenched her jaw and let out a scream.

Only when her throat felt like it was burning and about to

give out, did she stop. The echo of her scream surrounded her, carried on the waves of the loch, and by a sudden howling wind.

Her throat hurt, as did her numb fingers and toes, but the burning energy coursing through her was extinguished. Eilean stared up at the cloudy sky and let out a breath.

Why am I like this? she thought, letting the freezing water sink into her skin.

Only when she realized she was shivering from the cold did Eilean feel safe enough to leave the biting sanctuary of the loch.

Once back on dry land with wet feet and legs, Eilean didn't feel like leaving. She knew she shouldn't stay out any later; her parents would probably have noticed that she'd left by now. But still, she sat down on the beach, the stones stabbing her in the butt, and stared out over the waters.

She sat there for a long while. Every time she sighed, her breath formed a trail of mist in front of her face. Eilean didn't want to go back home. She didn't want to see Mamó like that again. She couldn't stand the idea of being a stranger to her. Eilean brushed away a stray tear and stood up. But it didn't matter what she wanted. She had to go. Besides, Mamó may not remember, but Eilean did promise to give her those sweets.

She was about to slip on her shoes when something strange happened.

Her pendant, the spiral around her neck, grew warm. Eilean stopped what she was doing, stood upright, and reached up for the necklace. It didn't feel warm to the touch now. Thinking she was imagining things, she slipped her shoes onto her cold feet and grabbed her socks and Mamó's sweets.

Heading up the bank, trying to ignore the chafe of her shoes, Eilean felt her necklace grow warm again. She stopped in place.

"That's… weird," she mumbled, reaching up to hold the wood once more.

Eilean glanced around, trying to figure out if she was just feeling an out-of-place warm breeze.

That was when she noticed it.

The fog had spread. Before, it had been at a distance, only covering a few of the smaller islands on the farthest side of the loch. Now it had spread to the beach, dancing over the stones and heading up the pebbled bank toward her. Like it was trying to swallow her up.

"What the—" Eilean started, until she was cut off by a cry.

"Help!"

Eilean, immediately alert, searched the beach for the voice. Nothing.

"Help me! Help!" the small voice cried, followed by the sound of frantic splashing.

Eilean squinted through the fog.

In the distance, about two hundred yards from the shore, a pair of hands raised into the air, waving madly. The wet head of hair appeared above the water again. The hands belonged to a struggling child.

"Shit!" Eilean cried, searching for someone nearby who could help. Where the hell had he even come from?

"Help—" The voice cut off.

Eilean whirled around, and for a horrifying second, she couldn't see the kid anymore. They came splashing to the surface again, clearly panicked.

She had no choice.

Dumping her items and throwing off her shoes again, she charged forward. Ignoring the stinging of the stones against her feet, Eilean leaped into the water. Unlike before, she submerged herself fully in the loch. Her entire body screamed at the sharpness of the icy waters by sending a wrack of shivers up and down her skin.

Christ. Balls. Fuck! she thought as she swam through the bone-chilling cold of the loch.

The kid's screaming and splashing were getting closer, but

so was the strength of the fog. She could barely see a foot in front of her. Eilean stopped swimming, unable to continue in fear that she could end up heading in the wrong direction.

"Kid!" Eilean shuddered out through her chattering teeth. "Shout for me!" She bobbed in place, turning frantically in every direction. "Where are you?"

Nothing.

Oh, God, I can't have been too late, Eilean thought. *They were shouting for me up until I stopped.*

Then, she felt something touch her foot.

Yelping in surprise, Eilean stared down at the water beneath her. She couldn't see a thing, the water too dark to see through, but she knew something had touched her.

Could the kid be underneath already?

Eilean threw her chin over both shoulders, hoping for a sign that she was close. Nothing happened. No call for help, no ripple in the water. Nothing.

"Crap," she muttered as she looked down at her reflection in the water. "Crap."

Eilean took a deep breath, then dove.

The waters of Loch Lomond had never been the clearest. While one could make out details that were in close proximity, without proper diving equipment, it didn't make much difference. But this time, it was as if Eilean had plunged into a room where all the lights had gone out. It was a terrifying feeling.

She kicked her legs and searched as low and wide around as she could manage. Eilean held an arm out in the hopes of feeling anything but eventually the need for air forced her to swim back up to the surface.

Just as she took her first breath, readying to dive back down again, something grabbed her foot and held on for dear life.

Eilean was so surprised she almost forgot to panic. She swallowed a great gulp of frigid water as the kid pulled her farther under. Kicking and thrashing, Eilean tried to remove their grip as best she could. She even tried to reach down and pry them off her leg. Nothing worked. Her last thought as the distant light above her faded into darkness cried out through the cold.

I'm not ready to die.

7

A WHOLE NEW WORLD (BUT LESS JASMINE)

EILEAN DIDN'T REMEMBER PASSING OUT. ONE MINUTE SHE was kicking and screaming as she drowned, the next she saw only black. She wondered if this was what death felt like.

Then she vomited up water.

Laying on her side, her nose and throat burning from being sick, she tried to gulp in air. She blinked her eyes rapidly to clear the tears, but her vision stayed blurry. Eilean could only just make out the green of the grass before she rolled onto her back to stave off the nausea. She stared up at the bright blue sky and wondered to herself: *what the heck happened?*

She concentrated on her breathing until she could inhale properly again. Eilean sat up and tried to find her voice. She needed to find that kid. Once she was upright and able to look around, Eilean had to pinch herself to make sure she was still alive.

Everything was a bright, luscious green, so bright that it made her eyes ache as if she'd just stared directly into the sun. It was like her surroundings were in a permanent state of spring bloom. Vibrant trees circled her around a clearing. Each ranged in height and size. The largest was an old and vast weeping willow. Past this luscious green land, in the distance, an entire world spread farther than the eye could see. But no two of what she saw were the same. The land was a kaleidoscope of color, blending more and more together the further into the distance she tried to see. Some parts changed from green to light brown, almost like a desert, with dunes rising so high into the air that Eilean wouldn't be surprised if they were touching the sky. There were even trees that reached so high up they disappeared among the clouds like something out of a giant's fairytale. She'd never seen a place like this before.

"This isn't Balloch..."

"You aren't as thick as you look," a gruff voice said.

Eilean jumped at the sudden voice. Spinning around to see who was there, she found herself staring into a pair of glowing white eyes.

Eilean shrieked and tried to back away, but tripped.

In front of her, standing on four legs, was a horse. Or at least, what used to be a horse. Its body was covered in sickly and scaly green fur. Its mane was made of decaying seaweed dripping with water. What was more terrifying—besides everything else—were the skeletal parts of its body.

Too stunned to stand, she crawled backward, her wet clothing dragging across the ground. The monster followed after her, showing off its razor-sharp teeth in a terrifying smile.

"Don't run, human," it said in a raspy voice that echoed, like he was speaking underwater. "You don't want me chasing you."

It was the chilling nature of his statement that made her stop. Eilean slowly pushed herself to stand as her heart pounded in her chest.

She reached up for her necklace to calm her panic, but quickly let go in surprise. Instead of the warm feeling of nature that would fill her when she touched it, the necklace shocked her with an ice cold surface.

"Where... where am I?" Eilean demanded in a shaky voice. "What am I doing here?"

Out of nowhere, a warm summer breeze brushed her skin, bringing with it a cascade of leaves that flew around her in a dance. The white-eyed monster snorted and nodded to his right. Nervous about having him out of her sight, Eilean quickly glanced to her left with the intention of turning right back. Before she could, something caught her eye.

Standing beside a clear flowing river was a woman swathed in green. She stood as tall as an oak tree, her shadow swallowing Eilean whole.

Her hair was tied in a delicate French braid with multicolored flowers sitting between each plait. The braid reached all the way down to the soft grass by her feet. The woman's skin was as green as the grass itself, if not more so. From the tips of her toes to the crown of daisies on her head, she looked like she had stepped straight from a children's fairytale. Even her outfit seemed ethereal. It was a gorgeously made dress of spun honey with cherry wreaths that held it all in place.

As Eilean breathed in, the scent of warm spring filled her senses. She smelled the flowers of the meadows she and her Mamó would play in when she was a child. She felt calmer, just as she usually did whenever she held her necklace.

The woman turned and locked eyes with Eilean. They were softer, but just as commanding in their green as the horse-creature's white. Though, unlike the horse, they didn't have that unnatural glow. Instead, they brought a warmth that reminded Eilean of the feeling her pendant gave her.

"Welcome, champion." The woman's voice was as gentle as cotton on the wind. "Welcome… to *Ar Dachaidh*."

Eilean, articulate as ever, responded by turning to vomit in a nearby patch of jasmine.

"I told you humans weren't worth the trouble," the horse-like monster snorted.

"Hush, Bhradain," the woman raised a hand to the beast. "The poor child must be overwhelmed. Your jibes will not help matters."

Eilean wiped her mouth and turned in time to see Bhradain —the *talking horse*—do the horse equivalent of rolling his eyes. As his white eyes rolled up to the sky in disdain, she fought the urge to throw up again.

On wobbly legs, Eilean walked toward the towering woman. She made sure to give the horse-creature as wide a berth as possible as she went.

"Who are you?" she demanded in as firm a voice as she could muster. "And how—how did I get here?"

An indignant huff escaped the horse-beast as he focused his beady, white eyes on Eilean. "I drowned you."

That stunned her.

"Does..." she swallowed hard. "Does that mean I'm... dead?"

"Oh my dear child, have no fear. You are alive and well yet." She lowered herself to the ground in front of Eilean, not that that made a difference, even sitting down she was far taller than Eilean. She had to hold her neck at an angle to look at the woman's face. "Humans are not allowed in our world except in certain circumstances. Your drowning was one way to draw you to us. The kelpie's methods are..." she grimaced slightly, "not the kindest way for one to arrive in our land, but it was where we found you."

Eilean had heard stories about the kelpies from her Mamó. Creatures of death and chaos that bring nothing but terror and cruelty to those unfortunate enough to meet them. She never thought they were real. None of it was supposed to be. Nor this terrifying. Eilean had always just pictured an evil horse when her Mamó told her the stories. When Bhradain bared his teeth at her again, she found herself wishing her version had been right.

"So, where am I?" Eilean kept one eye on the kelpie. "And why did you call me 'champion?'"

The Queen looked away at that, her smile and the warmth resonating around her fading. It was soon replaced with a heavy sadness that wilted the Queen's foliage into a dying brown.

"In your world, this land can go by many names. The Otherworld, *Tír nan Óg*, *Annwfn*, Avalon—but the name our home truly goes by is *Ar Dachaidh*," she said, drifting off in thought as she spoke. "This is the home to Gods so old that most have been forgotten. We are the Celtic Gods, the fae, and this is our realm."

Eilean probably should have reacted to that. She was either talking to a God or, if this was a prank of some sort, an incredible cosplayer on stilts. But all she could think about was the TV show *Merlin* and the Avalon they mentioned there. She'd caught the rerun of that show by accident one day as a kid and had loved it ever since. Morgana—the sorceress—had been her first crush.

"All right, time out." She raised her hands to make the shape of a 'T'. "You're a God? Or fae, or whatever?"

"Yes," the Queen said, her voice gentle like the seeds of a dandelion clock. "The land in which you stand is part of my domain and—"

"Okay, you've got to be pulling some kind of ultimate LARPing experience or something, cause this is bat-shit crazy." Eilean snapped, her voice betraying the panic that was returning. "What the hell is going on here? And *why* did you call me your champion? Am I like Arthur Pendragon or something?"

"Ar Dachaidh is in trouble, Eilean," the Queen said, her voice trembling. "And we need your help."

8

HOW ABOUT NO?

EILEAN STOOD GOBSMACKED. THIS SUPPOSEDLY ALL-MIGHTY Celtic God needed a seventeen-year-old girl with anger issues to help her? Eilean had to stop herself from pinching her arm to make sure she wasn't dreaming—or actually dead.

"Danu, my Queen." Bhradain came forward and lowered his head. "It's clear this human isn't right for the task. Let me throw them back and get another one—"

The Queen—Danu, as the kelpie had called her—raised a hand to silence him. Eilean took her chance.

"Look, Danu," she said, then changed up when a pair of fangs bared at her. "I mean, *Your Majesty*. I think your horse is right. You got the wrong girl."

Eilean stepped back from the Queen and gestured to herself. She was wearing a soaking wet oversized hoodie, no socks or shoes, and was barely keeping herself from hyperventilating as she spoke.

"I'm just a normal... mortal. I can't do anything special unless you want me to make you a trowel, you know, something you'll use in your garden." Eilean gestured to the vast land around them again. "Which is gorgeous, by the way, well done. My Mamó would love this. But, seriously, I think you've got the wrong person. I'm not a champion or whatever. I was just out getting my Mamó some sweets and…" The image of Mamó's distant gaze came to her. "Look, I just want to get back to her, okay? Besides, I'm the last person you'd want helping you. Hell, I don't even believe in the Celtic Gods; my parents are Catholic. I'm pretty sure they'd have me exorcized if I said I did." Eilean frowned. "I don't have anything to do with you, so—"

"That's where you would be wrong, Eilean MacAlistair."

Danu stepped towards her, shrinking before her eyes until she was level with Eilean's five-foot-seven height. The Queen pressed a finger to the spiral necklace that hung from Eilean's neck.

"Have you ever wondered why you set a spiral into your work?" Danu asked, her gaze rising to Eilean's. "Or why your Mamó gave you one and bid you wear it every day?"

Eilean wanted to respond and say it was because spirals were a pleasant image, but that would have been a lie. She remembered what her Mamó had told her the day she'd given her the necklace.

"*This spiral is more powerful than you know,*" Mamó had said as she did up the clasp. "*It protects your very soul from the cruelest of nights and brightest of days, and will never falter. You too must respect its gift by living the life it is protecting.*"

Eilean hadn't thought of Mamó's words much then. She was always spouting things like that to her. Old wives' tales and folklore stories were a staple in the MacAlistair home. But maybe…

Returning Danu's gaze, she played those words over in her head again and again. "How do you know all this?"

"Your family has been connected to this world for centuries, one of the few left with a history and power connected to the Gods." Danu leaned in closer. "It is why you have been brought here."

Eilean was not liking where this was going. She scanned

the area as subtly as possible to find an escape. Most of it was wood-like. Maybe she could hide among the trees if she distracted them.

"Look, I really don't know what you're getting at here but like I said, you've got the wrong person." Eilean found a low branch in an oak tree that hung above the river. If she climbed fast enough, she could get out of range from the evil horse. "I don't know how you know what you do, but someone gave you the wrong details."

"I do not think so," Danu said. "As you scanned our surroundings to escape—" *dammit,* Eilean thought, "what did you notice?"

Taking a deep breath, Eilean decided to play along. She'd been caught out after all. No point in angering a goddess or hallucination by trying to play dumb.

"You've a lot of vegetation and land mass that has been well looked after," Eilean began. "There's a lot of biodiversity here that looks like it helps keep everything thriving." She glanced to look around the wooded area. "Everything's so... natural. Like you've barely touched it at all. It's all just growing where it wants and balancing itself out. Like I said before, it's beautiful."

"What else?" Danu questioned.

Eilean hummed. "I don't know. Everything here looks pretty normal for a forest. Or, at least, a forest that hasn't been affected by pollution."

"What do you hear, Eilean?" Danu pushed, an urgency to her voice. "What do you see beyond the trees?"

Holding back a sigh, Eilean gave the land her full attention.

The trees were no higher than the ones at the loch back home, though unlike the uniformity of the bi-yearly trim, here they'd been left to grow free. Empty twig nests hung on their branches, and a muddied path of sparse hoof and paw prints lined the space between them. Eilean let out a breath and glanced back at Danu. "There's nothing there."

Danu stared at her. Her intense gaze made Eilean feel uneasy. It was as if she were waiting for her to get something.

And then it hit her.

"There's nothing there." Eilean took a step toward the tree she'd considered climbing and stared up at the bed of twigs. "The birds' nests are empty in spring; that never happens. And I've not seen any bees in the flowers either." Eilean turned to Danu. "How is this place still alive? Forests can't thrive without wildlife."

"And without my power, it would have faded by now," Danu stated plainly.

Eilean ran a hand through her hair. "Okay. But what does this place not having birds have to do with why I'm here?"

"It has everything to do with you being here," Danu said. "Last Spring. That was when our creatures began to disappear. My husband, Cernunnos, is the Lord of All Wild Things and, as they went missing, his fear of what it meant grew. As well as his illness."

Eilean nodded in understanding. Her Mamó had fallen sick last summer. She understood the pain that Danu was going through. It felt weird to have something in common with a God.

Danu continued. "Cernunnos went in search of his animals in the farthest reaches of our lands. Whatever he did, it returned them home—for a time. But he did not come with them. And without him, without his power, whatever had caused them to leave returned. And since then…" She gestured to the empty land.

"Okay, I swear, I'm not trying to be rude, but, again, what does that have to do with me?"

Danu grimaced. "When his creatures first returned, they had no recollection of what had drawn them to that place or how they were freed. All they can recall are the last words of Cernunnos. He called for a mortal to come to his aid." The Queen gazed down at Eilean. "And here you are."

Eilean swallowed hard. "This is real, isn't it?"

Danu rested a hand on her shoulder. "It is, yes. The Lord of the Wild has called you to him."

"But why now? I mean, you said this happened last spring, right? I just came back to Balloch. Shouldn't someone have dealt with this last year?"

"One tried..." Danu began but never finished her sentence.

"Okay, cool, so they failed, let's just get another clearly unqualified person to fix it. I mean, come on, like, why didn't you go after him?"

Eilean almost regretted the question the moment it came out of her mouth. Danu's eyes shimmered with what Eilean could only assume to be tears.

"I am all that is keeping this world, and yours, from collapsing," she whispered. "It is my magic and my domain over the natural world that is keeping the balance. If I were to leave, if I were to lose focus on keeping order..."

That was when Eilean remembered the fog over the loch. The trees and bushes that hadn't grown their springlike color. Scotland wasn't exactly known for its great weather, but that hadn't been normal. Eilean remembered then about the flood warnings, and even a forest fire from last summer, and wondered if it was connected somehow.

"I'm sorry, Danu, I didn't mean to imply—"

"It is fine, young one. But you must understand the urgency. It is why you are here." Danu rubbed at her temple. Eilean wouldn't have thought it was possible for a God to get a headache, but it seemed to be the case. "Things have changed with the impending Equinox. Each Spring we are reborn anew and regain the strength to continue our support of this world and yours. If Cernunnos does not return by then..."

"That doesn't explain why me, though. I'm nothing, I'm-I'm just a teenager, for crying out loud. I'm not important."

"And yet, you are no ordinary mortal." Danu offered her a

smile. "Only those with the blood of the Celts, connected to an ancestral power, can find us."

"Ancestral power? Danu, this is—"

"I know it is a lot, my child, but our time is short." Danu was close to tears. "Our rebirth arrives soon and if he is not freed..." She shook her head. "I must know... will you accept his call?"

Eilean bit her lip in thought. She had no idea how to feel about what was being asked of her. She didn't even know how to process that Gods were actually real. Only when Danu stepped away from her to give her space, did she find herself able to breathe.

She thought of what she'd seen here. Remembered the similar weird things back at the loch, the flowers that hadn't bloomed and the weirder-than-usual weather, and wondered if it was connected. Her Mamó would be able to tell what was going on, if she was herself.

That was when Eilean thought of the sweets in her shoe on the loch bank that she'd bought for Mamó. She may not remember her, but she couldn't leave her waiting.

"I—" Eilean swallowed hard. "I'd like to go home, please."

Danu and Bhradain blinked in surprise.

"I am sorry, Eilean," Danu said. "I am not sure I understand your answer."

"I'd like to go home," Eilean repeated as she nervously tucked her hands into her pockets. "I'm sorry. I-I'm not the right person for this. Please, take me back."

"Why you little—" Bhradain snapped, seemingly ready to tear her to shreds before Danu raised a hand to him. The kelpie stepped back, abiding the silent command. It didn't stop him from glaring at her, though.

"I understand, Eilean." Danu dipped her head in her own version of a bow. "I am sorry you feel this way. Bhradain will return you home, *safely and in one piece,* and we will not disturb you again."

Bhradain snorted angrily but said nothing.

Eilean wiped away a bead of sweat that had formed across her brow as the Goddess gestured towards the nearby pool of water. Her heart raced in her chest when Danu grew to her full height once more. The smile on her face did nothing to calm Eilean down.

"Hold your breath," Danu said, "and if you ever wish to return, go to the water."

Before Eilean could respond, she found herself knocked off her feet and plunged into the river's pristine water, drowning all over again.

9

THE NOT-A-CULT OF LOCH LOMOND

Coming back from a near drowning was as awful as it sounded. Eilean's throat burned. Her chest was tight, and she barely had enough strength to swim to the surface after Bhradain had abandoned her in the depths.

Breaking through the surface, she took in a huge breath, nearly swallowing the loch with it. Struggling with the weight of her soaking clothes, Eilean tried to catch her bearings. The fog was still heavy in the air but, in the distance, Eilean could make out the edge of the shore. She began to slowly swim toward it as she processed everything that had happened.

Eilean still wasn't sure if she'd imagined the whole thing or not. From how much her chest burned and how deep under she'd been, it was possible it had been a near-death fever dream of some kind. But the child had been nowhere in sight, unless Eilean had really failed to save them. She had no idea what to think. Nothing about what happened made sense. Eilean just kept swimming, hoping that when she got to shore and warmed up a bit, her frazzled mind would give her the pieces of what happened.

How was she going to explain to her parents why she was soaking wet? With how hard her teeth were chattering, she'd probably get pneumonia and ruin the entire trip. Eilean couldn't exactly be honest when she wasn't sure herself. She definitely couldn't claim that she was kidnapped by a Goddess and her bitchy horse. That was a sure-fire way to really get thrown into an institution—or at least grounded.

As she reached the shallows, Eilean was still thinking about what story she would need to tell when she noticed someone standing on the beach. She couldn't see who it was, but it seemed obvious that they were waiting for her, if the awkward wave in her direction was anything to go by.

Coming closer, Eilean recognized the girl.

It was the one from the shop. The one who, unexpectedly, was part of Chloe's lot. Though she had at least tried to get them to leave Eilean alone—Freya, she remembered she was called. Freya stood awkwardly, hands tucked into her jean pockets as she shuffled back and forth on her feet.

When Eilean clambered up the bank and out of the water, she noticed how quickly Freya stepped away from her. She tried not to feel offended as she worked to shake out the worst of the water from her hair.

"Did you follow me all the way from town?" Eilean asked as she slipped her shoes on.

"Yes," Freya said in a surprisingly gentle tone compared to the teasing one in the shop or her nervous one with Chloe. Her voice was so soft that it sounded like velvet. Eilean had no idea a voice could sound like that. "Unless you think I'm stalking you, then no."

"I don't think that."

"Then, yes." Freya tugged at a curl. "I, uh, I wanted to see if you were okay." She paused. "Are you okay?"

"Besides the near drowning I just experienced?" Eilean asked, snappier than intended. "Oh yeah, just swell."

Freya frowned. "Yeah, why were you in the water?"

"There was this kid, but then there wasn't, it's..." Eilean ran her hand through her wet hair. How would she be able to explain what happened when she didn't fully know? Had she imagined a kid and nearly drowned or had she actually met a God and a monster? She shook her head. "It doesn't matter–wait, you saw me in the water? Why didn't you come help? I was drowning."

It was quick, almost invisible, but Eilean had always been good at reading people. At the mention of going into the water, Freya's eyes flicked towards the loch and she swallowed hard. As soon as she'd reacted, Freya schooled her features.

Well, that explains that, Eilean thought.

"I'm not a lifeguard." Freya tugged at a piece of hair. "Do you need a towel? I have towels at home if you want one? You look freezing."

"Towel?" Eilean sounded like she'd never heard of a towel before. She tried not to close her eyes in embarrassment.

This is why she couldn't be around pretty girls.

"Yeah, usually used after a swim or a shower," Freya said with a cheeky smile. "Used to dry yourself. Great for stopping hypothermia for strange girls who decide to swim in ice cold lochs."

Eilean bit her lip, trying not to laugh. *She's got jokes. Great. I'm screwed.*

"I'm Freya, by the way. Though, I guess you already know that after what happened before." Freya tugged at one of her curls. "I'm sorry I couldn't stop them. That's why I came to see if you were okay."

"Oh," Eilean said. "Um, it's okay. I mean, I deserved it, so don't worry about it."

"What? No one deserves that. You—"

"I should probably head home. My Mamó's waiting for me." It was a lie, but Eilean didn't want to hash up her history. Besides, she was freezing. Moving would probably help. "Thank you for checking on me."

"My Granda's place isn't far from here." Freya blurted out. Eilean blinked at her in confusion. "He's got towels and a fireplace. You should probably warm up somewhere before trudging through town in soaked clothes."

"I appreciate the offer, but I can walk—"

"Your jeans will chafe if you walk all that way."

"I'll be fine," Eilean said as kindly as she could.

"Seriously, my Granda's place is just round the corner, it'll be better to dry off—"

"God, what's your deal?" Eilean snapped. "We don't even know each other."

"We went to school together before you..." Freya waved her free hand in the air in front of her. "Before you transferred."

That was a kind way of putting it.

"Which was years ago, so the point still stands." Eilean reached up to grip her necklace, anxiety building within her. Thankfully, the pendant's warmth and calming nature had returned, much to Eilean's relief. "Why are you helping me?"

Freya just shrugged. "Good karma, I guess."

Eilean raised an eyebrow. She couldn't quite figure this girl out. From the relaxed way she stood, hands in her pockets, shoulders pulled back into a posture no teenager had. Even her hairstyle, a collection of tight light brown Afro curls that came down just below her jaw, seemed to have been styled with ease. Eilean was as envious as she was drawn to her. Freya was objectively beautiful, no doubt about that. But she seemed to be incessantly kind, too. Unfortunately for Eilean, she was a sucker for the good girl.

"All right, fine. Where's your Granda's place?"

Freya turned and pointed toward the nearest grove of trees. "Just behind the trees there, in a small hut."

Eilean raised an eyebrow. "Your Granda lives in a cabin in the woods?"

"Yeah, he's a practicing Druid, so being in nature is kind of his thing." She glanced at Eilean. "Do you know there's still a lot of people in Britain who are pagans?"

Eilean just blinked at her. She knew about pagans but just from the videos of the people in weird outfits down at Stonehenge on the Equinox and Solstice. Eilean hoped this towel didn't come with its own white dress and demand for a virginal sacrifice.

Freya grabbed the rest of Eilean's discarded belongings from the beach, including Mamó's sweets, and started to walk away. "Come on, it's not that far. You'll be warm in no time."

"Riiight…"

I'm going to be murdered in the woods by a cult, aren't I? Eilean considered making a run for it, but seeing as Freya had her phone, jacket, and socks, she wouldn't really get that far. Especially not in soaking wet shoes and jeans. Besides, she was cold. *I'll just take the towel and go as quickly as I can.*

The two walked in awkward silence toward the cult hut. A few times Freya started to say something but stopped herself. For that, Eilean was grateful. She didn't have the energy to make small talk, not with everything that happened before still running in her head. Instead, she tried to focus on the surrounding environment.

Ahead of them, a man-made mud path appeared through the trees. Freya guided them down it, warning Eilean of certain trip hazards every so often. Eventually, the sight of a smoking chimney signaled they were close. As they were about to round a corner, Freya finally spoke more directly. "Uh, is it just me, or is that horse following us?"

"Huh?"

Eilean stopped and followed Freya's gaze. To her surprise, there was a stunning black stallion following a little way behind them. While it was confusing to see a lone horse in the middle of the woods in a town where no wild horses existed, there was something unnerving about this particular horse. The main one being that, as it walked closer to them, its hooves made no sound against the ground.

The horse stood taller than her 5'7" height, its head

towering above hers. When she cautiously placed a hand on its strong and muscled neck, she immediately pulled her hand away. Its coat wasn't the soft fur of a horse, it was wet and slimy. Like seaweed. As Eilean took in its appearance more, she noticed that it wasn't just a black stallion. It was an *all-black* stallion with even its eyes devoid of color. Eilean hadn't seen many horses in her life, but even she could tell there was something odd about this one.

"Humans are so slow."

For one, it could talk.

Both Eilean and Freya jumped back.

"Bhradain!?" Eilean hissed.

"In the flesh," the kelpie snorted in amusement. "Though please say it correctly. More emphasis on the 'A' sound. BRA-dane, not BRUH-dane. I am not your bruh."

Would it be animal abuse if I punched a kelpie? Eilean wondered. "What are you doing here? And… how are you so quiet?"

"Death is always silent." Bhradain bared his teeth in a grotesque smile. "I have been instructed to keep an eye on you, much to my disdain. My Queen thinks you are something special and in need of guidance. I think you're irritating and in need of dismissal. However, you may yet prove useful in some way." He glanced at Freya, bowing his head briefly. "You've even found yourself a Druid."

Turning to Freya, Eilean expected her to be freaking out. But what she saw was probably worse.

Freya's hands were raised in the air as if she were about to scream and run away. Instead, she began to wave them around, her whole body practically vibrating in excitement as she stared at Bhradain. She didn't look even remotely unnerved.

Who is this girl? Eilean thought incredulously.

"I know you…" Freya stepped forward excitedly.

Bhradain extended himself into a deep bow, the sort you

saw in horse shows sometimes. "I am glad to see you have grown up well, Druid, and pleased to be at your service."

"How do you know him?" Eilean asked Freya, ignoring the weird formality of the horse.

"He found me while I was lost in the woods." Freya reached out a hand to the now standing Bhradain and, after a pause, patted his neck. She didn't seem bothered by the slime. "I'd run off during my parents… during the funeral. And then this horse guided me back." Freya stopped petting Bhradain. "Why were you there?"

"I was passing by," Bhradain replied, his tail flicking behind him.

"You're a kelpie, though, right?" Freya asked. Bhradain nodded. "Have… have you seen my parents? You know, in the afterlife?"

"I do not cross into the realm of the dead."

"Oh," Freya said in a quiet voice. "That's okay. I guess if you're a kelpie, that means all the stuff my Granda talked about, with the Gods and the Otherworld, is real. And if that's real, then I can see them one day." Her energy picked back up. "Oh! That means I'm a real Druid then, right?"

Eilean couldn't believe what she was seeing. *How is she not freaking out about all this?*

"Wait," Freya turned to Eilean with an intense gaze that had Eilean considering running away. "If Bhradain is following you, then…" Freya stepped towards her. "Are you a Druid, too?"

Bhradain snorted before Eilean could even respond. "If only she were that useful." Eilean scowled at him, but he ignored her in favor of Freya. "Maybe I should have drowned *you* instead."

Freya's face paled at hearing that, but—as seemed to be her way—she deftly avoided the subject by focusing on Eilean.

"We need to see my Granda." She grabbed Eilean's hands in her eagerness. "Right now."

Eilean tugged her hands free from Freya's grip. She never liked being touched. And Freya's eagerness to do so knowing her past was more unnerving than she'd like to admit. But with Bhradain following behind them, she doubted she'd have the chance to run away from them both. For now, she'd stick with them. She still needed that towel, after all.

God, what a day.

10

TRUST YOUR ELDERS (WITHIN REASON)

The hut, as Freya had described it, was really more of a bungalow. Though from the wild flowers that grew all over it and the soft plumes of smoke rising from the chimney, it could definitely be mistaken for a set from *The Hobbit*—if it had been filmed in Scotland.

Eilean didn't even know this place existed, and she used to spend days exploring and hiking the land around the loch when she was younger. Though from the way the house blended into the surrounding nature, branches curling into the roof, vines crawling up the walls, it made sense that she had missed it.

"Granda made it himself," Freya said as they headed up the pebbled pathway to the front door. "Back when he was a teenager. It's been here since the 40's."

"He's got great craftsmanship," Eilean said, taking in the iron work of the knocker and handle.

"He'd love to hear that," Freya said, opening the door. "But maybe after you've changed." A hand clasped around her wrist, pulling her through the open door. Eilean yanked herself free at the doorway.

"Please stop grabbing me," Eilean snapped, harsher than she had intended. "I really don't like being touched."

Freya raised a hand in apology and stepped back. "S-sorry, I sometimes forget that some people aren't big on that. I'll remember it for next time." She went to the door. "Bhradain, can you wait outside for a moment?"

There was a soft nicker in response. With a smile, Freya closed the door and turned to Eilean. The two of them said nothing for a moment, just standing awkwardly. Then Eilean, shivering in her damp clothes, shuffled from side to side. "Uhm…"

"Right! Yes, a towel. First door on your right. There should be some towels in there, I'll get you some clothes to borrow."

"Thanks," Eilean said, waddling awkwardly to the room.

A few moments later Freya was knocking on the door and holding what appeared to be an old man's jumper, overalls, and a pair of Santa Dog boxers.

"They weren't used," Freya said quickly. "They were a Christmas present last year. I never took them out the packaging."

Eilean took the pile from her hands and before she could say thank you, Freya had closed the door. At least she wasn't the only one who felt awkward about the exchange. After drying and changing into her gifted outfit—Eilean started to feel a little bit more like herself. Or as much herself she could be when wearing an old man's clothes.

When she exited the bathroom and made her way down the short hallway, she found herself back in the main room of the bungalow. Freya was absent for the moment and, despite herself, Eilean began to snoop.

The house was open, with no walls blocking the view of a living room, dining space, and kitchen. Eilean instinctively found herself by the front door again, unsure if she should leave or not. She took in the space around her. There wasn't much to see really. A weathered couch, a single armchair, and a surprisingly modern television that hung above the fireplace. Even the dining area ahead of her only had a simple round table stood between the living room and kitchen. It appeared more of a dumping station than for eating. If the dinner trays tucked at the side of the sofa meant anything, it seemed Freya and her Granda spent more of their time eating in the living room than at the table.

The home didn't seem like a place made for living in. Books on folklore and mythology covered every surface space except for the couch and armchair. When Eilean took a step farther into the living room, she had to be careful of where she stepped so as to not trip on the books, or knock over one of the many potted plants. When she walked toward the kitchen, she realized that the junk on the table wasn't actually junk. In fact, as she peered closer, it appeared to be an altar. Unlit candles with figures and symbols drawn into the sides, multicolored crystals, and a strange smelling offering of some kind covered the place.

Is all this stuff magical too? Eilean thought as she reached out to touch one of the statues, before thinking better of it. No point risking the chance of being cursed.

That was when Freya and an old man appeared, heading her way from the open french-doors that led out to the brightly colored back garden. The older man had the tell-tale sun-kissed skin of a laborer, a well-groomed white beard, and a full head of white hair that framed his face. His striking blue eyes stood out as he watched her closely. Eilean figured he was Freya's Granda, mainly because he was the only man in the house, but when he offered her a smile did she know for sure. He had the same single cheek dimple.

"Wow, the overalls really suit you," Freya said, surprising Eilean.

"Uhm, thank you."

Freya grinned at her. "Eilean, this is my Granda. Granda, Eilean."

The old man reached out his hand to her. "Lovely to meet you, Eilean."

With only a brief hesitation, she took his hand. His grip was strong and fingers calloused. Soil was caked under his nails. From all the pots and the construction of the house with the vegetation, Eilean could see what Freya had meant about him loving nature.

"And you too, sir."

"No, no, no," he said with a wave of his hands. "No 'sirs' here. Please, just call me Walter."

Eilean wanted to protest at that. She'd always been taught by her parents and Mamó to address elders with respect. Never their first name. Though she supposed he was asking her to do it… it was a bit of a gray area. She ended up going with a mixed approach.

"Of course Walter, sir." Eilean cringed. "Uhm, thank you for letting me use your towels and borrow some clothes. I'll bring them back when I'm—"

"No need." Walter headed toward the armchair and sat down. "I have many just like it. If you find them comfortable, you are welcome to keep them." He gestured to the sofa. "Please, sit. You've been through an ordeal, I've heard."

"Oh," Eilean paused. "No, it's okay, I should head home."

Walter leant back in his chair. "Intent on forgetting what you saw in the Otherworld?"

Against her better judgment, Eilean frowned and took a seat on the sofa. Freya followed suit, but made sure to keep a comfortable distance between them. Eilean appreciated that.

"How do you know where I've been?" Eilean questioned. "I didn't tell Freya anything."

"You came out of the loch talking about hearing a child and were then followed by a kelpie, a carrier of the dead to the Otherworld, known for drowning its victims and taking them there," Walter smiled. "I put two and two together."

"How do you know so much?" Eilean asked.

"A story for later," Walter said, annoying Eilean to no end but she didn't argue back. Not yet, at least. "I believe you have a tale worth sharing more right now. If you wish to, of course."

Eilean wasn't really sure she wanted to. Eilean was still reeling from what happened. It didn't matter that there was a talking horse outside, part of her still questioned if what she'd seen was real. It was also pretty unnerving to be surrounded by people that she didn't know, who seemed to know a whole lot more about what happened to her than she did.

Maybe they can help me understand it all? Eilean wondered.

Not giving herself a chance to second guess, she told them everything that had happened. The sudden fog on the loch, the drowning child that disappeared, and then how she herself had been pulled under. To her surprise, she had no hesitation bringing up what came next. Walter's engaged gaze kept her talking. She told him about how she supposedly met a Goddess named Danu and that she had shown her her garden woods. It was at the end of the story, where she recounted the quest to rescue Cernunnos, that Walter's expression changed.

Where there had once been excitement and intrigue in his eyes, anxiety now took its place in the deep furrow of his brow and in how he tugged on his beard. That must've been where Freya got her nervous hair tugging habit.

Maybe she shouldn't have told him everything.

"Sir—" Eilean began, a slight stutter to her voice, "—I mean, Walter. I–I don't understand why they spoke to me about that stuff with Cernunnos. I mean, Gods should be able to deal with problems like that themselves, right?" She started to tug at her necklace. "Like, they said there was something about my ancestry but, what does that have to do with anything? And why would they ask a random kid for help?"

He stopped tugging at his beard and focused on Eilean. His eyes bored into hers, as if they were searching for something. It felt strange to have someone she didn't know staring so intensely at her. She clenched her fist around her pendant, searching for an excuse to leave, when Walter asked, "You're Ruth's granddaughter, aren't you?"

Eilean blinked in surprise. "You… you know my Mamó?"

Walter sighed. "A long time ago… we haven't been in contact for many years now. And it would be nearly fifty years since we…" He waved one of his hands in the air in front of him, just like Freya did. "We ended up walking different paths, I suppose you could say."

"Have…" Eilean started, but her voice was shaky. She thought of her Mamó in her chair, stuck in a time where no one could follow. She tried speaking again. "Have you been to see her since…" Eilean swallowed. "Since her diagnosis?"

Walter dropped her gaze, shame in his glossy eyes.

"I fear that my appearance may cause more problems than help," he said, sincere. "We didn't part on the best of terms. I admit, I was the reason we stopped talking."

"What happened?" Freya asked.

"Well." Walter scratched his cheek. "Let's just say, when your Mamó chose your Pa to marry, I wasn't the kindest." He rushed out the next part, sounding nervous, "Not because I loved her myself, Lord no, I was already with my dear Beatrice. No, it was more that, in marrying your Pa, she left a part of herself and her history behind."

That caught Eilean's attention. "What history?"

Walter chuckled lightly. To Eilean's surprise, the laugh sounded more like one of frustration than amusement. "I'm afraid that is something I cannae share."

"Granda—" Freya sounded disappointed.

He raised his hands in surrender. "I'm sorry, it's custom. I cannae break tradition. Your Mamó, Gods bless her, is the only one who decides when you are to know."

"But she can't tell me," Eilean pointed out, her voice still shaky. "Custom doesn't mean anything when the person's mind is gone."

Walter shook his head sadly. "I'm sorry, Eilean. It is a vow made among the Druids. The passing of familial knowledge should only be shared by family."

"Well I'm not a Druid, so why should I have to deal with vows?" Eilean said snippily.

"No, you're not, and neither is your Mamó, not really. But there is something special about your family line that connects you to the Druids. Your family helped many open their eyes to the truth of the world." He offered her an apologetic grimace. "I am sorry, but I cannae tell you more than that."

Eilean clenched her jaw. "Then *how* can I ever know?"

"If I know Ruth, somehow she will find a way. You'll just have to be patient for now."

I hate when adults do this, Eilean thought bitterly. *Why hint at something important if you can't actually tell me?*

"Fine," Eilean said sharply. "But that still doesn't explain what any of this God stuff has to do with me."

"Do you know much about the Celtic Gods and Heroes?" Walter asked.

Eilean shook her head. The most she knew about Celtic traditions were the folklore-based stories, like the Giants Causeway being made by Fionn Mac Cumhaill as a challenge by the Scottish giant Benandonner. But they were just fun stories to tell kids. Or at least, they used to be.

"Like most stories of heroes and myths, there is someone who goes on grand quests and adventures either for the Gods or against them," Walter began, drawing the girls in with the intensity of his words. "Whether it be because they were born special or the Gods choose them or because they act with great bravery or self-sacrifice that is seen by them, these figures end up becoming the heroes to save the day.

"Think about the stories we know," Walter said. "King Arthur, chosen by Caledfwlch, or Excalibur as we now know it, who goes on to be the hero of Britain."

"But dies young and betrayed," Freya interrupts to point

out. Eilean appreciated that even if she wasn't a fan of the implication Walter seemed to be making.

"Yes!" Walter exclaims, "and yet he is taken to Avalon, the Otherworld, to one day return in Britain's time of need."

Then why doesn't he take this crap on? Eilean thought, irritated.

She didn't care about this. There was no need for her to get a history lesson about old fairy stories which, sure, were now turning out to maybe be possibly true. That didn't matter to her. All she wanted to hear about was her Mamó. Perhaps Walter would know about this Morgan person she'd been talking to.

"Like I said, you are no Druid, that I do know." He scrunched up his features in concentration. "But there is something special within you, just like with Arthur. Something that drew you to the waters and to the Otherworld."

"A drowning child."

"Maybe so, but a part of you led you to that loch, whatever part that may be—"

"An old classmate I hurt by accident—"

"Did you feel anything before you saw the child?"

Eilean's protest died on her lips. She had. It was small, inconsequential, but she was about to leave when her necklace had grown warm against her chest. *Surely that's not...*

"When you stopped what you were doing and swam to save that child, you accepted Danu's quest to find her husband."

Eilean shook her head. "Anyone could have done—"

"And yet no one else did." Walter leaned forward. "Eilean, you were there at the right moment, saw the not-child at the right time, and met a Goddess who asked for your help."

"A dumb Goddess, clearly," Eilean said hotly. "I mean, I'm seventeen. What does a missing God have to do with me?"

Walter let out a laugh. "I don't claim to know a Goddesses mind, but only you can find out what Cernunnos' disappearance has to do with you."

"Can't they just, find someone more qualified? I mean, they

said someone had tried before, and they didn't succeed. I don't know anything about Gods or magic, how am I going to do any better?" Eilean got to her feet, sitting and talking was just making her more frustrated. "Maybe it's like Bhradain said, he should have taken Freya, or maybe you, at least someone who knows what they're doing and what's happening."

"Most heroes take companions with them on these journey's." Walter nodded, as if Eilean had made a good point without actually hearing what she'd said. "Even Fionn Mac Cumahill had a clan to support him on his adventures. And Freya would make an excellent addition, I'm sure."

"Oh totally, the Merlin to my Arthur. Let the comradic banter begin."

"You're a Merthur?" Freya asked.

"A what—?"

"Freya is a Druid, so, in a sense, yes," Walter replied, not noticing or just ignoring the sarcasm in Eilean's comments. "And if what you've said about Cernunnos is correct, you will need someone who has the power of healing, and a connection to nature."

And I'll bring my trowel, Eilean thought sarcastically. *Maybe I can dig the almighty God out of trouble.*

"Walter, sir, I don't mean to disrespect what you're saying but, I am not the right person for this. I know I'm not. A God's dying, and that sucks, but they need to call for someone else."

"Come with me." Walter said before leaving the room and heading for the back door. Eilean and Freya paused, shared a glance, and followed after him.

The garden was breathtaking. It reminded Eilean of her Mamó's own work. Colors and plant life of all kind surrounded them, some even climbed up the house walls in a remarkable pattern. If Eilean hadn't met a God, she would have thought she was imagining the image of a person-shaped figure climbing the vines that scaled the wall was in her head. Now she thought anything was possible.

"Cernunnos is the Lord of All Wild Things. He holds dominion over the land's animals and their safety. He and his wife, Danu—the Mother of Earth—are responsible for the changing of the seasons. Specifically, spring. Without them, our ecosystem, its animals and vegetation, the planet really, could collapse." Walter drew across the tips of the lavender bushes that lined the front of his garden. When he did, the purple that the name derived from, fell to the ground. Turning to dust. "I believe what you have told us is true. I have seen it by the loch, and right here in this garden." He knelt down to pick up the ash of the lavender. "Cernunnos is missing and with the Spring Equinox arriving in just three days… If he doesn't return, we will have far more to worry about than a few dying flowers."

Eilean tugged at her necklace. Danu had alluded to something similar. "But sir, that still doesn't answer my question of why they want a teenager to help them." Eilean's frustration showed in her voice. What could a teenager do to save a God? Call her mum and ask for help?

Walter offered her a sympathetic smile. "I'm sorry, but I don't have the answers for that. Only the one who called you does."

"Great, cool, got it."

Eilean didn't want to be rude but she'd had enough. Heading back through the back doors and toward the sofa. She could hear the patter of feet behind her as she went. She grabbed her pile of wet clothes and sweets that Freya had put in a bag by the sofa and pulled out her shoes. She didn't want to wear wet trainers but she would if it meant she could get out of here sooner.

"Walter, Freya." She turned to face them. She couldn't be *that* rude. "Thank you for the clean clothes and helping me not get hypothermia." She offered Walter an awkward nod. "I appreciate you not treating me like a child with an overactive imagination for all this Gods stuff, but," Eilean let out a breath of frustration, "I refused Danu's request. I said no."

The door burst open behind them, its wood splintering across the living room floor and covering the sofa, causing all three to jump away. Facing their newest arrival, Eilean had to bite back a growl.

There, glaring daggers at Eilean, stood Bhradain.

"You have severed my last nerve, mortal," the kelpie knickered angrily. "Danu may have let you refuse, but I had hoped you would have listened to your druidic elders. Even the non-magical kind."

"What is he saying?" Walter whispered to Freya, who quickly translated. Eilean noticed she left some of the harsher parts out.

"Go home, Bhradain," Eilean snapped as she stormed toward him. She considered shoving him out of the way, but with how muscular normal horses were, she didn't feel like risking a hoof to the gut. "And let me go back to mine. I made my choice. Find someone else."

Bhradain refused to move.

"I just want to go home to my Mamó," Eilean said in a far more pleading voice than she intended. "Just… let me go to her. Please."

The kelpie stared down at her. For a moment, his eyes flashed pure white like they'd been in the Otherworld. Then, with an indignant huff, he stepped out of the house and gave her room to leave. With a breath, Eilean turned back to the two Druids and gave them a sad frown. "Let me know how much it'll cost to fix the door and I'll try to cover as much as I can."

Without waiting for their answer, she left.

11

ALL YOU NEED IS A LITTLE PUSH

EILEAN KEPT HER HEAD DOWN THE WHOLE WAY HOME. EVEN as her feet complained at the chafing of her wet trainers, she never slowed down.

The moment she slipped through the front door, she'd expected to be told off by her parents for being gone so long; surprisingly, nothing happened. Walking past the open living room door to the left of the entrance, Eilean found her parents and Pa watching a football game on the TV. No wonder they'd not realized how long she'd been gone. Celtic was playing. They always had tunnel-vision when it came to Celtic.

Part of her knew it was good that, in the end, her parents hadn't been worried. That they wouldn't be mad at her for disappearing for however long she had ended up being gone. But the part that remembered how sad they were when they had to leave Balloch because of her, the part that still felt the pain when her mum flinched away from her with fear in her eyes, the part that knew her dad had considered sending her to a troubled kid's school… Those parts sparked within her as she watched them groan about a missed goal. Those parts reminded her that they were less stressed when she wasn't around.

They'd be better off without me, a voice inside her said. And Eilean couldn't disagree with it.

Leaving them alone, Eilean headed down the hallway to the farthest door on the right. The door was wide open, and Mamó sat in the same place and position as when Eilean had left her. Her green eyes stared out the window with her chin resting on her palm. The soft afternoon sun was catching her silver hair, making it appear lighter, almost white. Mamó seemed older in it.

"I've got your favorite, Mamó." Eilean came and crouched in front of the chair. "I'll make sure you get all the purple ones. I know you love them."

Mamó didn't respond. The only sign that she was even still conscious came in the form of a heavy sigh.

Eilean tried not to take the response personally. She knew Mamó wasn't being unkind. It was the dementia that was doing this. So, to keep herself sane, she opened the bag of sweets and began to sort them. The red, purple, and green went in one pile for Mamó. The yellow and orange to Eilean's pile. Eilean didn't really like the orange ones but she'd always pretended to, even as a kid, so Mamó could have her favorites.

Once she'd split the sweets, Eilean put Mamó's pile in the small bowl that laid on the table next to her chair. Sitting down on the floor in front of the armchair, just like she'd always done as a kid, Eilean unwrapped one of her own sweets and began to suck on it.

Mamó didn't reach for them. Didn't even acknowledge that they had been placed there. Her gaze stayed locked on the window, unmoving. Eilean followed her stare.

Outside the window lay the garden; the one Eilean and Mamó had worked on all the time when Eilean had lived in Balloch. The Bells-of-Ireland were the first thing Eilean could see, their soft green color caught the small rays of sunlight that broke through the clouds above and caused them to glow. Eilean wondered what about the flowers had gained her

Mamó's attention when, past the flowers and garden, she saw a black stallion standing behind the garden wall.

It was watching them. Or, more precisely, it was watching Mamó.

Eilean had mentioned Mamó in Ar Dachaidh and how she would have loved the place. Her conversation with Walter had told her of how connected to the Celtic Gods she was, though she'd seemingly stepped away from it when she married her Pa. Eilean glanced back toward her Mamó who was still staring out the window. She found herself wondering that, if Mamó had been in her position, would she have rejected the Queen's request? Eilean knew the answer immediately.

Then Mamó began to stir. She didn't acknowledge Eilean, only seeing the horse out front. Bhradain in his mortal world form.

"No," Mamó whispered. "It can't be."

"Mamó? Are you okay?"

She didn't answer her. Only staring at Bhradain who continued to stare back. Walter had said Mamó knew the Celtic world well. Did she know what Bhradain was?

That was when Eilean remembered what Freya had said. He had been at her parents' funeral. Kelpie's were carriers of death.

Is he here to take Mamó? Eilean thought, her breathing picking up in panic. *No, she's not that bad yet.* And then the worst possibility came to mind. *Is this a threat?*

Eilean grit her teeth. She leaned forward to rise, ready to storm out of the house and tell Bhradain exactly where he could shove his audacity, when Mamó suddenly gripped her wrist.

Her hold was tight and bordering on painful as she tugged Eilean back toward her. Eilean's heart raced. Sometimes people with dementia could get violent, she just never expected her Mamó to be one of them.

Eilean lowered herself to the ground in front of her Mamó,

hoping that in being lower than her she wouldn't be seen as a threat.

"Mamó?" she asked in a gentle voice.

When Eilean met Mamó's gaze, her heart almost broke. She looked terrified. Tears shimmered at the edge of her eyes as she searched the room for a threat Eilean couldn't see.

"Morgan, you cannae let her go," Mamó said, her tone low. "You cannae let them take her. You can't."

Eilean's mouth fell open. Mamó didn't sound confused like she had been earlier. She seemed afraid, but it was like she knew what was happening as she glanced out the window and toward Bhradain before catching Eilean's gaze again. There was no doubting that she was back. She was just speaking to the wrong person.

"Go…" Eilean started. "Go where?"

Mamó's grip tightened on Eilean's hand and she pulled her closer. "They have no right to put this responsibility on her, Morgan. Cernunnos can find someone else."

She knows. "How did you—"

"Make her stay here. Do not let them talk her into it."

"I don't understand what—"

"Promise me." Tears slipped down her cheeks. "Promise me they won't make her help them."

"Mamó, what do you mean?" Eilean asked in confusion. "How do you know what happened? Why do you want me to stay?"

Mamó stayed silent. She just stared at Eilean for a beat. That was when Eilean noticed her once clear vision clouding over.

"No, no, no, Mamó, what do you mean?" Eilean sat up and reached for Mamó's cheeks. "Tell me, how do you know about Cernunnos? Tell me, please."

She didn't get her answer. Her Mamó turned away from her and toward the window once more. Eilean could see the stallion still standing there, watching them.

Now Eilean had had enough.

Eilean stormed out the room. She shouted a quick "I'm going out" to her parents and rushed out the front door. The stallion watched her as she charged down the garden path toward him. Yanking open the metal gate, she stepped out and into the monster's space.

"What did you do to her?" she demanded.

"I did nothing." He flipped his slick mane. "Why? Did she say something to you?"

Eilean shoved the horse, sending him stumbling back two steps. Bhradain stared at her in surprise, his hooves *clip-clopping* back and forth for a moment before he stepped toward her again.

"Don't pull that crap with me. You tell your stupid Queen to stop screwing around and leave my Mamó out of it."

Bhradain's eyes flashed white. "Watch yourself mortal. You do not speak of the Queen that way."

"Then tell her to leave Mamó alone." Eilean's voice cracked. "It's bad enough that I have to see her like that, but to threaten me with taking her away? That's *not* okay."

The kelpie rolled his eyes. "I understand you know little of what we do, but I do not control who lives and who dies. Nor does my Queen. That is not our domain."

Eilean scoffed. "I find that hard to believe."

Bhradain stomped his hoof against the ground, the impact of it denting the concrete beneath him. "Believe me or not, I do not care." Bhradain forced Eilean to jump out of the way as he started to walk off. "I see no reason to remain if you refuse to see your use. Goodbye, mortal."

"Good riddance."

Bhradain snarled. "Watch yourself."

"Try me." Eilean's fists clenched.

"You are not worth the trouble."

"Whatever you say, mince-meat."

The kelpie rounded on her. The two stood face-to-face,

waiting for the other to make the next move. Electricity sparked at Eilean's fingertips.

"You're as bad as a pair of children."

Bhradain and Eilean turned in surprise toward the new arrival. Freya stood on the opposite side of the street, facing Eilean's home, her arms crossed across her chest. Her tightly-curled hair caught the wind, bouncing lightly in a way that drew attention to the soft browns and blacks of its color. She was wearing the same outfit as before, though this time with a light jacket and a backpack added to the ensemble. Freya looked like a cute hiker that you'd come across on the high hills of the lochs. She walked over to join them, checking both sides of the street as she did. She never uncrossed her arms.

"You both need to calm down and stop yelling at each other. Yelling never solved anything."

"But he—"

"I heard about your Mamó, but Bhradain is a creature of death. I doubt he'd have the ability to manipulate her dementia." Freya uncrossed her arms and raised them. "But, if he did, I'll help you beat him up."

Bhradain snorted in derision but said nothing.

"Thank you," Eilean sighed. "Uhm, what are you doing here by the way?"

Freya reached up to tug at her curls. "I came to say sorry about my Granda. I know he was a bit much earlier and that wasn't cool." She tugged at one of her curls. "I also wanted to check if you were okay."

"Oh." Eilean blinked. "Uhm, that's okay. I'm sorry Bhradain kicked down your door."

"I'm not," said the kelpie in question.

"Shut up," Eilean and Freya replied at the same time.

"Anyway," Freya continued. "I'm glad you're all right. You can ignore what he said." She tilted her head. "Well, not about the magic stuff, that's clearly right. But, you know, the going on this quest thing. It's not your responsibility to do it. It's..."

She brushed her hair out of her face. "It's pretty brave of you to say no."

Bhradain scoffed and Freya threw him a look.

"Thanks," Eilean said as she tucked her hands into her pockets. "I think my Mamó would agree with you."

"What do you mean?" Freya tilted her head. "Did she say something?"

Eilean rubbed at her temples. "She knows I was in the Otherworld, or, I guess, knows I was going to get there, somehow? But she told me not to go, and made someone called Morgan promise her." She shook her head. "It doesn't make any sense, how would she know what happened?"

Freya stepped toward her and reached out a hand. She stopped just before touching Eilean's shoulder, seemingly remembering what she'd said at her house. "I know I don't really know you but, whatever you do, it's your choice."

"Is it though, really?"

Eilean turned back toward her home. She could make out her parents and Pa through the living room window; it looked like Celtic had scored, if her dad leaping off the couch was anything to go by. Her gaze moved to the extension of the house. It was built in the early seventies as a place for Mamó to relax by herself. Even now it stood out from the house, like a combination of two Lego sets stuck together. It was through the extension's window that she could see Mamó watching her with that now familiar blank stare. Whether she actually was watching Eilean or not, she wasn't sure, but the sight of her eyes on her was enough to fill Eilean with the same warmth she felt when she touched her pendant.

Reaching up, she clasped her spiral necklace in her hands and felt the carving dig against the palm of her hand.

"What are you thinking?" Freya asked.

"That something isn't adding up." Eilean frowned. "My Mamó was talking to a Morgan even before I went to the Otherworld. Saying something about 'not my burden to bear'.

And now this…" she rolled her shoulders, feeling the tension growing within them. "I need to know what's going on with Mamó."

"What do you mean?"

"I'll go back to Ar Dachaidh." Eilean faced Bhradain who, to her surprise, seemed just as surprised as she felt at her decision. "I'll accept the quest."

"And I'm coming with you." Freya said matter-of-factly.

Eilean turned to Freya. "I know you said that before but, are you sure?"

"The Merlin to your Arthur, right?" Freya said. "Well, a Merlin in training, I guess. That's why I brought the first-aid kit, some snacks, and toothbrushes."

"Wow, you really prepared, huh?" Eilean said. "What I meant was, do you actually want to go? You remember how I got there, right?"

Eilean watched as Freya bit her lip and tugged at a curl. Her nervous habits were far easier to pick up than Eilean had expected. It seemed that Freya was quite the open book physically, even if she didn't actually say anything about her fears.

"Well, I do kind of owe you for not helping when you were, you know, drowning."

"Are you—"

"We've wasted enough time," Bhradain snapped. Grabbing Eilean by the strap of her dungarees with his teeth, he flung her onto his back like a sack of potatoes. Eilean nearly tumbled off by the sheer swiftness of it all. With Freya, he instead lowered himself to the ground. "Climb on."

Why didn't I get the courtesy? Eilean thought in irritation. Not that she cared about Bhradain favoring Freya. She didn't care what Bhradain thought at all…

The weight of Freya's body pressed against Eilean's back as she steadied herself on the kelpie. Eilean had to stop herself from shimmying away from her touch. She would have been okay with the light contact if it weren't for the fact that when

Bhradain moved, Freya quickly wrapped her arms around her waist.

"Sorry..." Freya said. "There's no reins or saddle, I didn't know what else—"

"It's fine," Eilean said with a tightened jaw. "You're fine."

Eilean reached forward to hold onto Bhradain's mane. It was as wet and slick as it had been before, which made getting a hold of it difficult but she did her best. If she was going to tug anyone's hair, she had no issue having it be Bhradain's.

The horse moved slowly at first and didn't say a word the whole time. Eilean was about to ask where they were going, when a pair of white eyes glanced back at her. His Otherworld form was returning...

"Hold tight, mortals." Bhradain smiled. "Your one-way journey to Ar Dachaidh is about to begin."

"One way?" Eilean and Freya asked in unison, the latter higher in pitch than her usual voice.

Bhradain never answered their question, and Eilean was too terrified to care. The monster was suddenly at a full-gallop charging ahead. Eilean only had a moment to think how he was going to get to the loch when she saw a large puddle up ahead.

Oh no.

Eilean held on tight to his mane as Freya's grip tightened around her waist. They only had a split second to scream when the kelpie leapt into the air and dove straight into the puddle.

All Eilean felt next was the crash of water against her skin before everything went black again.

12

EVERYONE HAS FEARS (NOT EVERYONE CAN FACE THEM)

Black dots covered Eilean's vision as she came to. She knew she wasn't dead, at least, she assumed she wasn't. It was still hard to tell exactly how this whole traveling to another world worked. But she felt very alive when she rolled over to vomit. Again.

"Is there a way to stop me from throwing up each time I come here?"

Bhradain snorted. "You could try not to."

Rolling her eyes, she wiped her mouth on her hand and then brushed it on the stoney ground. She stood up with a deep breath and tried to get her bearings. Eilean reached for her necklace and, finding it cold again, she knew they'd made it through. She'd have felt somewhat relieved if it weren't for the volcano.

"What the..." Eilean whispered as she took in the surrounding land.

Unlike the Ar Dachaidh she had seen when she'd first arrived, this place was completely different. There were no trees nearby. The closest ones Eilean could see were at least a few miles out. Instead of a luscious land of green and brightness, the terrain was covered in a gray haze that flowed from the nearby bubbling top of the volcano. This definitely wasn't where she had met Danu.

Eilean didn't have time to figure out what was going on or where the hell they'd ended up because, to the side, Freya was struggling to breathe.

Laying fetal on the ground, hair slick across her forehead in sweat and eyes clenched tightly closed, Freya trembled furiously as she tried to catch her breath. Eilean wondered if being in the water had given her hypothermia until she heard the choked sob.

Bhradain stood beside Freya in his Otherworld form of a green-scaled, white-eyed kelpie. He spoke in soothing tones and offered assurances of safety, but it was like she couldn't hear him. Bhradain pivoted to Eilean with a snort. Though he said nothing, his eyes said everything.

What do we do?

To be honest, Eilean wasn't sure. She'd had girls in her group therapy who suffered from panic attacks. A few of them had talked about how it felt and how it usually stopped. Some it was taking in deep breaths for five and releasing for five. Others talk to themselves, letting them know that they're safe. And some need to be held in a tight grip and talked to by others until it passes. The problem was, different people had different ways to recover. And Eilean didn't know what would work best for Freya.

"Do you have anything she could breathe into?" Eilean dropped down beside Freya, checking her over.

Bhradain grunted. "Do I look like I have pockets? No, I have nothing for her to breathe into."

"The sarcasm isn't helpful right now."

"And neither are you." Bhradain nodded to the hysterical Freya. "For the love of Danu, do something—"

"No," Freya gasped. Uncurling herself from the fetal position on the ground, she rested her head on the earth and stretched her arms out. If Eilean didn't know she was panicking, she'd think she was about to start a yoga pose. "Just... one s-second."

Freya took multiple gasping breaths she would hold for a few seconds at a time. She was trying to slow down her breathing but, from how her fingers dug into the dirt and her chest continued to heave, it wasn't working.

"What can I do?" Eilean reached out a hand to Freya's back but pulled away at the last moment. Her hands clenched and unclenched as she tried to think of how to help. She had no idea what Freya needed. "Tell me what to do."

Freya let out a shaky breath and sat back on her thighs. Her fingernails were coated with mud, but she clearly didn't care as she drew them through her hair. When she turned to Eilean, her brown eyes were glossy and red-rimmed. Her chin wobbled as she tried to hold back another fit of tears. She seemed trapped in whatever was going on in her mind. Eilean could understand that.

"C-can you hold me?" Freya stuttered out. "J-just for a bit."

With only a moment of hesitation, Eilean moved closer and sat behind her. She'd always been nervous about touching people, always afraid that she could end up hurting them by accident. But this is what Freya needed right now. Shuffling closer, she reached her arms around Freya's torso and took her hands in her own. She made sure not to hold too tightly, as though she were coddling a fragile egg. But would her loose hold be enough to comfort Freya? Eilean had no idea what to do from there, so she just started singing.

Coisich, a rùin, hù il oro
Cum do ghealdadh rium, o hi ibh o
Beir soraidh bhuam, hù il oro
Dha na Hearadh, hoch orainn o

It was the song "Come On, My Love" that Mamó always

sang to her when she was having big feelings. She would hold her and sing this quietly until Eilean calmed down. And with this song, she always did.

They sat like that for a long time. Eilean didn't even try to keep count as she held Freya's still shaking body in her arms. She could feel how hard Freya was fighting back against the panic from the deep inhales and exhales that filled the air around them.

Eventually, Freya's breathing started to work. Her chest no longer heaved in her need for air, her hands and body had stopped shaking, and even the panic-induced tears stopped. The embarrassment came soon after as Freya quickly but kindly pulled herself from Eilean's embrace and stood. Wiping her tears from her face, Freya offered her a sheepish smile.

"Sorry…" she whispered.

Eilean stood up. "Don't apologize. It's not your fault." She awkwardly patted her shoulder. "These things happen. Probably would've been better if we didn't have such a reckless driver."

Bhradain huffed in annoyance. Freya laughed loudly at that, the color coming back into her ashen cheeks. That was all Eilean needed to see to know that Freya was doing better.

"Do…" Eilean started awkwardly. She knew this was usually what you asked after something like this happened, but she wasn't sure if she should. "Do you want to talk about it?"

A heavy silence fell over them as Freya started to twist a finger through her curls. She didn't meet Eilean's gaze. "Maybe another time. But thank you… for the song and the…"

Eilean nodded and, to not make Freya feel uncomfortable, took a healthy step backward to give her a bit of space. She took the time to take in the surroundings once more. She knew she'd seen a variety in the landscape from Danu's land, Eilean just hadn't expected a volcano. To the side of them was a hot spring that Eilean could only assume was where they'd entered from. Though how they hadn't felt the heat of it, she didn't know.

"Where are we?" Freya said from behind Eilean, drawing her attention to her. Her voice sounded less shaky now.

Eilean rubbed at the back of her neck. "I have no idea."

Freya opened her mouth to say something when she suddenly froze. Her eyes were staring at something directly behind Eilean. At first Eilean thought she was just surprised about the volcano, until she noticed Bhradain bowing his head to whatever was behind her. Swallowing, Eilean slowly turned around and blitz-thought her way through exit strategies if it was a monster of some kind. Her Mamó had always told her stories about the Celtic monsters. What she had never warned Eilean about were tall, buff women.

"Freya and Eilean," the woman said with a smile that, if Eilean was correct, set off the volcano behind her. "Welcome to Mount Onyx. My name is Brigid. Shall we get started?"

13

DREAMS DO COME TRUE

If Eilean hadn't met Freya, she'd probably have considered this Brigid to be the most attractive person she'd ever seen in real life.

Everything about her screamed supermodel. From the way her makeup accentuated her brown eyes with smoky streaks and her cheekbones with a contouring skill Eilean only ever saw on professionals, it was clear she cared about her appearance. Even the leaf-wrap sling that held her left arm across her chest was color-coordinated to the same shade as her green silk dress. Yet the rest of her outfit seemed to contradict how she dressed.

Around her neck hung a pair of blacksmith goggles. The type that were often used to protect against the bright light of soldering metal, though from how loosely she wore them, it appeared they were more for aesthetic than practicality. But they were the expensive kind. The kind Eilean had always wanted. A leather apron covered her incredibly intricate gown. The kind Eilean used in her classes. It was splattered with burns, melted metal, and grease spots. Just like Eilean's always was.

"Where did you get your goggles?" Eilean stepped toward

the woman as if hypnotized. In the back of her mind she wondered if this was some kind of monster's trick, but she just had to know.

Bhradain snorted. "Mortals and their inane questions."

"Nonsense, Bhradain. I welcome the interest," Brigid spoke in a voice like butter. "I made them."

"For real?" Eilean asked. "How did you do that? I'd love to make my own. We just have the rubbish ones you get in a school science class."

"If I have the time, I shall write the instructions for you." The woman scratched at her cheek, smudging coal there. "You may need some training in magic first, there's a little infusion to get the translucence to work for the eye shield. Yours may need more protection, mine are more for the look than for safety."

"You are *so* cool," Eilean said in awe before realizing how lame she sounded. "I mean, this—"

Brigid laughed in the most delicate way possible. "Charm runs in the family, I see. Come now, this way. I've been waiting for you all." She waved a hand for them to follow her. "The soup will be cold by now, but I can warm it up easily enough."

"Wait, what was that about my family?" Eilean followed after the woman, Freya and Bhradain close behind.

The woman, who Eilean assumed must be a Goddess like Danu based on her taller-than-a-basketball-player size and appearance, didn't answer. She just guided them toward a small hut down by the base of the volcano. Streams of lava flowed beside it, but never breached the walls of the channel.

"Um, is it safe for us to be here, Miss Brigid?" Freya asked tentatively, glancing at the lava.

The Goddess paused. "I would say yes, but much of nature is unpredictable now." Brigid frowned up at the towering volcano. "LeLe has a mind of her own. She has not stepped out of line yet, but only time will tell."

"That's… reassuring," Freya swallowed.

The group kept walking. When the hut came into view, Eilean wondered if she'd died and gone to heaven. "This is your workshop!?"

Eilean ran ahead of the tall woman and the others, eyes wide as she took in the workshop every blacksmith dreamed of. The open doors held rows of handmade hanging racks that were covered in all the tools necessary for any kind of creation. Chisels, hand hammers, angle bits, spring swages, sledgehammers, and many more. And, if Eilean was right and the crosses on all the pieces were a smith's mark, they were all handcrafted. Just like the intricately made pieces that resided within. Swords, beautifully designed fences, shovels, chairs, candle holders, and even a collection of horseshoes.

Beside the shop lay an open forge. A furnace was raging near the lava flow and, from the steaming shovel that was propped beside the river, it seemed the molten rock was used as fuel for the fire. The forge appeared primed for use, burning charcoal at the ready.

"The forge is at temperature for you," Brigid said, stepping toward the forge that had been pulled right out of Eilean's dreams. "Your materials are ready; you just need to decide and begin."

"Awesome," Eilean replied, distracted. Then she clocked on. "Wait, what?"

Brigid's face shadowed. "We knew Cernunnos called for a mortal of the old Celtic line to come to his aid. I knew one would come and that they would need a weapon to protect themselves with."

"And you knew they'd be a blacksmith?" Eilean raised a brow.

"Oh, no, of course not," Brigid said. "But I follow my smiths in the mortal world to see their progress. I recognized my blessing's influence the moment Bhradain brought you to Danu."

"You've been… watching me?"

"As I watch all my smiths. You will learn much from Lawton. He and his family have had my blessing for generations. It is his work with you that notified me of your presence." Brigid frowned. "Though I suppose you may need a new mentor since returning home. I shall compile a list."

"Oh!" Freya shouted, interrupting Eilean and drawing the Goddess' attention to her. "Brigid! I remember you. Goddess of blacksmithing, wisdom, domestic animals, and er…" She tapped her head as if that would help her remember. "Fertility! I always forget that one, which is odd 'cause most Celtic figures have fertility connected to them in one way or another. But yeah, that's right, right?"

"Mmm" was all Brigid said, turning back to Eilean. "It has been a long time since I've had the chance to interact with a mortal smith. I have been watching your progress in your lessons. You have a good arm. It will serve you well in making your weapon."

"I–I don't make weapons," Eilean stuttered out.

"Nonsense." Brigid waved her hand towards the forge and a bench of different length and thickness Damascus steel appeared. "All good smiths know how to make a weapon. Or at least give it a go."

Eilean stared at the bench. She knew the material well. Most of her class used it because they, unlike her, had no fears about making weapons. Her, however? Her fists were enough of a weapon; she didn't want to know what she'd be like if she snapped with an actual one in her hands.

"Brigid, ma'am, I'm sorry, but I–I can't."

The harrumph that came from behind was so distinctly Bhradain that Eilean didn't bother to glance his way. She knew he would be like this. Eilean could only hope Brigid would understand. Smith to smith.

The Goddess stared down at Eilean. Her eyes burned like fire as she stood silent. "There is no room for second guessing in this world. You need protection, so make yours."

"You could teach me magic," Freya chimed in, seemingly trying to take away the tension. "If I can use magic, then we wouldn't need a sword to protect us, right?"

"Magic can only do so much." Brigid made a gesture and—in a terrifying moment—the ground beneath them shook. From the earth, roots rose up, curling together until eventually it formed a stool. Freya and Eilean glanced at each other in surprise. "Please, Druid, take a seat. You are not needed at this moment."

Freya's gaze dropped. She stared at the ground as she headed toward the magic stool to sit. Eilean didn't like how dismissive of Freya Brigid had been. Freya just wanted to help. And she really didn't like how hard she was pushing her to make a weapon.

"She's trying to be helpful," Eilean said. "You don't need to talk to her like that."

"Her help is noted." Brigid walked toward the materials table. "Come, you must be able to protect yourself, and your Druid. Let us make a sword."

"No."

The Goddess stopped. "Excuse me?"

"I told Danu we should have drowned another—"

"Silence, Bhradain," Brigid snapped. To Eilean's surprise, the kelpie did. Slinking off into the hut. Hopefully that meant she wouldn't have to hear anymore of his snark until they left.

"No, I won't make a sword." Eilean held herself tall, trying to make herself seem stronger than she felt. "I don't want one, I don't need one, and if you're so desperate for me to have one, you make it."

Lava burst from the top of the volcano, spitting out ash along with it. Whatever protections Brigid had put around her part of the land stopped both from reaching them here, but the explosion felt like a warning.

Brigid turned—a glow of red from the volcano surrounded her. It didn't make her look angry or even frightening.

Strangely, it made her seem vulnerable. As if the hues of disaster she couldn't control showed how small the Goddess was in the grand scheme of things.

"I do not understand you, young one," Brigid said, her voice gentle. "Nor do I understand this world I call home anymore. Things have changed since... things have become more volatile. I do not know what you'll meet out there. You need to be able to defend yourself—"

Eilean shook her head. "No, I'm sorry, but I can't—"

"Won't," Brigid interrupted. "It is not that you can't, it is simply that you will not."

"Fine," Eilean bit out. "I won't make a sword. Ever."

"I do not understand you." Brigid repeated. Her gaze wasn't one of malice, but of genuine curiosity. "You have skill within the craft, and yet you limit yourself to trinkets."

"Someone has to build belt buckles," Eilean said, reminiscent of what she'd told Mr. Lawton in her last class.

"Why do you not push yourself for more?" Brigid asked. "I am sure you, and your teacher, know that you are capable of far greater."

"I don't want more."

Freya stepped forward, joining them in the forge. "Brigid, she's told you she doesn't want a sword. Surely there's something else you can teach us that'll keep us safe here."

"There are many things I can teach you."

"Great!" Freya said with a smile. "Why don't you teach us that? Is it magic related? Merlin was always my favorite character. Oh! Could you teach me how to make a unicorn in smoke?"

Eilean let herself take a breath. Brigid's attention had been drawn away from her by Freya. The Goddess may not be interested in Freya, but maybe her pushing to be taught magic would be enough for Brigid to leave Eilean alone. She said it herself; there were many other things she could teach them. Eilean didn't need to make a weapon.

"Why would I do that?" Brigid raised an eyebrow.

"Okay, not that then, but something defensive?"

"No."

"But you just said—"

"I said there are many things I could teach you," Brigid repeated, "but it does not mean I will do so now. Magic may have its benefits, but in this world, you need more than that."

Eilean gritted her teeth. "Well, this is all we're doing. I am *not* making a weapon. If you can teach Freya magic, or hell, even me magic as a non-Druid, do that. Cause that's all I'll do."

The Goddess sighed. "Why?"

"I can just not want to make something," Eilean argued. "I don't have to give a reason."

"Yeah," Freya backed her up. It was odd, having someone who wasn't her Mamó on her side. "If she doesn't want to, she doesn't have—"

"Your support is kind," Brigid interrupted. "But your kindness will become corrosion. Just as your Granda's became yours."

A spark crackled at Eilean's fingertips. "Hey! That's totally out of order. You can't talk to her like that."

Brigid showed no signs of remorse beyond the tilt of her head. Eilean supposed she shouldn't be surprised. Her Mamó had told her tales about the Celtic Gods, and they were nothing if not complicated.

"There is much I do not know about my home now," Brigid said.

Freya glanced her way. Eilean didn't meet her gaze. Even she must now be wondering why Eilean was so against making the sword. She knew she was a blacksmith after all. Isn't that what blacksmiths make?

"You need to strengthen yourselves," the Goddess said again.

Eilean's hands shook. "Then find another way."

Brigid shook her head and headed for the table full of steel and grabbed a slab. The once regal and incredible seeming Goddess was now reduced in Eilean's eyes. All she saw was a bully. And Eilean hated bullies.

"We have one that is more effective in this world." Brigid brought the steel to Eilean, grabbed her hand, and put it to her palm. "Why are you fighting so hard against it?"

Eilean pulled her hand away as the spark that always lingered slithered down her arm and to her wrist, reaching out to the steel. She dropped it so fast it was like she'd been burned.

"Because I'm scared!"

14

THE SWORD IS NOT JUST A SWORD

THE TRUTH WAS OUT. EILEAN WANTED TO THROW UP.

"Ah," was all Brigid said in response, and that one word was almost more painful than anything else she could have said.

"So, yeah," Eilean continued, "that's… I can't make one. Teach us magic, or just Freya, if I've not got magic skills or whatever."

"There is not much I can teach there," Brigid said. "The rule of three is simple enough. What is not is how those three are bonded together. The elements chosen by the wielder must blend, and that is a roll of the dice, not something that can be taught. Which is why you must make this sword."

"I've already told you, I can't." Eilean dug her hands into her slowly drying jean pockets. "Now you've told us how to do magic, we'll be fine. So, tell us which direction we have to go."

"No."

Eilean had to stop herself from screaming. "What do you mean, no?"

Brigid hummed. "No, we need to make this sword."

"But… I mean, you heard everything I said. I can't."

"Won't, and a won't can easily be changed."

"But I can't—"

"Brigid," Freya spoke up, drawing the Goddess, and Eilean's, attention. "You can't keep pushing her; she's said no."

"I remind you again, Druid, with no intention of disrespect, you are not helping," Brigid replied.

Freya scowled. All forms of niceties fading away. "Pretty sure it's you who's not helping. Why force someone to do something?"

"Did you not face your own personal fears to come here?" Brigid asked. "You may not have been pushed to do so, your curiosity leading you here instead of an answer to a call, but you faced it all the same."

"That's different—"

"How so?" Brigid tilted her head. There was no malice in her voice. It was as if she was genuinely wondering the difference.

Freya's mouth opened and closed for a beat. "I still can't go near the water. The thought makes me want to throw up. Even getting here I..." She glanced at Eilean. "I had to be sung to just to breathe again."

"And now you're here on the other side of your struggle. Sometimes we must face our greatest fears to just acknowledge that they are there. We may not conquer them, but we may grow to understand them."

Eilean knew the Goddess was right, in some way. Freya had faced her fear for Eilean, and for the Otherworld, and here Eilean was, refusing to do the very thing that could, if Brigid was right, maybe protect them while they went to find Cernunnos. But that didn't change the facts.

"This is different," Eilean tried to argue. "I can't risk what'll happen if..."

If I have a weapon in my hands. Her mind wandered to the terrible potential futures of what her holding a sword would mean. *I can't risk anyone getting hurt because of me.*

"You love blacksmithing, yes?" Brigid asked.

Eilean frowned. "Well, yeah."

"Then think of only that." Brigid walked toward the materials table and picked up a charcoal covered notebook. "Follow my instructions and think of this as just another lesson in that which you love."

"But—"

"You will never be free of your fears if you do not face them." Brigid moved toward the forge, notebook in hand. "Use your love of the art, and then, maybe you will find yourself seeing this… *tool* in a new light."

The heat of the forge licked at Eilean's skin, warming her until her overalls were dry enough that she could move more easily. The warmth felt like home. Like she was safe surrounded by it. Eilean had always found that ironic, feeling safe in a place with fire and hammers. Yet, it was true. Being at the forge was… calming. As if the sound and heat that smothered her senses were blankets of safety. She couldn't explain it.

Maybe…

"Fine," Eilean said.

Brigid smiled. "Excellent."

"But, while I do that, you've got to tell Freya about Cernunnos and what we have to do."

The Goddess—in a very human manner—pouted. "I was to teach you—"

"You can do both," Eilean told her. "Besides, if this… if this is going to protect us at some point, we've gotta know why."

Brigid only hummed in response. A non-committal answer was all Eilean assumed she could expect.

"Forge is at temperature." Brigid gestured to the table lined with all the material Eilean could ever dream of. "Let's make a sword."

Eilean tried to ignore the thoughts in her head telling her this was a bad idea and scanned the line of material in front of her. They were all different sizes and thickness which would each provide a different outcome. She went for one that was about a meter in length and two inches in thickness.

"Why this one?" Brigid asked, her brown eyes lighting in curiosity.

"Excess length," Eilean said, holding the cool steel in hand. "It offers me more chances to work the material without the risk of making it too thin or short too soon."

Brigid nodded and gestured toward the fire pit. Eilean could see now what the Goddess meant by blessing Lawton. Her methods reminded Eilean a lot of him. He had always been more about an apprentice figuring out the answer and working on skills in one's own way than telling someone what to do.

Eilean slid the steel into the flame. "Tell us what we need to do."

"Remember to check your metal."

Eilean pulled the piece from the flame to see if it had heated enough. It hadn't. She pushed it back in. "So, where do we need to go and what do we need to do?"

Brigid stayed silent. Eilean could feel her eyes on her work. Not that she was doing anything beyond waiting for the metal to heat up. She chanced a glance to Freya, who now sat on the magic stool, watching the two of them closely.

"Brigid—" Eilean started.

"None of the other Gods noticed the problem," the Goddess said quietly. "Not to the full extent it had reached, at least. And once we had…" she brushed a hand over her injured arm, "it was too late. Cernunnos had already paid the price for our ignorance and now it is coming for us all."

"What's happening?" Freya asked.

"You noticed the missing wildlife, yes?" Brigid questioned Eilean. Eilean nodded. "Something is playing with the environment of this world and, as Lord of the Wilds, Cernunnos was most affected by it. It was why he went to find them."

Eilean pulled out the heated metal to work it once more. "Danu said something similar, but I don't get why we're here. She mentioned people had come before and they clearly failed. So, why can't you guys go to him? I know you said you can't, but, why? Like, why are you getting, you know, non-Gods to help? I mean, you've got kelpies at the beck and call—"

"I serve only one." Bhradain snapped, making Eilean jump. It seemed he'd recovered from his grumpiness over being told off by a Goddess. "I am at no one's call but hers."

Cryptic. "Okay, fine, but you're about. Same with the other Gods. Why couldn't one of you go save him?"

"Gods have many quarrels," Brigid said evasively. "We are kept to our own domains to prevent us from falling back into bad habits. Danu and Cernunnos are the only ones that can roam freely because of their responsibilities to nature. It has taken much for all of us to convince Danu to not go after him."

"Why can't she?" Freya asked curiously.

"We have already lost one God of the Wild; we cannot lose the last. There is no telling what natural disasters may follow."

"Oh," Freya said quietly. "So, um, that's why Eilean was chosen?"

Sweat trickled down Eilean's temple from the exertion of working the steel. Working in a forge was already hot work, but doing it by a volcano was even harder. She returned the slowly shaping metal to the fire.

"Of that, I am unsure," Brigid admitted. "All I know is the Lord of the Wild called for those of true Celtic ancestry to come to his aid and, as you said, while you may not be the first, here you now stand."

"Isn't it unfair to put the safety of the world on a teenager's shoulders?" Freya questioned.

Eilean paused.

"You are right; it is unfair," Brigid said directly, surprising the two teens. "But once the call is made, that is that. Now, focus on your work; you will need this sword for where you are going."

"And where is that?" Eilean questioned.

Brigid's gaze moved to the distant landscape behind them. Eilean followed her eyes but could see nothing but hilltops and trees. It was not Brigid who answered, though.

"To the end of this world," Bhradain said, his voice quieter than Eilean had ever heard it. "To where only Death is found."

"What does that mean?" Freya asked.

Bhradain returned to silence. Something that Eilean wasn't sure the kelpie was capable of. That put her on edge more than she'd have liked to admit. So, she focused on her work instead, as Brigid took over.

"Ar Dachaidh is a world of nature," Brigid responded. "While it may be an expansive world, it does have an edge. A place where all life comes to an end in one way or another."

Freya frowned and Eilean hammered away, just about paying attention as she tried not to think about what she was making. "That's still cryptic," Freya replied.

Brigid moved closer to Eilean, watching her as she worked. "Our world works in stages, like the seasons. Danu's land is spring, mine summer, and so forth. Your journey will take you through most of these realms, each changing so you can never truly be at ease—be careful of your metal." Brigid pointed to Eilean's fire pit. She pulled it out in time. "This world, I admit, is not a kind one. You will face more than just physical threats as you grow closer to the end of this world. You must be strong of mind to succeed."

"Good thing I'm in therapy," Eilean joked.

"This is no laughing matter, Eilean," the Goddess said. "Whatever has taken Cernunnos has built a barrier that is fighting to keep any that may save him out. The end of the world was a difficult place to begin with, a land near the resting place of the dead draws creatures of a similar ilk to it, but whatever being has Cernunnos is far stronger than any here have experienced."

"And you're expecting a kid to beat it?" Eilean bit out as she hammered at the metal.

Brigid didn't answer and, if Eilean were honest with herself, she was glad she hadn't. She didn't want to know. All she was here for was to figure out why her Mamó knew about Cernunnos. Maybe someone in this world knew her and had told her? Eilean considered asking Brigid about Morgan, but, as her arm began to ache, she decided against it. She had to focus on what was in front of her.

Only the sounds of the sizzling heat and the clink of her hammer against metal could be heard after that. Neither Eilean nor Freya seemed willing to ask any more questions. Too afraid to hear the answers. Eilean continued to work on her sword while Freya ate from a bowl of soup Brigid had silently provided. After that, Brigid stayed by Eilean's side, offering support and feedback.

"Not too thin now," Brigid said. "We want to be able to sharpen the tool and not have it chip." Eilean followed her instruction, hammering with less intensity to not flatten it too much. "You've a warp near the base; you need to reheat and reshape or it'll become unusable." She reshaped, fixing the flaw.

The closer her work came to the shape of a blade, the slower Eilean started to get. As much as she tried to focus on what Brigid had told her, the love of the work and not the piece, she couldn't get herself to think of anything beyond: this is a weapon.

Eilean knew she was getting closer to having something dangerous in her hands, and she was not remotely comfortable with that.

Trying not to think about it too much after normalizing and quenching, she focused on the next stage. Tempering. Steel could be incredibly fragile after hardening. So, to relieve any stresses, it goes back into the fire. Sliding the weapon into the oven, Eilean kept near the entrance to keep an eye on the color. A straw-like or bronze color is what she needed.

Heart-pounding with nerves, she stared into the fire. It felt like the world was fading out as she waited for the right moment to pull out her work.

"It is only what you choose it to be," Brigid speaks up, making Eilean jump back into the present. "See only what you want it to be. A tool, a decoration, or simply something you made only to show you could do it. It does not need to be what your mind tells you it is."

Ignoring her, Eilean pulled out the tempered blade. Letting it cool, and giving herself a moment to hydrate, Eilean moved onto the last two stages. Grinding and sanding to remove any scale and to polish and sharpen. That was to shine up the steel from all the heat treatment work and, as Eilean feared, make the blade more of a blade.

The moment she'd finished, hours later, Eilean stepped straight away from the blade and focused on the less frightening parts. The finishing touches: the hilt, guard, and pommel.

While she shaped the wooden guard, Eilean wondered how long she had been working. Most sword projects her classmates had done could take, at length, a week, and at its fastest, two or three days. Her body was aching, and she was close to finishing, but the sun in the sky hadn't changed position. It stayed bright the whole time, minus the smoke that rimmed the volcano's tip.

"Danu said that Cernunnos had until the Equinox before he regenerates or something, how much time do we have?"

Brigid glanced up at the sky. "A fortnight."

"Two weeks?" Eilean slid the pommel into place. "But, it… it was two days when we left Balloch. How is it longer here?"

"Time moves differently."

Eilean was getting a headache just thinking about it. "I know, I just… I thought it was a little more urgent."

"Just because you have time does not make the urgency any less."

Brigid stepped forward and picked up the now complete weapon. She moved the blade around, looked down its length with a sharp eye, and clenched and unclenched her hands around the handle. "Why the spiral?"

"Hm?"

The Goddess spun the sword around to show her the pommel. Carved into the cap at the base of the handle was the image of a spiral. The same spiral Eilean always put into her work. The same spiral that was on her now useless necklace.

"I suppose I did tell you to put yourself into the work," Brigid mused. "It is a fine craftsmanship mark. Even if the sword itself is rather crude." She ran a hand across the center of the blade. "You have also failed to work out enough of the imperfections within the center of the blade. Nor is it a particularly straight line."

Eilean was drenched in sweat. Her muscles ached in places they hadn't ached before. The overalls that had been Walter's were covered in ash and grime which meant her face likely was as well. She must've looked like a right mess and yet, at the critique of her work, that didn't matter.

Her hard work was useless.

"That's unfair!" Freya shouted from behind them. The two smiths turned toward her. "Eilean's spent hours working on this—"

"Brigid's right," Eilean cut her off. "I should have done better."

The Goddess nodded and offered Eilean back the sword. Or *her* sword, she guessed. "Do not be discouraged. You have found success in the attempt. You, young smith, created something you believed you never would. It may be imperfect, but, as you know, nothing is ever without fault. And contrary to what you humans often believe, few things are unfixable."

Eilean took the sword from her and felt the weight of the blade in her hand properly for the first time. Surprisingly, the sword felt comfortable in her grip. Even without the leather she'd wanted to include. The guard she had made laid gently against her skin, comfortable protection for her hand. The spiral on the pommel, her usual signature on her work, suited the sword well. Less like a signature and more like an ingrained part of its character. As she watched the light catch the sword, she couldn't help but smile. It may be crude, but it was something *she* made.

"What will you name it?" Freya asked her.

"Uh..." Eilean tilted her head. "I hadn't really thought about it."

"All swords have names, I mean, people even name cars," Freya lowered her voice. "And maybe naming it will make it feel a little less... intimidating."

Freya's words reminded Eilean of what her therapist had told her once. If you name your fear, you're one step closer to conquering it. Maybe this was just one of those things. Now she just needed to think of the name—

"Phobia," Eilean said, the name coming to her faster than she'd have thought possible.

"That is...," Freya started, a frown between her eyebrows that she was fighting to hide.

Eilean had expected a comment on her choice from Bhradain, but, still, he remained silent. He stood within Brigid's hut, and his gaze caught on somewhere in the distance.

"A fine name," Brigid interrupted. "Now, Druid, for your supplies."

As Brigid spoke to Freya, Eilean twisted Phobia this way and that in her left hand, feeling the movement of the sword.

She didn't know how to use the weapon, but she knew how they used them in TV shows.

Eilean reached out her right hand to hold the base of the handle, gripping it as if she were one of King Arthur's knights. A familiar ringing started in her ears as her hands shook. A flash of electricity shot from the tip of the sword toward her hand on the hilt.

Eilean dropped the sword.

Both Freya and Brigid stared at her in confusion. She didn't make eye contact with them. Afraid of what they'd see within her gaze as the electric feeling continued to thrum within her. When Brigid continued speaking, Eilean wondered if she was imagining the lingering charge on her fingertips.

"I have collected some water bottles and food you can cook on your journey. I have also left you my old tool-kit to keep Phobia well oiled so she may not rust or be damaged. It is all with Bhradain." The kelpie in question, though still quiet, stood with a saddle atop his back and a collection of supplies in a saddlebag. "For now, I think a wash and a change of clothes for you both are in order."

"Shouldn't we be moving on?" Eilean questioned. "I mean, we've wasted enough time here as it is."

"You are a strange one," Brigid said, surprising Eilean. "You refused Danu not too long ago and now you wish to move faster. Mortals are fickle creatures indeed."

Eilean clenched her jaw. "Fine, let's clean up then."

The two of them were sent to opposite sides of the huts to an unexpected changing room. Eilean's held a shower which, she assumed, was needed considering all her work. She was glad that the ash falling from the volcano was kept away from the forge. She couldn't imagine how long it would take to clean if she was ashy, too. Or how hard it would have been to breathe, surrounded by it all.

After changing, Eilean stepped out from the hut in her new outfit. The shirt had been heavier than expected, especially given it was a sleeveless top. It had only taken her a moment to realize that, if the feel of the material could be trusted, it had been lined with chain-mail. She didn't want to think about why that had been given to her. The other uncomfortable element of the outfit was the sleeveless top. Eilean didn't like showing off her arms. She tried to hide her physicality as much as she could. People who knew her were already distrustful. There was no need to make them more afraid. *What will Freya think when she sees me?* Eilean fretted, worried she'd make her uncomfortable.

It was why she had not worn the belt that Phobia would attach to. The sword was already sheathed inside a scabbard Brigid had given her. As she held the leather casing in her hand, she considered abandoning the item entirely but decided against it. She didn't want to risk facing a Goddesses' wrath. Thankfully for her, Bhradain had the saddle to carry their stuff. She could hang Phobia on him and never have to worry about it again.

"You look nice," Freya said from behind her, drawing Eilean's attention.

She almost forgot to breathe when she saw her. A cream cotton shirt hung loosely on Freya's body in a way that looked both deliberate and natural. She wore a pair of blue cotton trousers, evidently comfortable by the way she had tucked her hands into the pockets with a smile. Pockets made everything better. What stood out most to Eilean was how her hair had been pulled back into an intricate interlaced braid that showed off her face, accentuating her cheekbones and pink lips.

"Do I look okay?" Freya asked nervously.

Eilean smiled. "You look amazing."

Bhradain snorted a laugh, disturbing the moment. Eilean was pulled back to reality. She had a sword in her hand and was going, quite literally, into the unknown.

"Where do we go from here?" Eilean asked the Goddess.

"To the forest at the border of my land," Brigid pointed to a line of greenery a mile or two away. "Once you pass through there, follow the changing climates until you find the land of death."

"Yeah, you keep saying, going to the end, land of death, etcetera," Eilean said, irritated by the lack of a straight answer. "But you haven't actually given us a location. Where do we have to go?"

Brigid didn't answer this question. But Bhradain did, through a quiver of fear that Eilean never thought she'd hear from a monster. "The Withering Woods."

15

LOOK OUT FOR THAT—

Bhradain was a terrible tour guide. They had only been traveling for, Eilean guessed, around two hours and she already wanted to turn the kelpie into a minced kel-*pie*. Have a question about where they're headed? Receive a sarcastic comment. Ask about where to use the toilet? Cue eye roll. Question why he isn't carrying them to the Withering Woods? Get a lecture on the importance of rest for horses. The only time he would properly answer a question was when it came from Freya who happily walked alongside him.

"How long have you lived here?" Freya asked as she patted his scaly neck affectionately.

Eilean held back a shiver. She'd have thought Freya would have been put off being close to the kelpie when she saw his Otherworld form. His once beautiful black stallion image was now a nightmarish Cthulhu-like horror. Eilean couldn't remotely understand how Freya could so easily interact with him.

"That depends on what time you want to go by," Bhradain responded. "If I were to measure based on the mortal timeline, it would be around four millennia. By this realm, it would be since its creation… and even I do not know when that was."

"Huh," Freya said. "You sound young for your age."

This girl is so weird, Eilean thought. Freya was afraid of water and yet she seemed to enjoy the company of a kelpie. A watery death horse. How was she not unsettled?

Eilean definitely was.

Everything about this world felt… out of place. When the Goddess had first directed them toward this forest, Eilean had expected it to be similar to the ones back home. A nature reserve with hundreds upon hundreds of trees, rows of bushes, and woodland creatures. Sort of like what she'd seen with Danu. But no. Instead, it was a rainforest—a humid and oppressive feeling rainforest. Eilean usually lived for walking amongst nature, but right now she wondered if she just loved being in Scotland.

Eilean held back a sigh. She had enjoyed the folklore stories of the Celts and the Otherworld that her Mamó would tell her when she was younger. She would even beg to hear the stories. Yet, here she was, in the Otherworld Mamó had always talked about, and now all Eilean wanted to do was to go home. To go see Mamó, to understand what had made her so afraid before. To understand how she'd known about Cernunnos. To know who this Morgan she was pleading with was. Eilean hoped that maybe being here, taking on this quest or whatever, would help give her the answers.

She just had no idea how to go about finding them.

"Jesus Christ," Eilean whined quietly.

"Not around these parts," Bhradain snarked.

Eilean rolled her eyes. Eilean hurried forward to catch up with the other two, avoiding Bhradain's hindquarters. She wouldn't risk getting on the wrong end of those hooves.

Eilean tugged at her shirt. Sweat was already trickling down her chest and back uncomfortably. She was grateful for the sleeveless top until she considered the possibility of mosquitos.

"Why's it so hot?" she asked.

"Because it is," Bhradain replied.

Stupid goddamn horse.

"How long do you think it'll take us to get to this Withering Woods place?" Freya asked suddenly. Eilean had a feeling she was trying to play mediator between her and the kelpie.

Bhradain hummed. "That will depend on how fast the two of you can travel. We immortal beings can move faster than your human flesh allows you, so for me it'd be a day." He flipped his mane. "For yourselves, it could be much longer."

"I'm pretty good at running." Freya smiled at Eilean over her shoulder. "So were you, right?" She turned back to Bhradain. "We were always picked for the track races on sports day."

"Did you both travel around three hundred miles for these races?"

That stopped Eilean in her tracks. "Three *hundred* miles?"

Bhradain snorted. "Give or take. Our world is immeasurable, often considered to be never ending. It is difficult to know."

"You want us to walk hundreds of miles in two weeks? How many days does it take to get there, then? 'Cause there is no chance we're doing that."

The kelpie kept walking, ignoring her question entirely.

"Technically," Freya started. "For people who are fit like us, you know, in the health-sense, it's not as bad as it sounds. If we manage to walk about 21.42 miles a day, we could do it. It'll depend on the terrain we come across." Eilean raised an eyebrow at her. "Sorry, I ran a D&D campaign and worked stuff like this out for realism reasons. Silly stuff like this is what sticks in my brain."

"That's not silly," Eilean told her. "It's pretty cool."

"Yeah?"

"Yeah."

The two pause for a beat, enjoying the solidarity of being

able to comfortably be nerds together, before Eilean remembered the situation they were in.

"How is the journey, Bhradain?" she asked. "Is it all flatlands or?"

"It varies," Bhradain replied unhelpfully. "You will both have to adjust as we go."

"So you won't give us a ride because your horsy legs will get tired? But you expect a pair of humans to walk that length in two weeks, dealing with changes in terrain, and possible monsters along the way?" Eilean scoffed. "Yeah, 'cause that makes sense."

"I do not have the energy to explain my reasons to your minuscule mortal brain," Bhradain snorted. "That is the way it is. Accept it."

"Guys," Freya said gently. "This isn't something to argue over. Bhradain, it's a valid question. Why can't you carry us? Couldn't you at least part of the way?"

The kelpie let out a huff of frustration but didn't argue back with Freya. "While this may be the world I am from, outside of the water, I am not as strong. I cannot travel at the speeds I can within the waves."

"Can't you just jump through another puddle? Get us closer to the woods?" Eilean asked. Then she saw Freya pale and remembered her fear.

Bhradain, thankfully, made no comment. "There… there is something that has stopped me from traveling like I normally do in Ar Dachaidh." His tail flicked nervously.

"This is one of the things Danu meant about this place changing, isn't it?" Eilean asked.

The kelpie ignored her, whether for his own paralyzing fears or out of spite, she didn't know. "Either way," he said, "water or no water, you will want me at my strongest. There is no telling what monsters we may encounter. It is also why you should keep that sword of yours close to you and not on my back. Now, come on, we have already wasted two of our days for that sword of yours. We must get moving."

"Two days? But it didn't feel like—"

Bhradain gave her a look. Eilean closed her mouth. She'd been told by the horse, Brigid, and even Freya's grandfather about how differently time works here. She didn't need to give the kelpie a chance to give her a lecture.

"Okay, so 25 miles a day," Freya said, her voice high in pitch as if she were trying to lighten the tension. "We can totally do that. Damn, I should have brought my FitBit. I bet we would have broken a record."

"Totally," Eilean said, trying to put some enthusiasm in her voice. She could appreciate Freya's attempt. She fell back behind the pair to follow their trodden path in the grass. "So, which way do we go?"

"Just walk straight and you will find the right path," Bhradain said.

Eilean rolled her eyes at the philosophical-sounding words.

Freya and Bhradain continued on with their former conversation about the work of kelpies as if they'd never been interrupted. Eilean considered joining in. Her mum's voice reminded her that it's good to be sociable. Healthy even. But Eilean kept behind them. She was here for Mamó. No need to do more than the bare minimum. This wasn't a time to make friends.

"Have you read anything to do with the Otherworld before?" Freya said from beside her, making Eilean jump. She hadn't seen her move back to join her. "I know quite a bit from my Granda and books, so like, if you have any questions—"

"My Mamó told me stories," Eilean interrupted, cringing slightly at her rudeness. "Though she didn't tell me too much about the Otherworld. Just the usual hero and god stories, though she told me a lot about the symbols, especially spirals."

"Right, of course," Freya said apologetically. "Sorry, I

should have figured. That necklace of yours is a spiral of life image, right?" Eilean nodded. "Well, I guess it's technically the single spiral. The Triskelion is technically the main spiral of life, but I kind of like this one more. Like, the spiral itself means growth, while the gaps between the spiral represent life, death, and rebirth. So much more to analyze about it. Also, who doesn't love growth? I could do with another growth spurt."

Freya laughed at her joke and Eilean offered her a smile in return to not hurt her feelings. She was starting to get the feeling that Freya was the nervous talker kind of person. Eilean couldn't stand making conversation for the sake of conversation, but to be civil, she let her go on.

"Oh crap, you probably already knew all that." Freya tugged at her new braid. "Sorry, I just… well, I'm just really into this stuff. I've read so many books and heard so many different stories and interpretations that… sorry."

"It's fine," Eilean said. "I didn't know about the Triskelion stuff."

"Do you want to know about the other symbols I know about?" Freya asked.

"Maybe later."

The two of them walked in silence for only a few steps at most before Freya started talking again.

"I wonder what kind of plant life is here," Freya said. "It's very rainforest-esque. Do you think there will be anything dangerous? Like, human-eating fly traps or something?"

"I hope not," Eilean said. "From what I do know about the Otherworld, it's a place of chaos. But chaos doesn't necessarily mean, like, murderous monsters or something. I doubt there's anything that'll want to kill us."

"Not intentionally," Bhradain chimed in.

Freya and Eilean stopped in place.

"What do you mean?" Freya asked him.

"You are right that Ar Dachaidh is a land of chaos, while also being one of order. While nothing here will be openly hostile, accidents and anomalies can happen." Bhradain continued walking. "Just keep an eye out and you should be fine."

"Yeah, because that's reassuring," Eilean said with a roll of her eyes before following after the horse. She considered getting Phobia from his saddle bag, but she still wasn't ready to have a weapon in her hands.

She decided it was the smarter plan to just follow his path. That way, they would be in less danger of stumbling into any "accidents." Besides, Eilean didn't recognize many of the plants here. Most of her knowledge of botany from Mamó involved what they could grow in the garden or what they saw when exploring the lochs and moors. Sure, Eilean knew about Cacao and Monkey Brush Vines that grew in the Amazon, but there was nothing in this forest that felt familiar. Unlike in most tropical landscapes, this one didn't match.

While there were the usual bright, sometimes sickly green, colored leaves and plant life, there were no other colors around. No reds, yellows, or oranges that would usually be found in tropical atmospheres. There were some that seemed to have originally been brighter colors, but it was as if the color had been wiped clear from the leaves, like from a printer that had run out of ink. Black lines and smudges spread across those rows of vegetation. So much to see and so little understanding. Eilean made sure to avoid the plant life as best she could. As Mamó always said, "if you don't know it, don't touch it."

Eilean fully believed Mamó should've had a show like Bear Grylls but for plants. She'd even tried to film an episode for fun on her phone one year when she was younger. It turned out Mamó was not made for showbiz. She was as stiff as a board in front of a camera.

"What are you thinking about?" Freya asked, surprising Eilean again.

"Uh, nothing much, just something about my Mamó."

Eilean went silent and hoped Freya would walk away. She didn't. "You know, you can go walk and talk with Bhradain. I'm okay by myself."

"I don't mind walking with you."

Eilean rubbed at the back of her neck before dropping her arm to her side. "I know, but, I'm fine—"

"You're a solitary creature, I get it." Freya skipped ahead and spun around to face her, walking backwards. "I just want you to know I'm here to listen… or walk in silence. Whatever you want."

"Thanks, Freya," Eilean said as sincerely as she could, "but I promise, I'm fine."

It was clear that Freya wasn't convinced, if the narrowing of her eyes meant anything. Thankfully for Eilean, she dropped it. For now, at least. Eilean watched as she shrugged and spun back around, leaving Eilean to her own thoughts. Thoughts that were focused entirely on Freya as she tripped, heading right for a bush full of heart-shaped green leaves with jagged edges like teeth.

"If you don't know it, don't touch it," Mamó's voice came to her again.

But Freya was about to touch it. She was about to outright fall into it! Eilean sprinted forwards, grabbing Freya by the waist and yanking her away from the jagged-edged plant. She managed to keep her upright and in the center of the pathway Bhradain had told them to keep to.

Freya stared at her in surprise. "Eilean—"

And then the burning started.

Eilean couldn't even hear the scream she let out. She only knew she had because of the scratching that formed in her throat from how loud she must have been. The burning pain that welled up across her right arm, the one she'd grabbed Freya with, was so overwhelming that she could not feel, hear, or see anything but pain.

Reality turned into a dream. Or more like a nightmare,

with the heat that coursed through her. Sweat poured down Eilean's face. Or maybe that was tears? She didn't know.

The burning grew and now Eilean could hear herself screaming. The sound burst through the blur of pain and echoed so loudly she thought her ears must be bleeding.

Her breathing came in short gasps. Her heart was beating hard—violent and hammering. A weight pressed down on her, keeping her heart from pounding straight out of her chest.

"Bhradain," a distant voice said. "Get the medical supplies."

The voice sounded like Freya's.

A cold wetness on her burning arm drew her attention, but she couldn't open her eyes to see. The pain from heat and cold made her clench her jaw so hard she feared she'd crack her teeth.

"What do I do?" Eilean heard Freya say. "How do I help her?"

"Power of three, Freya," a distorted voice said. "Druid…"

Everything went quiet. Eilean felt something grab her wrist, holding her down. She tried to pull away, but she couldn't move. A warmth covered her arm in a sticky substance. Then she felt a tearing across her skin. A paste that tugged hard at her flesh and had her screaming all over again.

Remember how he screamed in agony, too? A melodic voice whispered into Eilean's mind as a relay of bloody fists, cracked jaws, and flashing lights overwhelmed her.

Eilean fell into unconsciousness.

16

SOMETIMES YOU NEED TO ACCEPT A HELPING HAND

WHEN EILEAN OPENED HER EYES, ALL SHE COULD SEE WAS a collection of bright dots. Blinking rapidly, she tried to remove the image before realizing it wasn't her eyes that were casting them. She was staring up at the starry-night sky.

Eilean had never seen stars like this before. Everywhere she looked, the sky above speckled with light. She tracked constellations she'd only ever been able to see in pictures: The Ophiuchus, the Hercules, even the Lyra and Corvus.

She had no idea how long she'd been staring blankly up at the starry sky when she heard a scuffle from beside her. Then, where the stars had once been, appeared Freya's face.

The stars framed her head, sharpening Eilean's awareness instantly.

"Are you okay? How are you feeling? Does anything hurt? Are you thirsty?"

Eilean couldn't make out much of Freya's features in the dark of night, but she could guess how she was looking by the sound of her voice. Scared and worried.

"Which one first?" Eilean asked in a voice that was croakier than she expected.

"Right, sorry," Freya said with a breath of relief. "Too many questions. How are you feeling?"

Eilean let out a soft groan in reply. Those three words seemed to have taken it out of her. She still tried, though.

"Wha..." was all she could get out.

"What happened?" Freya finished for her. Eilean could only nod. "Dendrocnide moroides. Or, as Bhradain unhelpfully described it, really bad stinging nettles."

Understatement much, Eilean thought irritably.

"A gross understatement," Freya said, as if reading Eilean's mind. "I mean, you were burning up from the pain and have been out of it for... well, I don't really know how long, but it got dark while you were unconscious."

Eilean tilted her head toward her right arm and, to her surprise, instead of seeing the damage that she had expected to be there, she found her forearm covered in a strange pasty material. A first-aid kit sat open nearby.

Freya caught on to what she was staring at and grabbed the bag. With it closer, the white plus sign that had been there once was now a tattered mess.

Freya shook her head. "My Granda will understand why I ripped it. I wish it had a lot more useful things in it though, I had to use strips of tape to get the stingers out." Freya continued to hold the kit in her hand. "It didn't seem to do much except hurt you more, so I had to figure something else out."

Eilean nodded, silently urging Freya to continue. She wanted to know what happened to her.

Freya tugged at her braid. "I, uh, used some magic."

Eilean was glad she couldn't easily speak, as it kept her from voicing her disbelief. Not at magic itself. She'd be an idiot if she thought it wasn't real. But at Freya knowing how to do it. Unfortunately, her facial expression spoke for her.

"Remember when Brigid mentioned the power of three?" She twirled her finger through her braid. "Bhradain helped me remember what that meant. Herbology and symbolism being the main parts. Symbols especially 'cause in Celtic myth—I mean, to the Celtic Gods, they're really important." Freya held up the tattered first aid bag. "Like this first-aid kit's symbol. It is similar to the *Ailm,* a symbol associated with healing. It's not exact, but I hoped it would work and it kinda did. That's why it's on your arm."

She really rambles when she's nervous.

"For the herbology, I got Bhradain to find something soothing. It's sort of like aloe vera but an Otherworld kind. I hope you're not allergic."

That's one short, Eilean thought as she stared silently at Freya, asking her for the answer.

Freya sighed. "Don't be mad, okay?"

If Eilean could have sat up, she would have. That was never a good thing to hear.

"You know the spiral of life we were talking about before?" Eilean blinked at her. "Well, that's real too. And very literal. Bhradain told me that the spiral starts at your first breath and then, as you age, it slowly unravels until it ends at your death. It's like your lifespan, I guess."

Eilean frowned. It didn't surprise her too much that the spiral meant something in the mythology. Or reality, she supposed. She just hadn't expected the importance of it all. Her Mamó had never mentioned any of these things in her stories.

"And for Druids and other Celtic descendants, our spirals will be stronger and give us the ability to perform magic." Freya smiled slightly. "Pretty cool, right?"

Eilean used what energy she had left to turn and fully face Freya. Something was still being held back. And that made Eilean anxious.

"Except for one thing," Freya continued after a pause. "Magic has a price. I had to use some of my spiral and infuse it into the other symbols."

Pain flared up Eilean's still healing arm as she forced herself into an upright position. She had a feeling she knew what Freya was getting at and she had no idea whether to be frustrated or furious.

"Don't hurt yourself," Freya said as she held an arm out toward Eilean as if she were prepared to catch her at any moment. Which, if Eilean's headache was anything to go by, could happen any minute. "But yes, if the look on your face means anything, I guess you got the idea. If I messed up the spell or whatever, there was a chance that a piece of my life-span could be taken away."

"What—"

"It didn't go wrong!" Freya blurted out. "I felt a warmth in my chest and let it go the moment I felt it start to grow hotter. I'm okay."

Eilean stayed uncomfortably upright, watching her.

"Okay, I may have been dizzy afterwards and drank all of our water and that's why Bhradain isn't here 'cause he's out getting more, but other than that, I'm okay. I promise," Freya tried to reassure her. "And more than that, you're okay, too."

That was when Eilean sank back to the ground and closed her eyes. She couldn't believe that a borderline stranger had risked her own life to help her.

"Why did you do that?" Freya asked. "Save me from the plant, I mean. Sure, I probably wouldn't have had someone to heal me, unless you've got magic too, but you didn't know what was going to happen. Or what could have happened."

Eilean didn't open her eyes. She may not have known that the plant would do this to her, or that it was dangerous at all, but she couldn't risk Freya getting hurt. She was only here because of Eilean, after all.

And if anyone deserves to get hurt, Eilean began, but stopped herself from finishing the thought.

"Well," Freya continued, "whatever it was, you saved me, so the least I could do was save you."

Freya's reassurances didn't do much to relieve Eilean's worries.

"I'm sorry..." she said quietly.

"Oh shut up," Freya replied, her tone one of exasperation, her arms folded across her chest in an attempt to seem firm. The kind smile weakened the image. Freya looked gentle like that.

"I wanted to help you," she said, "so I did. Now, please, stop being grumpy so I can enjoy the fact I just did freaking magic."

Freya moved out of sight and lay down nearby, leaving enough space for Eilean to be comfortable and for nothing to hit her injured arm by accident. She knew that she was being unreasonable in her response to Freya's actions. Freya was right; it was her choice to do it. Eilean had no right to be upset. If anything, she should be—

Eilean, carefully and cautiously, reached out her injured arm in the direction of Freya. When her hand found Freya's, she let out a breath. As gentle as a feather, Eilean squeezed the girl's hand.

"Thank you," she whispered.

Freya squeezed her hand back in reply.

As Eilean went back to watching the gleaming stars above, she noticed she hadn't removed her hand from Freya's. Gazing up at the constellations, her eyelids grew heavy and Eilean fell into a dreamless sleep.

17

QUESTS ARE EXHAUSTING

BRIGHT LIGHT GLEAMED THROUGH HER EYELIDS, WAKING Eilean, and the image of a skeletal horse right above jolted her straight into full consciousness.

"Jesus Christ, you have to stop doing that," Eilean said irritably as she sat up.

"Just checking you're still alive," Bhradain said casually. Eilean glanced up at him in surprise. It was the first nice thing he'd said to her. "It'd be frustrating to have to sever your arm to free Freya."

Eilean scowled. *So much for being nice,* she thought. And then she clicked onto what he'd said and became very aware of the tight grip on her hand.

Glancing over, Eilean found her arm still covered in the tattered first aid cover and bandage. Bits of her skin still glistened with aloe. To her surprise, she no longer wanted to cry over the pain. It still felt like a horrific case of sunburn, but the scream-inducing agony from before was gone. And there was Freya's hand in hers.

Eilean's instinct was to let go, feeling like she had crossed some sort of boundary by continuing to hold Freya's hand even while she was sleeping. Yet, as she tried to let go, Freya gripped on tighter and, worse still, opened her eyes.

Freya was clearly exhausted. Her previously bright brown eyes looked dulled and bleary, red lines streaking across the white. Her arms and chest were shiny with dried sweat, and her lips were painfully chapped. Eilean didn't remember her looking this exhausted last night. Though she supposed she only saw her shadow in the dark. Freya blinked heavily and glanced down at their enclosed hands. She let go instantly.

"Sorry," Freya said groggily. "I shoulda let go when you fell asleep. Are you okay?"

Eilean couldn't help it—she started to laugh. She wasn't really sure why. The situation they were in wasn't exactly laugh inducing. She'd been knocked unconscious by a plant, Freya had used her own energy to heal her. They'd barely managed to rest, yet Freya still remembered that Eilean didn't like physical contact enough to apologize and check if she's okay.

"Sorry, ignore me," Eilean's laughed tapered off. "I'm okay. How are you feeling?"

"Thirsty."

Eilean nodded. She was too. "Uhm, you said Bhradain was getting water, right?" She turned to the kelpie. "Did you manage to get—" A flask smacked against her knee after being kicked at her. "Thank—wait, how did you fill up a flask? You don't have thumbs."

"Use your imagination."

When her mind began to conjure the image of a pair of thumbs hidden beneath scaly hooves, Eilean refocused on the present. No need to give herself nightmares. Bottle in hand, and with only a moment's hesitation, Eilean helped Freya sit up and offered her the flask of water first.

"No, no, you first," Freya said with a wave of her hand. Eilean continued to hold it in front of her. "Okay, fine."

Eilean kept a hand hovering behind Freya's back and

watched her as she took slow sips of the flask. She felt an anxiety growing in her stomach seeing Freya look so unwell. She wanted to chalk it up to the intensity of the humidity. Eilean could feel sweat trickling down her back and forehead and see lines of it on Freya's chest. But with the breathlessness Freya was showing in between deep gulps, she knew the heat wasn't the only reason.

Freya let out a sigh of relief after she finished and then handed the flask to Eilean. The glare she gave her was enough for Eilean to not hesitate in drinking. They finished that flask and part of the second easily.

"I assume you will want me to refill these," Bhradain said irritably after Eilean lowered the half-empty second flask. "You humans and your need for hydration."

"Ah, yes, that pesky need for living. How terrible."

Freya laughed. "Bhradain, I know it can't be easy to fill but, please? We'll definitely need more water in this forest. This humidity is unbearable."

To emphasize her point, she tugged at her clothing in an attempt to cool herself down.

"Very well," Bhradain relented with a respectful bow of his head. "I will be back soon. Then we must move on."

Without another word, Bhradain disappeared into the nearby trees. Eilean found herself staring after him, wondering—not for the first time—why he was so attentive and kind toward Freya. She shook her head. She'd question why later.

"How're you feeling now?" Eilean asked. "You still look a little tired. We could probably ask Bhradain if you could rest more?"

"I'm fine," Freya replied. "Using magic was a bit more draining than I thought it would be, but it's okay. I'm alright as long as you are, too."

Eilean lifted her still bandaged arm. "Yeah, it only feels like a bad sunburn now. I'll be okay."

"I could do a little more—"

"No," Eilean said sharply. "You've helped me enough as it is, and you're already tired. A sunburn is fine." She tried to soften her tone. "Besides, if you do more, I may have to look after you and, well, I'm not first-aid certified."

Freya smiled. "I could teach you, if you want? I'm a qualified student medic."

"Scouts?" Eilean asked curiously.

"Nah," she smirked, "Air Cadets."

Eilean's eyebrows raised. "You're an Air Cadet?"

"Conversation for another time." Freya waved her hand. "So, what do you think we'll find on our way to Cernunnos? I know Bhradain said we're going to this Withering Woods place, where *Death* of all things lives, but, you know, that's going to be *way* too easy. I already had us meet a killer plant, but that's just boring really, what else do you think we'll see?"

"From what my Mamó told me about the Gods and stuff, my guess is nothing good." Eilean laughed humorlessly. "I mean, what mythological stories have good journeys or endings? A Goddess made Hercules kill his wife and kids and then had to do some terrible trials as penance."

"Or like Olokun, who wanted to wipe out an entire coastline cause the people weren't praying to them or respecting nature."

Eilean frowned. "Who's that?"

"Ah, they're one of the Orishas in Nigeria. My mum told me stories about them. They were more of a deity than a God but the story works," Freya said. "Now I'm wondering if they're real, too."

"Who knows?" Eilean replied. "Anything goes now, I guess. But yeah, Hercules and the coastline people, don't exactly make me excited about what's waiting for us."

"Maybe we'll meet some really cool folklore creatures like selkies or the real life Loch Ness Monster."

"You think Nessie is real?" Eilean asked.

Freya raised an eyebrow at her. "Eilean, we're in a magical world with Gods. *Of course* she's real. And I bet she's brilliant."

"Not if you wake her up early," Bhradain said as he stepped out from the bush. "She is not one to be disturbed."

Freya offered Eilean a self-satisfied smirk that had Eilean holding back her own smile. Of course, the Loch Ness Monster was real. Because this world couldn't get any more ridiculous.

"Are we ready to leave?" Bhradain asked.

"Yeah." Eilean nodded. "Though Freya needs to rest more, so if you can, you'll need to carry her for a bit of the way."

"What, why?"

Eilean turned to Freya. "You need to get your energy back. It'll just be until we're out of this rainforest." Eilean glanced at Bhradain. "We do leave the forest eventually, right?"

"Yes, only a few more miles and we will be out in the open once more."

"See, it'll only be for a little while."

"But you need to rest, too," Freya said.

"I'll be okay. I slept a lot already because of my arm. It may still hurt a little, but it's an arm—it's not going to keep me from walking."

"Eilean—"

"Freya," Eilean interrupted. "You looked after me last night—"

"You looked after me first."

"Well, now it's my turn again, okay?"

"We swap at the half-way point. No arguing. Even Arthur listened to Merlin about his health sometimes."

"Did you watch BBC's Merlin by any chance?"

Freya shrugged. "It had Katie McGrath in it."

Eilean couldn't stop the smile that spread across her face. The same reason she had for watching the show. Then she took in the slight flush of Freya's cheeks and wondered if it was for the *exact* same reason as her. "Okay, we'll swap places at the half-way point."

"Good."

Bhradain lowered himself to the ground and Freya climbed on. The only problem was, with Eilean's sword still attached to his saddlebag, the scabbard would bounce against Freya's legs. It wouldn't be the end of the world, but Eilean felt bad.

"I'll carry Phobia for now," Eilean said before attempting to joke, "just in case we meet Nessie."

Freya grabbed Phobia and held it in her hands. "Are you sure? You… you don't seem particularly comfortable with it. I don't mind it being kept in the saddlebags. I've got short legs, anyway."

She didn't really want to tell Freya the truth about why she was uncomfortable, but, after all she did for her last night, she should repay her beyond a thank you. Her therapist always said being vulnerable with others could sometimes help growth.

"You're right, I don't like weapons much," Eilean said. "I'm… I'm afraid of what I could do with them. They're made to hurt people and well, you know what happened…" She shook her head; that was too much to share. "I'll be okay. I can carry it for a bit."

Freya didn't move for a beat. Then she handed Phobia to her. "If you need to give Pheebs back at any point, let me know, okay?"

"Pheebs?"

"Right." Freya ran a hand through her hair, embarrassed. "Sorry, I, uh, it kind of came to me… Pheebs, short for Phobia. Sorry, it's stupid."

Eilean offers her a smile. "It's fine, I like it."

"Yeah? Do you think you'll use it?"

"Dunno." Eilean shrugged. "I kind of like Phobia, it… makes sense, I guess."

"I get it," Freya said. "Maybe one day."

Eilean didn't respond, focusing instead on attaching the scabbard to her belt. The weight felt immediate, almost as if she were carrying her fear on her hip. Though she supposed she was literally doing that.

Take it one breath at a time.

"Come now, it's time to go," Bhradain said as he began moving. "The River of Time may not be drying up anytime soon, but my patience certainly is."

Eilean followed after the horse and rider. "What's the River of Time?"

"It is the marker we must follow if we are to make it to the Withering Woods. All time flows to the end. And the end of time is what the woods border. If we follow the River, it will lead us to our destination."

"How far's the river from here?"

"Not far."

Eilean rolled her eyes. "That's not an answer—"

"If you keep asking questions, it will take longer." Bhradain flicked his tail at her. "Let us move on in silence."

"Bhradain," Freya said sharply. "Don't be mean."

The kelpie snorted and continued walking without another word. Eilean made sure to follow in silence this time. No need to poke the kelpie-bear.

As the trio walked through the forest, Eilean found herself drinking from her flask regularly. The humidity was as strong as ever and, once again, Eilean was thanking Brigid for the short sleeves. As they walked through the bush, the heat seemed to grow more intense. With the trees and wide leaves bearing over them, Eilean had hoped that it'd stave off the heat of the sun, but it just seemed to exacerbate it. To distract herself, she scanned the plant life around her, keeping an eye out for anything that seemed dangerous or out of the ordinary.

Just like before, she noticed the fading colors on the plant life. Spots of gray covered green leaves, tree trunks, and even patches of grass. Eilean knew plant life could end up with speckling colors, but gray wasn't natural. It was as if something was draining the color out of the forest.

"Does the forest usually look like this?" Eilean asked.

"Nothing is as it was before," Bhradain replied.

Eilean made a note to herself to be on the eye out for more things that appeared out of the ordinary. Or at least, as out of the ordinary in a world of magic, that is.

"Have you noticed this, Freya?" She glanced up and found Freya slumped against Bhradain's neck, snoozing.

Her face was buried in his seaweed-like mane which, as gross as Eilean found it, Freya somehow made look sweet. Her lips were parted slightly as she breathed softly—though occasionally the grunt of a snore slipped out. Eilean found herself biting back a laugh at the noise. Eventually she looked away from Freya's sleeping form, worrying she was coming across as creepy. Though she glanced back at her every so often, just to check that she wasn't slipping.

Freya may have told her to swap places at the half-way point, but Eilean knew she had no intention of keeping her side of the deal.

"Don't tell me when we reach the half-way point," Eilean said quietly to the kelpie.

"I had no intention of doing so."

18

SOME SECRETS SHOULD BE KEPT QUIET

EILEAN WAS SWEATING BUCKETS. NOT ONLY WAS HER PALE skin red with sunburn and sticky to the touch from how hot it had gotten, her injured arm was starting to ache again. As were her feet.

"How much longer till we get there?"

"The same amount of time as the last time you asked," Bhradain replied.

"Which is?"

"An hour."

"And how long have we been walking?"

"Fifteen minutes."

They walked side by side in silence for some time. Or at least, it felt like some time.

"Are you sure it's only been fifteen minutes of us walking?" Eilean asked. "It definitely feels a lot longer than that."

"Good thing your feelings do not determine time."

"You're an arse."

Bhradain huffed. "No, I'm a kelpie."

"Why do you not like me?" Eilean asked. "Like, what have I actually done that has you being so grouchy with me all the time? You aren't like this with Freya."

The kelpie came to a stop, jostling Freya slightly before he rounded on Eilean, his white eyes brighter than she'd ever seen them. "That is none of your business."

Eilean raised her hands. "All right, calm down. I was just asking."

"Don't."

"I won't," she snapped back.

Bhradain started walking again. "Good."

"Good." Eilean followed after him.

"You both need to stop," a croaky voice said from the kelpie's back. Both Eilean and Bhradain froze.

Eilean glanced up at Freya while Bhradain's ears flicked back toward her, waiting for her to speak. Freya was pushing herself up into a sitting position on his back while rubbing at her tired eyes. "If you'd both stop arguing and pay attention, you'd have heard it."

Eilean frowned and looked at Bhradain, who seemed just as confused, until his ear twitched to the left of them. He was clearly picking up on something in the distance. Eilean tried to listen for whatever the others had heard.

It took her a second, but she heard it. The sound of rushing water.

"Thank the Gods!" Bhradain exclaimed before rushing off. Freya quickly grabbed onto his mane and held on for dear life.

Eilean had to run after the two of them, to the complaints of her aching feet. Careful to avoid the vegetation as she followed Bhradain's hoof-printed path, Eilean stepped out into the sunshine. The sudden brightness forced Eilean to blink her eyes quickly to remove the silver dots that filled her vision. Once cleared, she saw it.

Right beside them, splashing against the edge of the forest they had just left, was a vast river as bright and blue as the sky above. The water and sky seemed to join as the river flowed out toward the horizon. It was as if the river and the sky had blended together to become indistinguishable.

They'd reached the River of Time.

Eilean had always thought the lochs in Scotland were breathtaking with their natural beauty, but this was entirely different. It was like no place she'd ever seen before. A river that was untouched and unblemished. A river that had been left to its own devices to flourish.

The surrounding land had grown wild and healthy. Plants of all kinds lined its shoreline and grew, tickling the tips of her fingers as she moved closer. A wood stood to the right of her and it was larger than anything she'd ever seen. The tips of its trees reached the edges of the clouds in the sky, and the length of the forest went farther than Eilean could see. Even the rocks that sat at the edge of the woods were large—the size of a car, at least. Anything could be hiding in the giant wood, ready to use those boulders, but Eilean tried not to think about that right now as she took in a deep breath.

The air and the water was so fresh that it was almost overwhelming after coming from the humid intensity of the rainforest. Standing by the edge, Eilean tried to see across to the other side of the "river." She wondered if this could even be called such; it felt more like a vast ocean with a distant land that she could only just make out on the horizon.

"Wow."

"Yeah…" Freya agreed in a shaky voice.

With Bhradain at her side, Eilean glanced up to find Freya no longer there. Behind them, rucksack on, and stepping away from the water, Freya was struggling to keep it together. Eilean had entirely forgotten Freya's fear until then.

Hanging her sword back on Bhradain's saddlebag, with no word from him to her surprise, Eilean moved away from the river bank. "Best to stay away from the water. The ground's a little slippy from the mud."

Freya offered her a grateful smile.

Bhradain stomped his hooves on the ground, moving himself away from the waters edge. "Yes, let us keep moving."

The kelpie walked away from the river, giving it a wide berth. For a creature that comes from water… that drew Eilean and Freya's attention.

"What's wrong?" Freya asked him.

His tail flicked behind him. "The River of Time leads to the Land of the Dead, and with the Withering Woods just past this forest, there are beacons of death on all sides. Beacons that draw monsters. And yet," he glanced at the river, "my kind, the carriers of souls to the Land of the Dead, are not within the water."

Eilean followed his gaze to the river. Beyond its flow, nothing within it seemed to stir. It seemed unnaturally empty. "They could be out doing their job?"

Bhradain shook his head. "There are more of us than you would think. We exist not just within the Celtic lands, but beyond. For the River of Time to be empty… something is not right."

"Do you think this could be connected to Cernunnos?" Freya asked.

"I do not know what to think," he replied, continuing to walk ahead. "All I know is we must keep going."

The two girls followed after the kelpie who had moved to the center of the field, the sky high trees the same distance away from them on their right as the river was to their left. No one spoke for a time—until Freya piped up in a quiet voice.

"You… you said people who've died are brought here, right?" she asked, a longing in her voice that surprised Eilean. Until she remembered about Freya's parents.

"Yes, including your parents," Bhradain replied, distracted. "I escorted Diane and Ewan myself."

Freya froze. "What?"

"Two fine spirits they were." Bhradain nodded in thought as he continued walking. "They were pleased to know that, one day, their daughter would join them in this world and they would know who she is. It was an honor to carry them."

Eilean and Freya had both stopped moving. Eventually Bhradain noticed, stopped, and spun round to look at them, confusion in his gaze.

"You…" Freya started. "You were the one who took my parents?"

"Their accident was not my doing, if that is what you are inferring. I was the one who carried them into their next life."

"And you didn't think to tell me?" Freya ground out.

Bhradain turned away from her. "I did not know how."

"And you thought dropping it on me like this was a good way?"

"It seemed relevant to the conversation at—"

Freya moved toward him. "Was all that stuff in the woods after the funeral a game to you?"

"No, it was not," he replied, his voice taut as if he were holding something back.

"Why, then?"

Bhradain started walking away. "Let us move on. The land here is not as it was, we should not dawdle for long."

"No." Freya stormed after him. "You tell me what happened. Now."

Eilean rushed after Freya and, in as kind a tone as she could, said, "Maybe we should discuss this later. If something's off here—"

"I need to know," Freya said through gritted teeth.

"I know you do—"

"No," Freya whispered, tears forming in her eyes. "No, you don't know."

"You're right, I don't," Eilean said, keeping her voice calm. "Bhradain dropping this out of the blue was crap, and I'm sorry. But if this place is a beacon for monsters, and there are currently no monsters here for a reason that even Bhradain doesn't understand, we can't risk drawing attention to ourselves. Please, just, until we're safer, wait—" Eilean glanced up as a shadow grew over Freya's head.

A single tear fell down Freya's cheek. "Eilean—"

Before Freya could finish, Eilean was ramming her clear of a flying boulder.

19

IN A FLASH OF A GIANT'S EYE

Freya and Eilean tumbled *hard* toward the riverside. Eilean's arm ached and Freya groaned from beneath her. But at least they hadn't been crushed. If they hadn't moved, they'd have been pancakes beneath the boulder.

"Are you okay?" Eilean asked, breathless. "I didn't hurt you, did I?"

Freya's eyes were wide, but she shook her head no. Eilean released a sigh of relief and got the two of them up and standing. Mud sucked at their feet and their clothes. Eilean felt the chill crawl up from her toes to her calves until eventually they were numb from the cold. She and Freya continued to push through the sticking mud to get away from the water's edge.

Eilean thought they were out of danger. She was wrong.

"Look out!" Freya pulled Eilean back to the ground.

The two of them nearly went tumbling off the bank and into the water. A second boulder sailed overhead and splashed into the river, sending up an explosion of water, soaking them both. The chill of the mud that had sunk into her bones was nothing compared to the icy bite of water.

"What is going—"

Eilean turned in the direction that the boulders had come

from and considered diving them into the river then and there, Freya's fear be damned.

A giant, an actual *giant,* stood glaring at them from the edge of the woods. He had huge beefy arms, which he was already using to grab another boulder from the treeline and lift it above his head. His legs, just as muscular, held his towering height and boulder with ease. He didn't throw it this time. She guessed he was holding it as a very real threat of what he could do.

But it wasn't the giant's height that terrified Eilean the most. He looked like a living nightmare—or, one of those overly aggressive bodybuilders, if bodybuilders were two double deckers tall. All of that was terrifying by itself, but it was his eyes that unnerved her. He only had one. Not in the way a cyclops might, it was clear he'd once had two. His working eye was wide and golden in color, like a honeycomb. The other empty socket was a scarred mess, like it had been burned away. Eilean's own eyes ached in sympathy at the sight. But that sympathy only went so far with that humongous boulder in his hands.

As he held the rock high in the air, the giant took one step forward as the ground shook under his foot.

That was when Eilean saw Bhradain at the giant's feet.

"What… what do you think he's doing?" Eilean asked.

Freya swallowed, her gaze still on the giant. "I'm sure he's talking him down or organizing safe passage or something."

"Yeah, yeah, let's go with that."

They couldn't hear what was being said but from the way Bhradain's neck stretched upwards and how his hooves tapped up and down, a sign of anxiety Eilean remembered learning about from one of the horse books she'd read as a girl, she could only guess he was talking to the giant.

"I think Bhradain's distracting him," Freya noted. "Maybe we can make a run for it while he does. We can hide from the giant among the trees, right?"

"I think so," Eilean said. "It's worth a shot. Are you feeling strong enough to run?"

Freya nodded, and the two, after an intake of breath, bolted. Part of Eilean felt guilty about leaving the kelpie to the giant but, unlike them, he knew this world. She guessed he knew what he was doing and, if not, well… she wouldn't think on that part too much right now.

"Why should Balor care for this world's safety?" The giant boomed just as the girls made it to the treeline. "What has Cernunnos and Danu ever offered Balor beyond the continuance of my suffering? Has Balor not been punished enough?"

That sparked a memory for Eilean, something from one of her Mamó's stories. Something about him having a daughter that made him lose an eye. She really wished she was better at remembering these things.

They still couldn't hear Bhradain. Freya motioned for them to keep moving, staying further inside the treeline and out of sight until they were close enough to hear him. That plan probably would have worked well if not for the squealing whinny of Bhradain as he slammed, back first, into the trees meters in front of them.

He fell, hard, to the ground, and didn't move or make a sound after that.

Quaking steps vibrated the earth as, Eilean realized, the giant moved toward the kelpie to finish the job. Bhradain may be a pain in the ass, but she wouldn't let this happen. Without thinking, she ran out from the trees.

"Stop!" Eilean yelled, running at speed in the giant's direction. She could just make out Freya among the trees running alongside, heading for Bhradain. "Stop, you can't do this."

The golden eye locked on her. Eilean slowed down and stared up at the large man.

"You have had Balor's pardon once before, Ruth," the giant said coolly. "Balor will not allow another until Balor receives what Balor is owed."

"My name is Eilean, moron," she snapped back. Ruth was her Mamó's name.

"No matter." Balor waved his hand. The motion caused a heavy breeze to pass over Eilean's skin. "You will not die today. The kelpie, however, has insulted Balor too many times."

Glancing ahead to Bhradain, Eilean saw Freya at his side. Her hands, glowing in an orange light, moved over his body. Starting with his spine. Bhradain's eyes were closed and, beyond his labored breathing, he didn't move. Around them lay the scattered items from Bhradain's saddlebag. Including Phobia. Meeting the giant's eye once more, Eilean took in a shaky breath of her own.

"I… I can't let you do that."

Balor laughed. His laughter shook the ground beneath her feet. Eilean thought she was going to throw up.

"And who are you to stop Balor?" he said.

Eilean's gaze dropped to Phobia once more. Only a few quick strides and she'd have her. Eilean knew this was crazy. She had no training with a sword against a person, let alone a giant the size of a double-decker bus. But she had to do something.

She bolted. And the ground behind her exploded.

Thrown off her feet, Eilean tumbled forward. To her insane luck, she landed near Phobia. Glancing behind, she found where she had been standing was now a burning crater.

"Balor will not miss again."

Eilean grabbed Phobia off the ground and gripped the hilt with one hand.

"You are going to let us pass," Eilean said, trying to keep herself from stammering. "Or… you'll regret it."

Balor took one step closer, his large feet now only ten yards away. He smiled down at her, showing off his gruesome teeth. Eilean could only imagine what he had eaten for his teeth to be stained red and yellow.

"Balor will make your friends' deaths swift," Balor said. "You, Balor, will do no such favor."

Fingers trembling, Eilean drew Phobia from her sheath so fast that the blade sang. She felt the weight of the sword and dropped the scabbard to the ground. Staring up at the towering figure above, Eilean had to fight to not drop the weapon and run. This was insane. Certifiably insane. Her whole body shook. Vomit crawled up the back of her throat, which she had to swallow down. Eilean inhaled and, stupidly, charged.

Eilean had no idea what she was doing. Swinging her sword at his feet wildly, she desperately tried to keep herself from getting crushed. Eilean felt like a child with relighting candles. The more energy she exerted trying to do any kind of damage to the giant, the more invigorated he became, while her arms ached painfully.

"I grow tired of these games," Balor said, barely a wheeze of exhaustion in his words. He kicked in her direction. Eilean only just missed being catapulted into the sky by ducking to the ground like a possum playing dead.

The wind of his foot brushed over her, rippling the material of her clothes viciously. His foot came back down and, remembering she was still alive, Eilean rolled out of its pathway and got to her feet. Glancing back at Freya who, now covered in sweat, was still working on Bhradain. The kelpie had yet to open his eyes. Electricity thrummed in Eilean's veins.

I need to give her more time.

"Well," Eilean shouted out, barely able to contain her panting breaths. "I'm… I'm not done with you yet."

Eilean was sure that, if the giant could have rolled his eye, he would have. Instead, he went to squish her with his foot. Without thinking, Eilean raised her hands, bracing to protect herself from the impact.

Balor let out a cry that echoed around them as he stumbled

backwards, the sole of the foot he intended to crush her with, bleeding.

Eilean nearly dropped Phobia from her grasp when she saw the blade. Blood poured down from tip to hilt, winding down into her hands. Eilean never wanted to draw blood from someone. Not again.

Yet, as she watched Balor, now walking on the ball of his left foot, come toward her again, Eilean knew she couldn't hesitate. Bhradain was still unconscious. Freya had looked close to it with how much magic she was using. She needed to get Balor to back off so they could get out of here.

With a shaky breath, Eilean tightened her grip on Phobia. Flickers of blue appeared across her vision.

I'll get you more time.

Everything came in flashes after that.

It felt as if she were moving in slow motion. Or the world around her was. She vaulted forward, dodging the giant's car-sized feet as he went to kick her. She slashed across the flesh of the inside of his foot, drawing a prolonged bellow of pain from him. Blood poured down and over her hands before Balor wrenched away. The ground shook as he stumbled, and she knew she couldn't stop.

She ran behind him, aiming for the Achilles tendon of his right foot. He raised it before she could get there. But he had another he hadn't protected. The cry of pain shook within her mind as much as the ground did as he placed his right foot back to the ground. Eilean sliced through it with ease. Blood splattering onto her cheeks.

Unbalanced and in agony, Balor fell.

But Eilean didn't stop. She climbed atop him, drawing her Phobia across his stomach, his chest, and—when he tried to swat at her—his arms and hands as well.

Eilean didn't know how long she had been slashing and stabbing at him by the end of it. She felt the blood as it coated her fingers, wrists, and face. And she could still feel the bubble of excitement from flowing through the movements with Phobia in her hands. The blue sparks were still crawling up her arms from when she'd swung, again and again. The more she'd struck, the more intense the flow of electricity had become in her veins, making her stronger. She knew this all had happened, could see it in her mind. But she didn't remember doing it. She just knew that, to her eternal shame, Eilean had loved every second of it.

Now she stood atop Balor's fallen form, her sword pointed at his eye, as he begged for mercy.

"Eilean?"

The blood-soaked sword dropped from her hands and tumbled from Balor's chest to the ground below. Eilean stared at her hands. Just like Phobia, they were stained with his blood.

Just like they had been with David.

"Eilean," Freya called out to her again. "Let's go."

Turning to her voice, Eilean found Freya beside the giant's body. Freya held her hands up in a placating manner. The teachers at her school had done the same thing after she'd broken David's jaw. They'd corralled her away from the other students so she wouldn't hurt anyone else. Those looks of terror still haunted her.

Freya didn't look afraid, but that was somehow worse. Instead, she just looked nervous with the way her eyes kept flitting to the frozen whimpering form of Balor. Eilean was without a weapon now. He could crush her if she didn't get moving.

Obeying Freya's words, she slid from the giant's torso, hitting the ground with a thud that knocked the wind out of her. On all fours, she gasped in deep gulping breaths. Next to her lay Phobia, coated in layers of blood. Eilean couldn't look at it without feeling physically sick. And so she was.

"Eilean!" Freya cried out, but it wasn't her who came to Eilean's side.

Hooves appeared in her blurry line of vision. Eilean couldn't even register the relief at knowing whatever Freya had done had worked. She just wiped the vomit from her mouth and forced herself to look up and face those judgemental white eyes. To her surprise, Bhradain stared at her with only calm alertness.

"Get up, Eilean. We have to get moving."

Eilean didn't question him. She didn't have the energy. Standing up on shaky legs, she held onto Bhradain's neck to keep herself upright. He didn't seem to mind.

"Now we run," Bhradain said.

She was still weak on her legs, but the thought of seeing Balor—who still lay whimpering over the damage she had done to him—was enough to push herself faster. Both Bhradain and Freya were as exhausted, if not more so, than her, but they ran fast enough to be at her side the whole time. She glanced at each of them as they ran and wondered why they were still with her.

Eilean was just as much a monster as the one she had left in tears.

20

TIME IS RUNNING OUT

Blood coated Eilean's vision. No matter how many times she wiped the bloody sweat from her face, her hands and vision were still glazed red. She kept running, with Bhradain and Freya right behind her.

They rushed through the woods, not stopping until the trees grew sparse to their left, exposing the River of Time once again. Only then did Eilean slow down. Only then did she find a way to rid herself of the blood on her hands. Or she would have, if Bhradain hadn't stopped her.

"I'm sorry," he said quietly. "But the River of Time cannot be contaminated."

Eilean wanted to push. Desperate to clean herself of the now dried brown stains, but she just didn't have the energy for it.

"Let's keep going," she said in the end. "The more distance..."

Bhradain nodded in agreement and began moving. Freya wasn't as convinced.

"Do you want to—"

"No," Eilean responded, knowing what she was going to ask.

The three of them continued moving without a word. Freya walked beside her in quiet support that Eilean desperately didn't want right now. Especially not from Freya.

She didn't want to hear that she'd saved them. Didn't want to hear about how she hadn't done anything wrong. Eilean missed the disgust and anger that was given to her. She'd take Chloe and her gang's assault or her parents' disappointed gaze over Freya's admiration. There was only so much understanding that she could take before she snapped.

Right now, all she wanted to do was go home. Of course, she didn't say that out loud—Eilean didn't feel like getting chastised by a judgmental death horse. So she stayed quiet. And so did they.

Eventually, darkness fell. They continued on, the only light that guided their way from the moon and twinkling stars, shining above and reflected in the river beside them. The grass was even and easy to walk along, but there was too little light to truly see where they were going.

It was in the dark and quiet that Eilean's mind spiraled as she tried to piece together what had happened with Balor. It felt like she'd had an out-of-body experience. Flashes of her attack flared in her mind, but she was never in the action. She was just watching herself from a distance, going feral. Eilean couldn't believe she'd lost control so easily. She worked so hard not to lose her temper and yet, all of that training had gone to waste. Twice. And with a strength she'd never had before. Eilean couldn't understand how she had managed to do all of that, and to a giant!

Until she remembered the spark that had coursed through her the moment she drew the sword.

It was a sensation that she felt whenever rage or fear coursed through her; as if such overwhelming emotions were second nature to her. That spark came when she'd destroyed her bedroom after a particularly brutal argument with her parents as a kid. It came in P.E. with a football clearing the whole field and slamming into the goalie's stomach after seeing them picking on a year seven kid. And that feeling had taken over her when she broke David's jaw.

It was as if letting the anger out was scratching an itch that she couldn't reach. Eilean could never admit that before—not even fully to herself. But there was no arguing that that's what happened with Balor. She'd let herself be consumed by the spark of rage.

And she'd *liked* it.

"Hey, wait up!" Freya's voice sounded far away.

Surprised at how far ahead she was, Eilean stopped and turned. She could barely see Freya and Bhradain in the dark.

Freya jogged up to Eilean with a still panting Bhradain at her heels. A gap in the trees allowed moonlight to catch Freya's features, highlighting the bags under her eyes and chapped lips. Bhradain looked just as haggard, with his coat covered in white patches of sweat. It seemed he had not lied about the downsides of being on land for long periods of time.

"Could we rest?" Freya asked in a voice that sounded close to a wheeze. "It's too dark to keep walking. Plus, I don't know about you, but giants and running have tired me the hell out."

Eilean wanted to protest. Bhradain had said they had to follow the whole river to make it to the Withering Woods. It may be dark now, but she was pretty sure they were nowhere near the end of the river. If they kept going through the night, they could at least get a little closer to their end goal. The sooner they got there, the sooner Eilean could leave and put this whole mess behind her.

"Come on, you could probably do with some sleep, too." Freya offered her a gentle smile. "I'm sure your arm will thank you for it."

Awareness made her arm throb again, and Eilean had to bite back a hiss of pain.

"Yeah, sure," Eilean said with a nod. "I'll go grab some wood and make a fire."

"I can come with—"

"It's all right," Eilean interrupted. She attempted to offer her own version of a reassuring smile, but failed miserably. "I won't be gone long."

Before Freya could stop her or insist on coming along, Eilean was speed walking away again. The energy from what she'd done to Balor still lingered. She needed to do something with her hands. Maybe snapping some twigs from a tree would help dull the itching spark of power that still remained.

"Remember to check that the tree isn't sentient before chopping it for wood," Bhradain called after her.

This world is ridiculous, Eilean thought as she headed into the woods. The muted voices of Bhradain and Freya trailed behind her as she slipped past the trees and set to work.

Eilean considered checking the trees at the edge of the wood as she would get back to camp faster, but found she didn't want to. She needed more time with her thoughts, away from the others.

With the *whoosh* of leaves and the creaking of tree branches around her, Eilean set to work. Remembering Bhradain's comments, she tapped on a trunk.

TAP. TAP.

"Hey, anyone there?" she asked, feeling ridiculous. Eilean wondered if Bhradain was messing with her. Until a face appeared beneath her hand.

Eilean yelped and jumped back in surprise.

"Could you not?" the grumpy tree said. His branch arm bent and made a shooing gesture at her. "Some of us need our beauty rest."

"And *they* definitely need it," another said with a laugh.

Eilean turned to find more branches bending to cover a strangely carved tree face. Their laughter as they held their imaginary stomach sounded like the cracking of twigs.

"Watch it!" Grumpy shouted.

"Well, it's true," Giggles replied.

Truly ridiculous.

It took some time, but Eilean managed to find trees that didn't talk back to her. And thankfully, scattered around the silent grove, there was an array of branches and twigs of all sizes. Now all she had to do was break them into smaller piles to make firewood. As with most things in this world, it turned out to be a lot harder than she first thought. With her arm still throbbing, it was difficult to use her full strength to snap them. After a fourth failed attempt, Eilean swung the meter long branch in her grasp against a tree.

SNAP.

She had a few cuts on her hands and one on her cheek, but she didn't care. A few little stings were nothing. Besides, now she had her first two pieces of firewood. Eilean lifted the next and swung it against the tree, releasing a breath of relief at the crack. She ended up with a lot of scratches, some of which caught her still healing arm, but Eilean would rather fall out of a tree and get hurt than have to use her sword again.

Eilean had seen Phobia back on Bhradain's saddlebag when they stopped. A part of her hoped that it would have been abandoned back with Balor. Luck never seemed to be on her side. Perhaps she could leave it behind when they headed out in the morning.

With enough wood to last the night, Eilean headed to where the others set up camp. As the trees were still sky high, the once useful moonlight became about as helpful as carrots, with only small beams of light reaching through to show the path. Eilean was grateful for the sound of the river to guide her way back.

She walked slowly. She didn't want to face any of the questions likely waiting for her back there. Like, how was she feeling? What happened? And, if Freya had seen them, what were those blue sparks? She didn't know how she'd answer them. Even now, she could still feel the blood trickling down her fingers.

Eilean hoped that the walk into the woods would help burn off the remaining sparks within her. She didn't think jumping into the river here would work the same way as the loch back home.

So, she wasted a little time by taking small steps. Until she felt the hairs on the back of her neck stand up straight.

Dropping the wood, Eilean spun around and held up her fists. Nothing in the air had changed. The breeze was still only just brushing the leaves in the trees. But Eilean had felt something.

"It means someone is walking over your grave," Mamó had told her when she was eight. "That strange cooling sensation on the back of your neck, the one that comes out of nowhere." Her eyes had sparkled with mischief. "It means, somewhere in the distant future, someone has passed over your grave."

Eilean huffed out a breath of annoyance and lowered her fists. This place was putting her on edge. The sooner she got out of here, the better. This world wasn't good for her.

The flicker of flame helped her find her way out of the woods. And reignite her irritation.

"What was the point of me getting firewood if you were going to get your own?" Eilean said, far snappier than she intended to be. She dropped her wood on the small pile that had already been collected.

Freya held her hands in front of the fire. It almost irritated Eilean more that she didn't react to her petulance. She could do with someone yelling at her. Making her feel as bad as she should feel. Instead, Freya only sighed.

"You were gone for ages," Freya replied. "I was cold." Brown eyes lifted and locked with hers. The flicker of the fire made them look fiercer than Eilean had ever seen them. "Your arm needs rewrapping again."

Eilean looked down at her arm to find the aloe smudged off, the tattered first-aid kit wrap hanging off her wrist, and her skin as red as a fresh sunburn.

"Oh."

Bhradain snorted. "An astute observation."

"Shut up," Freya said sharply. Surprising both Eilean and Bhradain. "Sit down, Eilean. Let me take a look at it."

"It's fine—"

"Sit. Down."

Eilean sat down. She may have wanted someone to snap at her because of all the damage she had caused but she no longer wanted that person to be Freya. The glint of frustration she'd seen in those warm brown eyes was something Eilean didn't want to see again. Especially not directed at her. If she ever ended up on Freya's shit-list, the shame might keep Eilean from ever returning to Balloch again.

"Give me your arm," Freya said as she grabbed the first-aid kit.

Eilean didn't argue as she held out her right arm to Freya and let her left soak in the warmth of the fire. It was a nice sensation, to have the heat of the flames fluttering against her skin. She hadn't realized how cold she was feeling until she felt the warmth again.

"Ow!" Eilean shouted when the sticky substance was slapped onto her arm. "Jesus, a little warning."

"I've found the more you expect something to happen, the more painful it ends up being." From her tone of voice, Eilean could tell she wasn't just talking about medicine. "Now sit still."

"Wait." Eilean pulled her arm away. "You're not going to do any magic, are you? Just the aloe will be fine." She had no intention of sucking any more life force from Freya.

"It keeps hurting you, Eilean," Freya said softly. "It's the least I can do after you saved us from Balor."

Eilean's jaw twitched. "That's not what—"

"Yes, that is what you did," Freya interrupted. "You stood up for me with Brigid, took a death plant for me, and gave us time to escape Balor. That's saving in my books. It's a hero in mine, too. Now give me your arm."

"Freya—"

"Arm."

Eilean put her arm back in Freya's grasp. It still took her by surprise that Freya didn't flinch whenever they touched. It was refreshing, if a little weird. The only other person who didn't do that was Mamó and Pa. But they were grandparents, so it didn't count.

A warmth spread along her arm, jolting her to look back at Freya. A glow illuminated her face, shadowing it in a way that had Eilean unable to turn away. A soft orange light, like the one Eilean had seen being used over Bhradain's body, fluttered over Freya's skin and onto hers. Every so often, Freya whispered words so quietly that Eilean could only guess it was some kind of spell helping the magic work. Listening closely, Eilean heard the Scottish Gaelic. It made sense that the language of old would be used for Celtic magic. When the light managed to flow without the need of an incantation, Freya spoke up properly.

"You don't remember me being there, do you?"

Eilean blinked, confused. "What do you mean? Where?"

"You..." Freya's voice cracked. She cleared her throat. "You remember the rumor about the gay kid in school, right?"

Eilean remembered. She'd not been out at the time. Hadn't even told her parents yet out of anxiety. When she heard the rumor, she kept her head down as much as possible to avoid drawing attention to herself in case they figured it out. She'd never known for sure how her schoolmates would act toward someone who was gay, but at twelve, she wasn't going to risk getting caught out.

Freya glanced up. "Well, I was the gay kid. Well, bisexual kid."

Eilean had felt a vibe from Freya since their reunion on the shore, so she wasn't surprised by that. She just hadn't expected this part of it.

"I'd told Chloe my secret in the girls' toilets and, well, someone had overheard us. The rumor spread pretty quickly. Everyone was speculating about who it could be. Including my friends. I was always grateful that Chloe kept it to herself until I was ready to say anything." Freya's frown deepened. "But the others had their own theories about who it was. Including David."

Eilean was aware of Bhradain moving around them, but she couldn't focus on him or anything else. She didn't know this story, but she knew the ending. And she feared how Freya would tell it.

"I was always surprised Chloe never ratted me out to him. Those two had always been close. I guess I sort of expected her to say something. So when she didn't, I was confused." Freya glanced up at Eilean. "She's still not a great person and, honestly, I should have stopped being friends with them a long time ago, I just..."

Sometimes the fear of being alone is scarier than being with those who aren't good for you.

"Then came Kathy Baker," Freya said hoarsely. "A girl who not only wasn't queer but also had no one to protect her. And I did nothing to stop them. I let David find Kathy in the playground, let him call her a slur and shove her to the ground. And I just watched." Freya brushed away a tear. "But you didn't."

Eilean felt disgust rise in her. She'd put a kid in the hospital. She'd broken his jaw, his nose, and her own fingers with what she'd done.

"You were my hero, you know?" Freya glanced up at her. "You stood up for someone you didn't even know."

Eilean couldn't speak.

"I know it isn't a good thing exactly, but you were the first person I knew who stood up for someone like that. I admired you for it." The light faded from Freya's hands and she gripped onto Eilean's arm, almost sensing that she was going to pull away. "Not for what you did to David, *never* that. But you stood up for someone when you didn't have to. That's what I admired."

Freya let go of Eilean, having said what she wanted to. Eilean moved away from her the moment she could. She had no idea how to process what Freya had just said. Laying down on the cool earth, Eilean stared up at the dark sky above them, like she did at home. She'd never had someone talk about what she'd done like that.

That was when she realized.

Eilean stood up with a start, making Freya jump in surprise.

"Bhradain," Eilean said. "Look up at the sky."

An anxious nicker met her ears, and she knew that meant he was seeing what she was seeing. Or rather, what she *wasn't* seeing.

"What is it?" Freya asked.

The stars were gone. All that could be seen was the moon floating alone in the inky blackness of space. More of a city scene with an empty night sky filled with light pollution.

Eilean searched the sky for any possible sign that she was wrong. She squinted her eyes so tight she managed to give herself a headache. But there was no denying it.

For a brief moment, there was a flicker. A flicker so violent that it looked like the stars were fighting to come back. As quickly as it came, it was gone.

"It's happening..." Bhradain said quietly, drawing the two girls' attention. "Cernunnos has been gone too long. The stars have gone out."

21

HISTORY WILL CALL THEM MONSTERS

Eilean had wanted them to keep moving after that. The stars had gone out, things were getting worse quicker than Bhradain or anyone had expected. She could only assume that they had a few days before things went from worse to catastrophic, equinox or not. To her surprise, it was Bhradain who rejected that idea.

"You need to regain your strength." He pawed at the ground nervously. "The stars will still be gone tomorrow. Pushing yourself more than necessary will do us no good."

She considered arguing, but didn't see the point. Bhradain was as stubborn as she was. If he said they weren't going, they weren't going. Besides, Freya had passed out asleep the moment it was clear they weren't going anywhere. Magic seemed to really take it out of her. Eilean had made sure to give her the extra blanket once she was fully out.

The empty sky stared down at Eilean in a sickening reminder. She couldn't stop looking up at it. It felt… unnatural to see nothing but the moon up there. Glasgow had enough light pollution to cloud most of the stars at night, but she could still see the glimmer of some of them. And in Ar Dachaidh, lights had filled the sky. Now it was empty. Utterly.

Eilean laid her head back down and continued staring up. "What happened to them?"

"The same as what is happening to the rest of Ar Dachaidh," Bhradain said with a waver in his voice. "Much has been fading here. Even before Cernunnos went missing, this world has been off-kilter. Only Cernunnos can help us figure out why. I am sure of it."

"And for some reason, a seventeen-year-old girl is the answer to getting him back? Fantastic."

Bhradain snorted. The noise wasn't dismissive or unkind, but unsure. "I am afraid I cannot explain why you were chosen. I do not understand it myself. That is a question for Cernunnos."

"So I gotta find the guy to ask him why I was chosen to find him?"

"In a manner of speaking, yes."

"Fab."

"You did not sense anything when you were at the loch, correct?" he asked, curious. "Often a kelpie's trick comes out of nowhere, but if there was something that—"

"My necklace," Eilean said, reaching up to hold her pendant. "My necklace grew hot, I guess? Twice. One when I was heading up the bank to leave."

"And that is when you saw my child form?"

"Still messed up by the way," Eilean told him, to which she received a huff of, she guessed, dismissal. "But yeah, it made me stop and then I heard you."

Bhradain stood silently for a moment. "Has that happened before?"

"No." Eilean frowned. "At least, not in my world. Could that have been the sign? Like, Cernunnos is reaching out to me through my necklace?"

"I do not know," Bhradain said. "But it is the only answer we have for now."

Eilean sighed. Nothing about this trip made any sense. "Where do we go from here?"

"We are not far from the entrance to the Withering Woods," Bhradain said quietly. "There is only one more being we must meet before we can enter. And she is not the… easiest of creatures to engage with."

This time, Eilean didn't keep her irritation to herself. "Ah yes, because the giant and the murder plant wasn't challenging enough. Why are they making things difficult for us?"

"I do not claim to understand the laws of the Gods or their methods." The kelpie pushed himself up to stand. "But even if we had not met Balor on our travels, we would have to deal with this creature. It is her land that we are passing through."

Eilean pushed herself up to sit and face him, no longer facing complaints from her once injured arm. She'd have to thank Freya properly when she woke up.

"You know who we're meeting?" she asked.

Bhradain's tail flicked nervously behind him, and he didn't meet her gaze. "She and I are very similar creatures," he began carefully. "Yet, I hold only a quarter of the power she does. It is her land we are entering, and it is her permission we must get."

Leaning her arms on her thighs, Eilean stared curiously at the kelpie. She'd seen him nervous before when it had come to Freya, but this felt different. Every so often, his eyes flicked toward the river, as if he was considering jumping in. It took a second for Eilean to realize that he was afraid.

"Who is she?" Eilean asked.

He shook his head, his mane flicking from side to side. It seemed like he was trying to shake off the fear. "She is Death."

Eilean blinked at him. Had she heard him correctly? She knew creatures of death existed; there was one standing right in front of her, after all. Yet in his words was something more final. More terrifying.

How could a creature of death be afraid of death itself?

"What do you mean, 'She is Death'?" Eilean asked.

"You will understand when you meet her. We should be at her doors within a few days." Bhradain shook his mane, splashing Eilean with unexpected water. "Do not be afraid. She is only a messenger. It is only what she will warn you of that you have to fear."

"That's reassuring," Eilean said, trying to keep the sarcasm out of her tone. She rubbed at her eyes, considering the possibility of them having to get moving soon. "How many days do we have left?"

"You mortals need your rest," Bhradain said. To Eilean's surprise, it was not said with his usual disdain. "We have enough yet to make it there in time."

"Okay, that's good."

A small noise came from Freya, drawing Bhradain and Eilean's attention to her. She rolled onto her back, still asleep, grunted, and then began to softly snore. Both Eilean and Bhradain let out a sigh of relief at not disturbing her.

With everything that had happened—between Freya and Bhradain, and then with Balor—Eilean hadn't even checked to see how she was doing. She'd used magic again, and Eilean knew how that could affect her. But no, she'd only been thinking about herself. Hell, she'd barely even spoken to her since everything went down. All the effort had come from Freya.

"We've both been bad companions to her," Eilean said quietly.

"I suppose we have."

"Why did you tell her about her parents like that?" Eilean asked, before quickly adding. "Not that you shouldn't have, but like, it wasn't the nicest way in the world."

Bhradain sighed. "I had not thought it through."

Well, that's obvious.

"And that stuff with her after her parents' funeral?" Eilean stared up at the horse. "What were you doing there?"

"I heard her crying."

Eilean tilted her head. "How did you hear her?"

The kelpie lifted his head to stare up at the dark sky, his monstrous body catching the light of the moon, illuminating his green algae skin in a ghostly manner. "Her parents spoke of her their entire journey to the Isle of the Dead. It is rare I hear humans speak to me with such love for another. When they speak to me at all."

"You were curious about her."

Bhradain bowed his head. "I should have let her be."

"I think she'll forgive you." Eilean glanced at Bhradain. "It may take some time, but I think she will."

"Not many do." Bhradain moved around the fire and toward Freya. "To know that a creature of death was with a loved one the moment they passed is never easy to bear. I would not blame her."

"I think she'll surprise you," Eilean said. She watched the kelpie settle on the ground nearby Freya. "Just give her time."

Bhradain didn't respond to her. All she heard was the wet sound of—what she assumed to be—the kelpie's snores. With the warmth of the fire still beside her and the knowledge that both her companions were resting, Eilean stared up at the empty sky and fell into a dreamless sleep.

22

DEATH: SHE GROWS NEAR

Eilean.

A horned figure stood before her, covered in a black putrid liquid that swallowed its mouth, face, and hands. It struggled to reach out to her, the thick sap pulling at its limbs so much it could hardly move. It called out to her. Its voice was hollow and raspy, but she could hear her name from it as clear as day.

Eilean.

She reached out to the figure and touched its hand, and all she could feel was pain. A burning acrid pain that filled her lungs until it suffocated her.

Eilean woke with a gasp. Sitting upright, she tried to catch her breath as her mind focused on the reality around her. It was still dark, which surprised Eilean, and the stars were still missing, which frightened her.

"Are you okay?" Freya asked from the other side of the now-extinguished fire. The embers' glow revealed brown, guarded eyes and anxiously crossed arms, but the way Freya leaned toward Eilean showed she was still worried.

"Yeah…" Eilean started to lie and then, remembering the voice in her head, changed her mind. "Well, minus the nightmare."

"What was it about?" Freya asked before adding, "if you want to say, that is."

"I don't remember much," Eilean said. "There was a shadowy figure and, when I touched them, it hurt. Like I was being burned or something. Kind of like what the plant did to me but, worse. It was... weird."

Freya just nodded in understanding. "I used to get weird nightmares like that when I was scared," she said quietly. "Though mine usually had my parents in them instead of a shadow."

"Do you know what it could mean?" Eilean asked.

"My therapist said my nightmares came from my misplaced guilt about their deaths." Freya tugged at her braid and stood up. "But every dream is different..."

Eilean got to her feet and kept her eyes on Freya. "I'm sorry that you felt that way when you were young."

"It is what it is." Freya shrugged, taking her focus away from Eilean and to her things. "Anyway, we should get ready."

"Freya—"

"Come now, mortals," Bhradain snorted, ruining any possible chance Eilean had of apologizing to Freya. "The day is upon us, and we must find the entrance to the Withering Woods."

"I wanted to go last night—"

"Let us be going."

Eilean grumbled to herself. Freya laughed a little, which gave Eilean some hope that she hadn't ruined everything.

As the three of them headed into the woods once again, Eilean wondered when the sun would rise. She knew this place was odd with its timing, but it felt a little strange to still be in darkness. Opening her mouth to ask Bhradain, she took in the kelpie's darting gaze. Up to the sky, around at the trees, and back up to the sky again. It seemed Bhradain was just as aware of the lack of sun as she was. As they continued to walk, and the moon continued to shine, Eilean realized this was just another sign that something was wrong in the Otherworld.

Darkness surrounded them, casting shadows across the trees and bushes and turning them into terrifying figures. Every so often, Eilean had to remind herself that they were just trees. But, in a world where some of them might not be, it didn't offer her much comfort.

Eilean could still hear and see the river to the left of them, which meant they were on the right path according to Bhradain. Yet, the farther into the woods the three traveled, the more changes Eilean started to notice.

Where there had once been sky-high trees with thick green leaves and flower bushes showcasing a kaleidoscope of colors, there were now only withered leaves and lifeless trees. Leaves pooled along the grass, wet with moisture, to the point that they stuck to Eilean's shoes. The air had a bitter taste of rain, as if at any moment a storm could follow. Trees, now at a normal height, stood with bare branches; the few leaves and flowers remaining an autumn red. Even the smell of the forest had changed. Instead of the floral smell of the bushes and flowers, now there was a sharp pungent scent of rotting leaves that seemed to stick to her like the foliage on her shoes. A chill trickled down Eilean's back as a gust of wind caught her, wafting leaves into a miniature cyclone before settling once more on to the ground or among the trees.

Tree branches drooped down and looped together. Limbs entangled in a twisted mess that caused cracks in the branches and bent tree trunks into strange angles. One pair of trees looked as if they were caught in mid-battle. The thinnest was bent toward the ground, its branches hooked around the trunk of another and seemingly pulling it down with them. It was a marvelous sight of nature, but terrifying all the same.

"Can trees physically attack each other?" Eilean asked as they walked around the warring oaks.

"Only if they have something to fight for," Bhradain replied.

Eilean made sure to give the thicker trees a wide berth after that.

With the darkness never letting up, the farther they traveled into the forest, the more difficult it was to see. Eilean wasn't sure how long they had been walking. She'd attempted to use the moon above to track the passage of time, only to realize that it hadn't moved from its peak in the sky. It was as if time had stopped, but everything else kept moving.

Or maybe it was only them who continued to move. She'd not yet heard any of the trees speak during this part of their journey. The one time she'd knocked on a trunk to ask if she could climb over them, she was met by silence.

"You will not hear their voices here," Bhradain had said from ahead of them.

"Why?" Eilean asked.

"They are trapped in limbo, stuck in-between Cernunnos and Danu's world and that of Lady Death."

Eilean remembered what Brigid had said, however long ago that was now. Ar Dachaidh seemed to change seasons the further you traveled.

"Autumn," Freya said. "They're in limbo because we're in autumn."

"Yes," Bhradain responded quietly. "We are close now."

In front of them lay a thick forest wall. While the wood had already been dense, this section took the cake. It had brambles and thorns lining the ground, so they couldn't even consider crawling. The only part they could find that gave them a way through to the other side was a tree split like a high "V".

"That's going to be… interesting," Freya said.

Bhradain stomped a hoof. "I may need some of your items removed from my back. I do not think I will fit through with them."

Eilean took Freya's backpack and slipped it on. She'd always been good at climbing trees, having loved doing so as a kid when she and her Mamó explored the loch. She figured she could handle the heavier weight. Besides, she really didn't want to hold that sword again. Freya took that.

"Thank you both," Bhradain said.

Then he leaped over the tree with ease.

"Show off," Eilean muttered, heading toward the tree.

It was about ten feet or so up to the "V" point and, after a steadying breath, Eilean started to climb. It wasn't easy, especially with a backpack, but there were various thick growing branches on the side or dips that Eilean could grab onto or stick a foot into so she could climb up. She thanked her blacksmithing for giving her the upper body strength to do it.

When she reached the top where the tree split, she turned back to find Freya struggling to climb up after her. It seemed as if she were trying to follow Eilean's steps, but from the way her arms shook, she didn't have the strength for it. And it didn't help that Phobia was digging into her ribs as she climbed.

Then Freya slipped and fell a good five feet, hands scraping along the uneven bark.

"Freya!" Eilean quickly climbed back down the tree and rushed to Freya's side, where she sat in the dirt.

Cuts from the tree dotted her palms, drawing blood. They didn't have the first-aid kit with them and the cuts would need to be cleaned soon to avoid any possible infection.

"Bhradain, wait!" Eilean called out, hoping the kelpie would hear them. "I'll need the kit when we get to your side."

Eilean put a cautious arm around Freya's waist and helped her to her feet. "Are you okay?"

Freya's face was flushed, and she was clenching her jaw so tightly Eilean was surprised she wasn't hurting herself. Eilean understood that look. Frustration. Frustration at not being able to keep up and needing help.

"Pheebs being a pain, right?" Eilean asked, trying to get a smile at Freya's preferred name for the weapon. "Here, I'll take her for now and then, when you get to the top, I'll throw it up to you. Sound like a plan?"

Without a word, Freya unhooked the sword from her waist. She'd slid the scabbard into her belt loop, stretching the material to make it fit. It explained why it had jabbed her in the side so easily.

Freya handed Eilean the sword. Eilean had to fight back a shiver at the small spark of electricity that returned to her when she gripped it. She hooked the sword back onto the material strap attached to her belt and got to work.

Neither of them spoke as Eilean bent down and offered her hands for Freya to step on. After only a moment's hesitation, a muddy boot pressed against her palms and a hand rested against her shoulder. Freya bounced a little and then Eilean lifted, taking her weight to get her off the ground and against the tree. She then slid beneath Freya and continued to push until she could slide one of her feet into the dips. Higher up, Freya had less work to do to get to the central point of the trunk.

With a swiftness that surprised even her, Eilean climbed up again, the sword only causing minimal struggle for her. Without pausing, she climbed down the other side and reached up as Freya lowered herself down. It was strange how easily they could work with each other in silence. She didn't need to tell Freya when to slide forward, when to let go of the tree, or how to help Eilean keep balance.

After Eilean lowered Freya to the ground, Freya turned. What little moonlight was left to them reflected in her gaze. After a beat, Freya stepped out of Eilean's hold. Eilean hadn't realized she still had her hands on Freya's waist until she broke away.

"Thank you," Freya said quietly.

"You're welcome."

"Here." The first-aid kit fell at their feet. The girls looked over to see Bhradain standing nearby. "There is no need to risk an infection when we are so close to the end."

The kelpie began moving and, after opening the antiseptic wipes and getting the worst of the mud and blood off, the two girls followed after him.

The rest of their walk continued in pensive silence. Every so often, Eilean glanced over at Freya and took in her furrowed brow. Eilean was surprised she hadn't imploded after everything that had happened. Bhradain's info dump and Eilean's emotional instability—they weren't exactly easy to be around. Eilean was just about to speak up and offer an apology for everything when a burning in her neck had her yelping in surprise.

"Eilean?" Freya asked, concerned. "You okay?"

Lifting her pendant away from her skin, Eilean shook her head. "Bhradain, it happened again."

"Your necklace?" he asked.

"Yeah, it's—"

She looked up to tell the kelpie more when something white caught her eye. In a thick grove of trees just ahead, branches were bare and devoid of color entirely. Except for one. Frost caught the tips of twigs and grass, drowning the brown in a crystalized white. When Eilean stepped closer, her breath started to come in puffs. Her sight may be dampened by the darkness, but there was no mistaking the arctic atmosphere. They were no longer in autumn.

"We're here," she said quietly.

"Yes." Bhradain pawed at the ground. "We are ready to find Death."

Not literally though, she said in her mind to any cosmic being that may be out there. *I don't want to die young.*

࿋

She was going to die young. Specifically, of hypothermia. The hair on her arms was permanently raised, her jaw ached from her attempts to stop her teeth from chattering, and she had to hold her hands across her chest because Brigid had somehow not considered weather changes when giving her this outfit. She could barely walk with how slippery the grass was with frost and snow.

"How m-much further?" Eilean stuttered out.

Bhradain didn't answer for a beat. "I am… unsure."

"Do you know where we're going?"

"Death is where you least—"

"That's not an answer," Freya responded bluntly. "How do we get to her?"

Bhradain came to a stop and sighed, his breath pouring out in smoke. "I do not know."

"How do you not know?" Eilean demanded. "You're a monster of death too, right?"

"She is different from my kind," Bhradain said quietly, lowering his head. If Eilean didn't know better, she'd say she'd hurt his feelings. "It is complicated, and finding her is just as much so."

"Okay, cool, great. By the time we find her, we could actually be dead." Eilean let out a heavy breath.

"That is not my fault—"

"Bhradain," Freya interrupted. "Can you look for her while we just move around here? We need to keep warm, and you're a lot faster than us."

The kelpie didn't argue back. "Take the blanket. It'll keep you warm."

"And you couldn't have given us the blanket sooner?" Eilean snapped.

"You didn't ask for it."

Freya took the blanket from his side saddle without a word. Bhradain watched Freya as she walked away from him, a look of sadness in his gaze. He bowed his head to Eilean and vanished so fast that Eilean barely even saw him leave.

Wrapped in the blanket, the two of them moved slowly around. Freya said it wasn't safe to stop moving when they were this cold. Safer to keep their blood flowing this way. Eilean wasn't going to question her. She'd saved her life, after all. In more ways than one. It's why she owed her one.

"Uh, so there's something I think you should know—"

"I heard you guys talking."

Eilean stopped moving, which meant Freya did too. "You what?"

"When I rolled over, I was waking up," Freya said. "Then I heard what you said, and, well, I decided to eavesdrop. Sorry."

"Uh, no, it's okay."

"Bhradain wasn't… torturing me," she sighed, "but still, I don't know, I just… I can't think about it. He didn't do it, I know, but he was still with them."

"I know," Eilean replied, "and you don't have to figure it out now. You only just learned about it."

Freya nodded. "It's… it's not usual that a creature of death gets interested in mortal love, is it?"

"You know more about Celtic myth—or reality, I guess—than me."

The two of them fell into a heavy silence. Eilean was about to recommend they start walking again to keep warm when she was interrupted by her pendant pulsing with heat once more.

"What the—"

It was then she noticed the changes.

Around them the trees that had laid still and bare now curled toward them, highlighted in the moonlight. Their branches curved in terrifying angles, reaching out as if they were waiting for the girls to step too close. A fog billowed toward them, carried across the earth by the sudden chilling wind until it blurred the sight of the ground beneath them. Dropping the now frozen-solid blanket, Eilean and Freya took a step toward the growing cloud to investigate. With each step they took, the fog swallowed their feet, covering them in white powder and leaving traces of frost behind.

"What's going on?" Freya asked in a shaky voice.

"I don't—"

A spine-tingling scream burst out of the darkness, swirling among the trees, echoing along the wind and burying deep into their skulls. Eilean felt the cacophony forcing its way into her mind, rattling her sense of self until all that remained was numbness and fear. It felt like hundreds of screams were echoing all around her, but she could only hear one voice.

Falling to her knees in the ice, Eilean covered her ears with her hands and closed her eyes tightly. It didn't matter; the echo of the screams pounded in her eardrums. A trickle spilled down her palms. It might've been blood, but she didn't want to risk removing her hands to look.

The screams finally faded, and Eilean collapsed to the ground. Her breathing was heavy and she was covered in sweat. Her legs were weak and shaking, but she tried to get to her feet. Once she was up, she wiped the blood covering her palms onto the front of her pants and took a heavy breath.

"Freya?" Eilean croaked out. It felt like she'd been the one screaming at how sore her throat was.

She turned around to find Freya cradling her head in her hands on the ground. Eilean came to her side and hovered a hand above her back. "Freya, are you okay?"

Freya's hands shook as she removed them from her ears. "What was that?"

Eilean had no idea. She looked around, hoping for a sign, but all she saw was the fog, terrifying trees and—

"Gravestones."

All around them, up against the trees, dotted across the ground, standing above the fog, were graves. A chill ran up her spine at the thought of dead bodies beneath her feet.

Freya got to her feet and moved closer to one of them.

"There aren't any names on them." Freya said, confused. "Aren't there usually names?"

"These are the lives that have not yet passed," came a disembodied voice.

Eilean's hand jumped to Phobia's hilt. Freya had nothing to protect herself with. If she needed to shield Freya, she wouldn't hesitate to draw the blade.

"Who's there?" Eilean shouted in an attempt to be brave. The crack in her voice wasn't helpful.

Ahead, the trees began to part. Branch arms reached down to pull their roots from the ground, cracking and splintering their wooden bodies. With each tug, the trees moved themselves backward. It was as if they were running away. The fog at their feet receded at a speed that had both Eilean and Freya stumbling backward.

The fog sped toward two tree trunks standing side by side. There mist collected between the trees from top to bottom in a creepy, smoky mirror-like image. And as quickly as it had risen, the fog dropped and faded, leaving behind a dark hole—and a woman.

The woman walked toward them slowly. Her skin was paler than the moon, translucent and sickly as it hugged unnaturally against her bones. She wore a white strapless dress that fell loosely around her body, reaching just below the knees. Her hair was long and dark, framing empty black-pit eyes.

"What..." Freya started. Eilean commended her bravery at being able to speak first. "What are you?"

The woman paid Freya no notice. Her solid black eyes were fixed solely on Eilean.

"You know what I am," she said in a gentle whisper that echoed all around them, resonating in an unholy refrain.

It was the scream that had Eilean thinking back to Mamó's stories. The scream from a woman who looked like death. She knew what and who she was. She was the one who decided the fate of those who would die. No amount of begging or pleading would move her. Once her third scream was heard, it was only a matter of time.

"You're the Death Bhradain said we'd meet." Eilean tugged Freya behind her. "You're a Banshee."

The Banshee smiled, her teeth pure white and blinding. "Welcome to my home," she whispered. "I have been expecting you."

23

HEED DEATH'S WARNINGS

It's never a good sign to hear that Death has been waiting for you. Eilean thought it was probably the worst thing anyone could hear. Except maybe her scream.

"What do you want with us?" Freya stepped toward the woman in either an act of courage or stupidity. Probably both.

The Banshee laughed. It was a strange sound, closer to the noise that a dying vacuum makes than actual laughter. "I want nothing from you. It is you who wants something from me." The Banshee bared her teeth in a smile. "You may call me First, for I am the first of the Banshee. Second mistress to Death."

Oh great, Eilean thought as she gripped her sword's hilt tighter. *There's more than one of them.*

"What do you mean we want something from you?" Eilean questioned. "You're Death, right? You're the one guarding the entrance to the woods?"

First stared at her. Eilean tried to get a read on the creature, but the blankness in her eyes and the stillness of her body betrayed nothing. "Yes, I guard the entrance."

"So, we have to do something for you to get through, right?"

"No."

Freya, with her hands tucked under her armpits to keep warm, stepped closer. "Then why do we have to meet you to get there? Can't you just tell us where the entrance—"

"It is through this door," First interrupted, gesturing with her pale hand toward the two trees where she had entered.

"The black hole?" Eilean asked, staring at said hole that resided between the two foggy trees. "Great, cause that's not ominous at all."

The dying vacuum laugh wheezed out once more. "You amuse me, Eilean Ruth Elsbeth MacAlistair."

Ice filled her veins at hearing her full name. She never heard her full name. Last time it was probably used was at her Communion when she was seven, and all she cared about that day was the bread and Ribena. Hearing it now, from a creature of Death, felt… ominous. Eilean gripped tighter on her sword hilt, trying to ignore the sparks tickling her fingertips. Now was not the time to lose her cool.

"So we just walk through the hole?" Eilean asked her. "No tricks, just walk right in, no problem?"

First stared at the fog made door. "You may walk through that door," her gaze returned to the girls, "but your line knows more than most that nothing is without cost."

Eilean had to stop herself from rolling her eyes. *Of course.*

"All right, lay it on us." Eilean let go of her sword and crossed her arms. Freya was giving her a look that read very much as a warning. She was, after all, sassing the most well-known Celtic creature of Death. "What's the catch? Another giant? A God who we've got to do a side quest for? What is it?"

Freya had been right to try to warn her.

In a blink, First stood a hair's breadth from Eilean. Her already translucent skin had faded even more so, showing the white of her bones. An unreadable blankness on her face twisted to the state of a silent scream. Her dark hair flung back, as if trapped in a wind Eilean couldn't feel, forcing Eilean to stare straight into the pit of her eyes. A pit that wasn't as empty as Eilean had first thought.

Within her gaze, Eilean saw her death. Or deaths, she should say. For her ending seemed to be in flux. In one version, she lay in a hospital bed, old and haggard, clearly having lived a full and long life. She was surrounded by, she assumed, her children, who were saying goodbye to her as her eyes closed. Another, she was older, maybe in her forties. Freya was by her side, which confused her. Bhradain too, which was even weirder. She didn't know what was happening. She didn't look like she should be dying, but she could feel it. Feel the life being drawn out of her until the woman in front of her let out her final breath. Many versions appeared in the Banshee's eyes, and Eilean saw them all. Only when Freya pulled at her arm and stepped between the two did the visions fade.

"What are you doing?" Freya snapped, a crack to her voice the only sign of her fear.

First bowed her head, almost as if she were apologizing. "Answering your question."

"W-why did you show me that?" Eilean managed to get out.

"You must know what could come to pass," First replied, her tone no longer passive but urgent, almost anxious. "Once you pass through to the Withering Woods, you will face a test that will change the course of your future."

Freya raised her hand. "Why is there a test?"

The Banshee shook her head. "I do not know. There is something in the woods, something that has captured Cernunnos, that is making its own rules for my part of the world." First's skin paled further. "And now I can no longer enter all of my domain. Something is keeping me away."

"How are we meant to pass through, then?" Eilean asked, a tremble to her voice the only sign she was still affected by what she'd seen. "If you can't, how can we?"

"One of your kind has passed through already."

Freya and Eilean glanced at each other. Danu had said something about her not being the first. She had assumed that meant the person who'd come before had failed. But, if they'd made it this far, what happened to them that they couldn't save the God?

Eilean thought back to the futures she'd been shown and shivered at the thought of what the first person to come here had gone through. Mamó's stories of the heroes from Celtic myth, and others, often had their ending in death or everlasting misery. Whether it be Arthur and Excalibur, a King prophesied to die before completing his mission. Or Cúchulainn who was told he would be one of the greatest remembered heroes but, as a result, would die young. She thought of her Mamó back home and felt a fear that she was about to become one of the people in her stories.

"Those who shine bright can burn the fastest," Mamó would say. Eilean could only hope she hadn't shone enough yet for that to be true.

"Do you know what tests we could expect?" Eilean asked.

"This land is home to the most terrifying of creatures, ones who have no qualms about harming a mortal that crosses them with tricks and games. Whatever may be controlling the Withering Woods, they have many beings to choose from."

"Lovely," Eilean muttered. "Well, I guess we've got our own terrifying–" She glanced around, suddenly aware that they were missing a member of the team. "Where's Bhradain?"

"I have kept him away," the Banshee said quietly. "His kind hold no love for me and mine."

"But," Freya spoke up, "aren't you both creatures of death?"

First offered her bared teeth as a smile. "Yes, and yet we are still different. He is a carrier and bringer of death; I am a predictor. We may be connected in some ways, but my abilities spread beyond mortals. Even creatures of death fear it."

Well, that's reassuring, Eilean thought.

"When can we have him back?" Freya asked, surprising Eilean. She and Bhradain weren't exactly on great terms.

"Soon," First replied. "There is one more thing you must know."

"Oh, great. There's more."

First raised an eyebrow at Eilean. She kept her mouth shut after that. "Make your choices wisely and know that what you want is not always what you need."

Before Eilean could even question the Banshee's cryptic words, the woman collapsed into a pool of mist. A white gravestone appeared where she had once stood. It had no name on it, like all the others, but as the words of First played in her mind, she could only guess what name might appear there if she failed.

The clopping of hooves reached them soon after the Banshee had left. From the trees came a breathless Bhradain. He looked exhausted and borderline panic-stricken.

"What happened?" he panted.

Eilean pointed toward the wall of shadow that lay in front of them. Wisps of black mist slithered out into the air before fading away. They couldn't see anything beyond the smoke—and part of Eilean thought that was a good thing.

"We found Death," Eilean said bluntly.

Her voice was unnaturally steady, considering how terrified she felt. She could feel Freya at her side and sense the same fear from her. When she chanced a glance, Eilean found Freya biting at her nails. A new stage of anxiety had been unlocked, it seemed.

"What now?" Freya pulled her thumb away from her mouth as if recognizing what she was doing. "Do we just," she waved a hand toward the shadow, "walk through and wait for the test to appear, or?"

"Test?" Bhradain questioned.

"Apparently something's going to distract us or something."

Eilean shrugged. "I don't really know, but there's one way to find out."

Bhradain snorted uneasily behind her. "Sword-wielders first."

Of course.

Taking a deep breath, she took a few steps toward the shadowed entrance. The closer she got, the more she noticed the depth of it. The darkness within seemed to get darker and deeper than a simple misty doorway. As she stared, it seemed less like a door and more like a never-ending tunnel.

She could feel Freya and Bhradain behind her, waiting for her to take the first step.

Hand hovering over Phobia's hilt, Eilean breathed in deeply through her nose and stepped forward into the darkness.

24

THE PAST WILL HAUNT YOU

THE DARKNESS DID NOT STAY DARK FOR LONG.

Strange visions crossed Eilean's mind with every step. She saw herself receiving an apprenticeship offer from Mr. Lawton and her parents, smiling with pride. Another vision showed her with Mamó, who looked healthier than ever as they worked together in the garden. It was as if the two of them had never been separated. She even saw a vision of her family all together, no fighting, no resentment, just... happiness.

Then the darkness faded and took the visions with it.

"Wait..." Eilean reached out to the visions that felt like memories. But she knew they'd never happened, even if she wished they had. Blinking her eyes quickly, she found herself on the other side of the shroud.

Freya and Bhradain stumbled through after her, both looking as disorientated as Eilean felt.

"Did you...?" Freya started asking as she glanced around her. "Did you see something?"

Eilean nodded and turned to Bhradain. "What was all that?"

"I am unsure," Bhradain said uneasily. "It is not often that monsters like I experience visions like this." He shook his head. "What did Death tell you?"

"That..." She ran a hand nervously through her hair. "That we would be tested before we could make it to the woods."

Bhradain shook his mane. "That did not feel like a test."

"What would you call what just happened?" Freya asked quietly, wiping sweat from her brow.

"A trick." Bhradain glanced around as if he were waiting for confirmation. "For it should not be this easy to make it to the Withering Woods."

Whirling around, Eilean came face-to-face with a dark, foggy forest that towered into the sky.

Just like the graveyard, a grove of wintery trees spread far and wide before them. They blended together in a way that made it hard to distinguish which branches belonged to which tree or even how deep the woods went. Unlike the frozen land they were in before, here they had returned to the autumnal feeling of empty branches, mulch covered earth, and the sharp tangy scent of dying plant-life. Or at least, Eilean hoped it was the scent of dying plants.

"That's..." Eilean walked toward the trees, focusing on a gnarled and curled tree archway in the center. "That's a creepy-looking entrance."

The archway was similar to the one they had passed through but was filled with thick gray smoke, smoke so thick that Eilean had almost mistaken it for a concrete wall. What stood out as particularly strange to Eilean was the fact that none of the smog was spreading beyond the trees. It was like it was trapped there.

She stepped closer and reached out a hand. "Weird."

As she pulled her hand back, a waft of the fog came with it, flowing up to Eilean as she took in a breath. She instantly started hacking and coughing. The bitter smell of car exhaust and the taste of rotten food filled her senses. Eilean stumbled away from the smoke.

"What happened?" Bhradain asked her.

"That's... that's not fog," Eilean coughed.

Through her blurry vision, she glanced up at Bhradain, who stared at the wood. "Something has polluted the land."

Out of the corner of her eye, Freya walked toward the arch. Was Freya trying to get a closer look out of curiosity? Before Eilean could warn her, she disappeared into the smog.

"Freya!" Eilean yelled after her.

Both she and Bhradain ran toward the entrance. Eilean hesitated for only a moment, remembering the burning in her nose and throat, before pushing through her fear and charging after Freya.

Her eyes burned instantly, making them water. She had to hold back a cough as the acrid smell enveloped her senses. Covering her mouth and nose with her hand and closing her eyes, Eilean blindly stumbled forward, desperately searching for Freya. She'd lost Bhradain the moment they'd stepped through. She was all alone and had no idea what to do.

Risking the pain, Eilean removed her hands from her mouth and took a breath.

"Freya!" she choke-screamed. Immediately, her throat started to burn as she breathed in the toxic air. It reminded her of the time she tried a cigarette one of her classmates gave her, as if she'd tried ten of them at once. "Bhradain! Freya!"

A shadow appeared in front of her and she felt a tug at her shirt, finding herself suddenly airborne. Seconds later, she was gulping in clean air and feeling the frost-covered ground beneath her feet. She took a deep inhale and almost cried with relief at finally being able to breathe without pain. As she regained her sight, she saw Bhradain nearby coughing, from the ache at her side and how close he stood to the smoke arch in front of them. She could only assume he was the reason she'd escaped.

That was when she caught sight of Freya lying on the grass

at Bhradain's hooves. Without thinking, Eilean crawled toward her.

"What happened?" Her voice sounded hoarse from the smoke inhalation, but the intensity in her tone was still clear as day.

"I... I don't know." Freya coughed. Her voice sounded as dry as a fifty-a-day chain smoker. "There was this voice, it was... it was calling for my help."

"A trick." Bhradain shook his head. "There's always a trick."

"Why didn't you say anything?" Eilean asked Freya, ignoring Bhradain for now. "It could have been a trap or..." She shook her head. "Whatever you heard, you should have said something."

Freya rolled her eyes. "Don't think you can lecture me about talking, but yes, I know. I should have."

"Sorry, I—" Eilean started but Freya raised a hand.

"You *need* to stop apologizing. I'm just saying, if this friendship is going to work, there's gotta be a little tit for tattas." Freya frowned. "Wait, that's not the way you say it."

Eilean let out a stunned laugh. She hoped Freya thought the laughter was over her mistaking the joke, and not the utter surprise at her comments.

She thinks we're friends? Eilean thought. She probably shouldn't have been confused by the idea. Everything Freya had done since trying to stop her friends from harassing her was supportive and kind. She had tried to comfort her after the Balor fiasco. Eilean could only guess that that was the sort of thing friends did. But when Eilean started thinking about what she'd done for Freya in return, she wondered if it could really be called friendship. She'd not exactly been the easiest to be around.

"Either way," Freya continued, drawing Eilean out of her thoughts, "I don't think I could have told you even if I wanted to."

"What do you mean?" Eilean asked.

Freya rubbed at her throat. "It was weird, it's like I couldn't *not* follow the voice… like I didn't have control of my body. I was barely aware of you guys around me."

"Is that normal?" Eilean asked Bhradain. He was from this world. Maybe he could explain it.

"Nothing that we have seen is normal." Bhradain looked around them nervously. "Something does not feel right."

"But the woods are here," Freya croaked.

Eilean helped Freya up to her feet. "Yeah, but we can't get through them."

"Could this be the test? Like, maybe we have to figure out how to get rid of the smog or we help someone and, if we do a good job, the smog goes away?"

The two girls turned to Bhradain, who offered them the horse equivalent of a shrug. If their guide in this world was clueless about what was happening, Eilean feared what may be coming their way.

"Let's…" Eilean started nervously, "let's just try and find our way around. Maybe it doesn't cover the whole place?"

"Worth a shot," Freya said. "Hopefully, the test or whatever doesn't come right away. I'm exhausted as it is."

"If you've jinxed us, you're buying me chocolate when we get home," Eilean said in an attempt to be playful.

"Deal," Freya coughed and then spat out a chunk of gunk. "Oh, that's gross."

"We'll walk slowly," Eilean said. "No point rushing when we don't even know if we'll find a way in."

Freya offered her a grateful smile and started walking. Eilean and Bhradain followed after her, using the now visible moon's light above and the strange glow of the woods to see the path in front of them. There wasn't much space between the woods to their left and the tight clump of trees to their right, but they were able to walk side-by-side well enough. As the sound of Bhradan's hooves clip-clopped against the softmudded ground, Eilean's thoughts returned to what Freya had said about them being friends.

Wouldn't it be nice to have a friend? A melodic voice whispered into her mind, forcing Eilean to stop in place.

"Eilean—" Freya's voice faded away as an image came into her mind.

She, Mamó, and Freya sat out in the garden with a pot of tea and biscuits as they talked and laughed together. Her Mamó looked better; her eyes were no longer glazed over, but alert and alive. Eilean watched as Freya and Mamó laughed together. It was such a nice sunny day. Eilean could feel the warmth of the sun on her skin and smell the lavender in the garden. It felt so real.

And what of the day she gets tired of you? The same voice said, their words as soft as butter.

The vision changed to a darker hue. Freya watched Eilean lose control again. She wasn't sure what it was about though, with her, it could be anything that set her off. Eilean watched as fear and horror filled Freya's eyes at the sight of a blood covered Phobia in her hands as she used its blade to hack at an unknown figure's body. She watched herself as this Eilean smiled, blood coating her teeth, as she continued to slash at the body needlessly and with a joy that had her feeling sick. She watched as Freya turned and ran away.

Another vision followed. Mamó was crying out in terror. She didn't know who Eilean was. She was screaming, calling for someone to save her. Eilean was holding Phobia in her hands. Mamó was afraid of her, believing she was there to hurt her. Eilean wasn't sure if she would or not. Why does she have the sword in her hands? Her parents appeared and screamed at her to leave. Eilean fled, knowing that when Mamó dies with no memory of her, that it's a good thing. Because who would want to remember a monster?

They're all better off without you.

"Eilean?"

You don't deserve to find happiness in this world.

"Eilean!"

Hands shook hard at her shoulders, but Eilean couldn't draw away from that voice.

But perhaps I could fix it all for you. Its words were like music to her ears, echoing within her mind. *I could take away that one mistake. You only have to ask.*

"Show yourself, beast!" Bhradain bellowed.

The voice slipped away from her head. Then, so did the vision. Blinking rapidly, Eilean found herself back in the forest with Freya and Bhradain standing protectively around her.

"What…" she stuttered out, "what happened?"

Neither answered her question as Bhradain called out into the surrounding emptiness. "Face us, you coward!"

"Now, now, Bhradain," a soft purr of a voice drifted out from the trees. "That isn't very kind, is it? Surely, an old friend like myself deserves a proper welcome."

25

LET'S TURN BACK TIME

From the trees behind them a beautiful woman stepped out. With eyes a sharp fluorescent blue and hair a glittering array of blonde, brown, red, and silver, it was clear she wasn't human. She was petite, almost pixie-like when combining her shape and size. When Eilean noticed her pointed ears, she found herself wondering if she really was a pixie.

Completing her ensemble was a musical instrument held delicately in her hands. Eilean thought it was some kind of old-fashioned harp until she remembered images of the God Apollo from her history class and realized it was a lyre.

"Lady Liana Shade of the Leannan Sìth, at your service, dear hero." She threw Eilean a dazzling smile that left her speechless. "Did you enjoy my gift to you? It was a wonderful sight, wasn't it?"

"What gift?" Freya asked.

Eilean turned away from Liana Shade and toward Freya. For a second she was sure she heard a growl come from the woman, but when she glanced back, all she saw was her smiling face.

"I don't really know..." Eilean told Freya honestly.

"Why, haven't you figured it out?" Liana Shade asked. "I showed you a glimpse of a better life."

"What do you mean? Those things you showed me they aren't… real." Eilean faltered. "Are they?"

"Oh, they can be," Liana Shade drew her fingers across the lyre. It was a single chord, and yet Eilean was sure it was the greatest sound she'd ever heard. The first tune of a song she didn't know she needed. "Did the vision bring you joy? That is my one mission—"

"Don't lie!" Bhradain trotted in front of Eilean and Freya, blocking them from Liana Shade's sight. "Your trickster magic will not have them. I will not allow it."

Liana Shade laughed a dainty laugh that made even Bhradain step back in confusion. "I find that rather rich, coming from the beast who took this lovely young child's parents away."

Even Eilean could feel the tension between Freya and Bhradain that followed that. It was a sore subject, one she was surprised Liana Shade knew about.

Bhradain snorted. "Unlike your kind, I do not take life that is not meant to be taken."

"We shall see."

Her form faded. And though she could not see where she'd gone, Eilean had a feeling she wasn't far away.

"'Cause that's not suspicious at all…" Freya said with a nervous laugh. "Are you alright? You kinda spaced out or something before. Do you think she did something to you?"

Eilean bit her lip. "I don't know. Her voice sounded familiar, but… it doesn't make sense. She showed me a happy vision and a sad one. Why would she show something like that?" She turned to Bhradain hoping he'd have the answers. "What even is she?"

Someone who can make your dreams come true… Liana Shade's voice whispered into her mind.

"Eilean?" she heard Freya ask.

Allow me to show you my offer. Her words were like a soft lullaby, lulling Eilean into oblivion. *I will grant you your greatest desire.*

EILEAN COULD SEE HERSELF. HER YOUNGER SELF. SHE WAS back at the school in Balloch when she was twelve.

She was walking toward the playground for lunch; her backpack hanging casually off one shoulder. Just like how the cool year-elevens wore them. She had ham sandwiches for lunch and she couldn't wait to eat them.

Then a kid crashed into her and sent both of them tumbling to the ground.

"Hey!" Eilean pushed the kid off her. "Watch it."

When the girl locked eyes with her, Eilean took in the tear-stained cheeks and scuffed bloody knees from the gravel beneath them. She was in the same year as Eilean, but Eilean had never learned her name. She only knew what the girl looked like because she was one of the few other redheads in the school. Eilean thought she might be on the girl's football team. Or maybe she'd just played that one time at lunch? She didn't know.

"Come on, don't cry," Eilean said as she helped her to her feet. "I didn't mean to yell at you, you just ran into me and—"

"Careful, Kathy," a voice nearby mocked. Eilean turned to find the year-nine thug David next to them. "You don't want the uniform to get ruined, do you?"

He had his posse with him, just like always. Eilean wondered to this day how he'd managed to get so many people from different years to follow him about. He wasn't the nicest guy out there.

"David, it's not me, I swear—"

"You know, the more you say that, the less I believe you."

David shrugged like somehow Kathy was bringing this on herself.

Eilean didn't want anything to do with this. She quickly started to make her exit when she heard it.

"I swear it's—" Kathy started to say, but was cut off with a sudden *oof* after David pushed her to the ground.

"Don't touch me, you filthy dyke."

Eilean remembered what happened next. She could picture her fist crushing his jaw as if it were yesterday. She didn't want to relive that. So she turned away from the picture. She closed her eyes and hoped the image would just go away.

It can. You can make it go away. Right now. The voice of Liana Shade returned. *You can change this forever. Just walk away. Leave the girl and go on to live your life as you should have. See what you will gain if you do.*

The image changed to the one she had seen in the shroud.

She'd never left Balloch at this time. She still lived at home, repainting the front door and window boxes with Mamó every spring and autumn, changing the flowers to fit with the new theme. A warm red for love, mixing red geraniums, azaleas, and poppies.

Mamó wasn't sick in this version of her life. She never had to face the stress and anxiety of her son and granddaughter leaving her behind because of what Eilean had done.

Eilean would take up art at school. The same school she had to leave because of what she did. Here she had friends, friends who liked the things she did and didn't fear her. They had weekends together at the movies, going shopping, having sleepovers, normal teenage girl stuff.

Her parents stayed at the jobs they loved and never quietly resented Eilean for losing them. Her dad and her had even taken up playing football together. Not for a team or anything, but just because it was something fun they could do together. They still argued. She was still a teenager after all, but there was no doubt they loved her. Because she hadn't ruined everything for them.

She had a life. A life where she isn't the problem. A life where she could be normal like she always wanted. A life where Mamó was herself and where Eilean was always with her. Learning Gaelic, learning botany, creating art for her walls. A life Eilean had always wanted.

Take my offer, child, Liana Shade whispered, her voice a caressing rhythm that guided Eilean toward the answer. *Take it, and it will be like all of this never happened.*

Eilean saw herself walking away from David. She picked up her backpack and ignored the crying girl on the floor. This wasn't her business; she wasn't going to put herself in the firing line. Why would she?

"Don't listen to her!" a familiar voice shouted.

Surprised, Eilean turned back to the image of David advancing on Kathy. She glanced at the group of friends behind him, who quietly tried to get him to stop. One face among the group stayed guiltily silent, unable to look at what was happening in front of her. She felt familiar.

Keep walking, Eilean. Liana Shade's voice returned. This time her voice was hard, dangerous even. *Change your fate.*

"She's a liar. Do not trust a word she says."

The voice sounded male. There was a hiss to it that somehow didn't sound human. She looked around for who was talking and again found no one. Was she just imagining things? Eilean listened to the Leannan Sìth once again and turned away to leave. She could hear the cries of the girl she was abandoning echoing around her, and guilt built up in her heart.

It is not your responsibility. Liana Shade said in an excited whisper. *Keep going. Leave the playground and our deal will be sealed.*

"Eilean!" the female voice from before shouted. This time, Eilean recognized her.

Spinning round and back to the impending attack behind her, Eilean caught sight of Freya. She couldn't make out her face well enough: the details of the tarmac at her feet, David with his hand raised toward the girl who didn't deserve it, and the faceless audience that watched on were too strong. A fog billowed around Freya's form, making her hard to see. Eilean wondered if she was real.

The fog moved closer to her, and the image of the playground swam like a watercolor painting. A pair of warm brown eyes appeared from within the cloud, the only solid thing Eilean could see.

"You can't leave," Freya cried. "I know why you want to. I know you hate what you did to David that day, no matter how cruel he was. I know you'd give anything to change it, but you can't."

She lies, Eilean. Liana Shade whispered into her mind, her voice gentle like a lullaby. *It is her own guilt at not stopping David that guides her. She only wishes you to continue for her own selfish gain. Do not trust her. Only I can change your past.*

Liana Shade appeared beside her and smiled. "Just take my hand, and it will be done."

She held out a hand to Eilean—a hand that shone like diamonds in the sunlight above them. Eilean couldn't help but be drawn to it. She reached out her hand…

"No!" Freya screamed.

Jumping in surprise, Eilean turned toward the image of Freya. She was solid now, her form stabilizing in a way that made no sense.

"Why?" Eilean asked her. "This will fix everything."

"Yes it will," Liana Shade said, then reached her hand out closer to Eilean. "You will have everything you always wanted. Just take my hand."

"And she'll die if she does!" Freya snapped at Liana Shade. "You'll suck the life out of her." She looked back at Eilean. "It's what her kind do to their victims."

"They are not my victims," Liana Shade sniffed. "They

choose willingly. Eilean, can you truly tell me that you would not like to be with your Mamó? To have never left her side?"

Eilean's heart sank at the image of her Mamó's tearful face five years ago when Eilean had to wave goodbye from the car. The look in her eyes as her mind faded back to emptiness only a few days ago. She'd not known who Eilean was. Maybe if Eilean had never left, she'd know her.

"Take my hand, Eilean, and you will never have to see that look in her eyes again. You will be with your family. You will be happy." Liana Shade's smile was all teeth. Eilean thought she saw the hint of fangs there, but she didn't look again. Her eyes focused solely on the hand in front of her. "You will no longer be a monster."

Eilean reached out.

"Now!"

A sword appeared in Eilean's periphery, swinging down right in front of her.

"No!" Eilean screamed.

The hand of Liana Shade was sliced off. As the limb fell to the floor, it started to fade to dust; just as the fae did. The image of the school playground and the pre-teen form of Eilean disappeared, revealing the forest around them and the faces of the two people who had just ruined everything.

26

THE COST OF A CHOICE

"WHY?"

It was only one word. But when her eyes flitted from the ground, to her empty scabbard, to the two figures in front of her, both of them stepped back.

Good, she thought.

"She..." Freya stuttered out as she held the sword weakly in her hands. "She was going to kill you. B-Bhradain said the Leannan Sìth are monsters. They drain the life from their victims after preying on their insecurities and dreams to talk them into agreeing to it."

"It's true, Eilean," the kelpie said from Freya's side. "If she had not—"

Eilean stormed toward Freya. As much as Freya tried to hide it, Eilean still saw her flinch as Eilean shoved her hand out. "Give me Phobia." Freya only briefly hesitated in handing it over. Somewhere deep down inside, that hurt. But Eilean powered through, too angry not to. "I was going willingly."

"You didn't even know what you were doing," Freya murmured. "I... you were being tricked by her. She'd have hurt you if—"

"So what?" Eilean snapped. "She was letting me change my past! Any risk is better than living with what I did."

"You don't mean that..."

Eilean looked down at the sword in her hand. "You don't know anything about me."

"It's not good that you're feeling this way," Freya said gently. "When we go back, we could get you some help." She carefully reached out a hand toward her.

"*Don't* touch me."

Freya pulled her hand back and raised them in surrender. "I'm sorry, I—"

"Eilean, you need to calm down," Bhradain interrupted. "She just saved your life."

She let out a bitter laugh. "Saved me? No, you *ruined* me. You took away the one chance I had." She tore off the necklace, the rope snapping easily at her harsh grip. "The one chance I had to be normal and not need a damn necklace to keep me sane."

Freya stepped toward Eilean again. With a shake of her head, Eilean stepped back and away from her, watching the tip of her sword drag in the mud.

"Why did you stop me?" Eilean asked in a voice so quiet she wasn't even sure Freya could hear her.

"Because you deserve to live."

Eilean looked up and locked eyes with Freya. Both of their eyes shimmered with tears. Turning away from her Eilean swallowed a lump in her throat.

"You should have let me go."

Before Freya could get another word in, Eilean turned and ran.

She didn't know where she was going, or what she would do when she got there. All she knew was that she needed to find Liana Shade. She was her only chance at changing what she had done.

So Eilean ran. Ran through woodlands, not caring for the branches that tore at her skin, or the mud that sucked at her shoes. Ran down random paths that appeared to her as her feet pounded on the ground. Ran through mist as it swept up around her waist and frosted Phobia with ice. In the back of her mind she knew they still had the deadline for Cernunnos, but she just couldn't bring herself to care. She'd told them she was the wrong person for this job. Now she was just proving her point.

Tears started to fall. They blurred her vision and caught in her throat, making it difficult to breathe without a sob following.

All Eilean could picture were the memories of her *what if*. Each one haunted her as she ran. She could still feel the could-have-been memories on her skin. The heat of the sun during her lunch with Mamó and Freya. The weight of her dad's hand on her shoulder as he smiled proudly down at her. She could even taste the coffee on her tongue from a casual day out at a café with no fears of hurting anyone following her.

Her feet hammered the ground so hard it sent shockwaves through her legs and up her torso until her foot caught a root and the world turned on its side.

She slammed into the earth, tumbling and rolling until sliding to a halt with a thud. She didn't move to get up. She couldn't. The weight of her tears held her down. Her hands pulled her shirt, her nails scraping against her chest. She didn't know what she was doing. All she wanted was for the pain to stop.

She didn't want to be a monster. Didn't want to be this way. Why couldn't they have just let her take the deal?

Mud soaked into her clothes, cooling her skin until shivers joined her sobs. Eilean didn't care. Didn't care how long she laid there. Didn't care how cold she was. Didn't care about anything.

She cried and cried until her tears stained tracks down her

neck, pooled at her clavicle and dripped into the mud below. Then she cried even more. She cried until there were no more tears left in her, until she felt numb. Darkness and dirt surrounded her, but it didn't matter. This was where a monster like her belonged.

27

CRYING IS THE KEY TO (INSERT INSPIRATIONAL QUOTE)

SHIVERS WRACKED EILEAN'S BODY AS SHE LAY LISTLESSLY IN the dirt. Her tears had long since dried up. Only waterless sobs and chokes remained as she curled tightly into herself on the cold, muddy ground. She was lost and Liana Shade had not shown herself. Eilean knew she had to get up and keep searching. She just couldn't move.

Eilean could still feel her pendant in her hand, digging into the skin of her palm so hard she'd be surprised if she hadn't drawn blood. Bringing the necklace up to her eye line, she looked at its spiral design.

I'll fix this Mamó, she thought. *I'll find a way to go back and fix it. I promise.*

She'd wallowed enough. She had to get moving. It's what her Mamó would do. She was a woman of action.

Taking a deep, steadying breath, Eilean uncurled herself out of the ball she'd formed and forced herself to sit. Then a patch of smog glided past her vision.

Eilean scurried backward and away from it—she remembered the burning in her throat and nose when she'd inhaled the toxic air last time. It was only then that Eilean noticed where she was. And when she got to her feet, she found herself wondering how the hell she was alive.

Smog surrounded her. It hung so thickly in the air that when she raised her arm out in front of her, she could barely see it. It reminded her of those pictures they'd been shown at school of the London Smog back in the fifties.

How have I made it all the way out here without choking? Eilean looked around, trying to figure out where she was. As expected, she couldn't see a thing. *I didn't even manage less than a minute before. How have I done it this time?*

Eilean cautiously began to move forward, holding out a hand in front of her to make sure she didn't walk into anything. Though she had been breathing without a problem, Eilean still measured her breaths, just in case.

The ground beneath her feet was rock solid. At one point, the earth softened. Her pendant started heating in rapid bursts when Eilean's shoes began to sink beneath the surface. In panic, she started jumping and leaping to get out of the mud and to a solid surface. Eilean only just about made it, nearly losing a shoe in the process.

Still taking careful steps, Eilean waved her hand in front of her until she felt something solid. Or at least, it felt solid at first. Then an oily liquid began to suck at her hand, the wet, cold material slipping between her fingers and sliding down her wrist.

Eilean tried to pull her hand free. She yanked it but all she could feel was the liquid tightening its hold on her. Dropping her pendant, she used her other hand on her forearm to yank even harder.

It worked. She went flying to the ground. Letting out a sigh of relief, Eilean went to get to her feet. Instead, she collapsed back to the floor and retched.

Crumpled on all fours, Eilean gasped for clean air but there wasn't any to be had. Spluttering coughs came as the toxic waste choked her. She felt like she was burning from the inside out. Her eyes turned blurry and tears fell down her cheeks.

Her curling fingers felt the wood of her pendant. Desperate to feel its familiar comfort, she grabbed it and pulled it into her chest.

And the tightness in her lungs loosened.

Eilean stayed tucked into a ball on the ground. Afraid of what would happen if she moved. The stinging in her eyes and pain in her throat faded slowly, and she lifted her head from the ground.

The smog was still there, still floating around her and obscuring her vision. Yet it wasn't affecting her.

Taking her time, Eilean got to her feet. Standing fully, she looked around. How on earth was she breathing in this smog? It was only in the shine of the distorted moonlight above did she see it.

A layer of fog swirled around Eilean's skin but avoided touching her. It was as if there was a protective barrier keeping it away. But only one thing had changed when it had rushed in….

"I wonder…" she whispered.

Crouching down, she pressed the pendant spiral on the ground directly in front of her. And then lifted her hand.

She choked as the toxic fumes flooded into her lungs. She snatched up her necklace once more.

Eilean looked over the necklace as she stood. It hadn't protected her when she'd rushed in after Freya, so why was it doing it now?

"This place makes no sense," Eilean snapped.

The necklace grew hotter in her hand, as if it agreed with her. Eilean stared down at the pendant, confused.

"How…" she started to ask her necklace before realizing how ridiculous this was. "Christ, I've gone mad."

The wood in her hands grew colder, just like it had been the whole time in the Otherworld. Eilean frowned down at the spiral and followed the carving with her eyes. There was nothing about the pendant that stood out as different as before. It looked the same as it always did. Although she had felt it grow warm a few times before, like in the forest just before the fog and gravestones appeared, she'd not really thought about it much. She'd had other problems, after all.

"Can you..." she started again, feeling mad at herself. "Can you understand me?"

A tepid heat pressed against her skin. Eilean let out a dubious laugh. This all felt too ridiculous to be true. Yet as her thumb brushed over the carving and she felt a warmth follow her movements, Eilean couldn't help but smile. As mad as she felt doing it.

"Do you know who I am?" she asked. Again, the same heat appeared against her hand. She guessed that was the necklace's way of saying yes.

"Do you know what I want to find?"

Warmth.

"Can you take me to her?"

The pendant grew hot again, but unlike before, only part of the necklace was warm. The right side. Eilean turned in the direction of the pendant in case it was reacting to something in the atmosphere. But there was nothing there.

Warmth came again, but this time at the top of the necklace. Eilean looked ahead into the foggy unknown and then back down to the spiral. "You want me to go forward?"

Warmth touched the center of her palm.

Eilean ran a hand through her hair. Following a heat-powered necklace wouldn't be the craziest thing that had happened these last few days. Maybe it was showing her the way out.

"All right," she said nervously. "You're the magical pendant. Lead the way."

Eilean followed the pendant's guidance until she reached a stream. It appeared shallow enough, so she lifted a foot to step in, but the pendant seared hot. When she looked down, she saw how steam rose from the water. Eilean grabbed a nearby stick and dipped the tip into the liquid. When it came out, part of it had melted away.

Eilean used another stick to figure out how wide the stream was by seeing if she could feel the edge of a bank at the end of the branch. She thanked her lucky stars when she did. It didn't feel far—about five feet wide, Eilean guessed. She took multiple steps back as a run-up, just in case, and leaped across.

As she traveled farther, more warnings came from the necklace as it guided her: bogs of oil where she could have easily drowned, and even an ignited bush that she barely avoided. It was only when the muscles in her legs started to ache that Eilean realized how long she'd been walking.

"Wait," she stopped in place. "I thought you were taking me to Liana Shade. Shouldn't she have appeared by now?"

The necklace stayed silently cold.

"Where are you taking me?"

Coolness again.

Is this a trap?

She placed her hand on the hilt of her sword and took a step forward. Something wet brushed against her face and Eilean let out a squealing scream. She drew Phobia one-handed and swung the blade wildly.

"Get back!" Eilean yelled, attempting to frighten off whatever had touched her.

Eilean let out a sigh of relief when she realized it had only been the drooping branches of a weeping willow that had touched her. She moved the vine from her face and immediately recoiled.

The willow tree was smothered in a black and brown oozing liquid that slipped down its branches. She'd not noticed it before because of the thickness of the smog but, slowly, the smokey haze appeared to be fading away, showing the tree's sorry state.

Branches had snapped from the weight of the ooze. The usual green of the willow vines wasn't visible to the eye, the only color that could be seen was the black of the thick liquid. When Eilean wiped the muck that had been left on her face and rubbed it between her fingers, it felt thick and gooey. Against her better judgment, she brought her hand to her face and smelled it. She gagged at the intense, chemical-like smell. It reminded her of the quenching oil they used at the forge, but worse.

The pendant began to heat up in single blasts. Eilean figured it was letting her know that she had reached her destination. Where that destination was, she had no idea. She couldn't imagine that Liana Shade was here.

Using her sword to hold back the branches, she stepped through the gap in search of the woman who would fix it all. Instead, she saw a large figure leaning against the tree. It was hard to see in the low light, but its antlers and ghoulish shape made it clear. Eilean had found the wrong monster.

Scrambling backward, Eilean tried to make a run for it, but slipped on a patch of tar-stained dirt. Covered in the oily material, Eilean desperately tried to get to her feet.

Then her necklace started pulsing heat once again.

Does it want me to stay here?

The pendant heated up in succession in response.

Eilean glanced back at the creature. To her surprise, it hadn't moved from its position. A spot that, if she was right, had the figure staring right at her.

Maybe this creature can help me.

Getting to her feet, Eilean reached for Phobia's hilt and held onto it. She didn't know what this figure was like and, as much as she didn't want to hurt anyone—or thing—else, she would be ready to defend herself if necessary.

Stepping closer, the image of the figure began to drift apart, becoming clearer. Eilean realized it wasn't one giant creature, but three. A tall man, a deer with giant antlers, and a tightly coiled snake. The three of them were covered in the oily substance, much of it covering the animals' eyes and mouths. The man, who was the only one moving, worked tirelessly to remove the toxic liquid from the animals, but with his own skin and hands enveloped in the oil, he could not do much.

Safety be damned, Eilean sheathed Phobia and moved quickly toward them. She needed to get them out of the goo. Images of those environmental videos showing penguins and baby seals poisoned by oil spills replayed in her mind as she made it closer to the center of the tree where the three of them sat. Eilean couldn't let animals suffer like that. She had to do something.

When she got closer, she stumbled to a stop as she realized it wasn't the deer's antlers she'd seen. The man, who sat at seven feet tall, had a pair of horns sticking out the sides of his head. Just like the deer's actual antlers, they were in poor shape. All three of them were, but none more so than the horned man.

"Are…" Eilean swallowed hard as she looked up at the giant man. "Are you okay, sir?"

His furry legs were covered in bald patches, with clumps of hair scattered in the surrounding goo. His great antlers, which stood high and grand above his head, were cracked and covered in the black ooze of the willow tree. So much of the liquid had dripped down onto his face that it had bleached his eyes to a solid white in blindness. And the animals that sat with him looked no better.

The man-beast smiled vaguely in her direction. "I will be well, Eilean. Do not worry about me. It is I who has worried for you." He lowered his head. "I am sorry for what you have suffered in coming to my aid."

"What…" Eilean stumbled back. "What do you mean? An-and how do you know my name?"

He smiled at the question, wincing when the action caused his cracked lips to begin bleeding.

"I am the one you have come for," he said, his voice rough and tired, like every word he spoke was torture. And they probably were. The air here was thick with toxicity, which crept away from Eilean but had no issues swirling around the others. "I am Cernunnos."

28

WHEN A GOD REFUSES

"WHAT THE HELL WERE YOU THINKING?" EILEAN SHEATHED her sword. "A teenager to save you? Really?"

Eilean didn't expect that to be the first thing to come out of her mouth. She seemed to be making a habit of confronting immortal beings, even though she knew they could likely end her on a whim. Luckily for her, Cernunnos didn't seem to be doing well.

"I made that call in desperation, but did not choose who would answer it." Cernunnos coughed roughly into his hand. When he pulled it away, Eilean saw specks of blood on his ooze covered skin. He sighed wearily. "Even immortals fear death."

"I didn't know Gods could die."

Cernunnos leaned forward and tried to brush the fresh ooze from the deer's face, but, with his declined vision, he kept missing. "Nothing can live forever."

"What can I do to help?" she asked. She couldn't stand to see creatures in pain.

Eilean looked around in hopes of finding something to help brush the muck from the God and animals' stoic faces. It was a gloomy sight to see them being smothered in the tar. Eilean may have been protected for some reason by her pendant, but even with it the heat she felt in the air, touching her skin, made it clear that this forest and the creatures beneath the willow tree were suffering. And from the way the deer was gagging, the air was still as toxic as the ooze. Eilean remembered the metallic taste in her throat and the smell of petrol as she choked after letting go of her pendant. She couldn't imagine endlessly suffering from it.

"You can leave."

Eilean stood silently for a moment. "I'm sorry, *what?*"

Cernunnos began coughing again. The cough was so rough that more blood speckled his lips and the fist that covered his mouth. He turned away and spat a clump of tar onto the ground. Leaning back against the tree, he let out a sigh that crackled painfully.

"I was selfish in my actions when I called to the Celtic bloodline." He offered her a sympathetic smile. "You are not the first descendant to come to my aid. And I have already taken too much from yours."

"What are you talking about?" Eilean asked, her voice rising with frustration. "Did the person before me die here or something? Is that why I'm here?"

Cernunnos stayed quiet. Eilean looked over at his deer and snake and found them watching her. There seemed to be intelligence in the creatures' eyes, and Eilean wondered if they were understanding everything she said. This time, she didn't stop herself from reaching out to clean away the muck that slid down and into their eyes. As her fingers were about to brush against the fur of the deer, whose head was closer to her height, the oil that coated its skin did something unexpected.

It leaped out at her.

Eilean jumped backward, yanking her hand away. A touch of oil had caught her finger and she couldn't stop the screech of pain that bubbled in her throat as her skin burned. Rubbing the finger against the material of her shirt, Eilean watched as the cloth itself began to burn.

With her blade, she quickly cut at the edge of her shirt and tore away the piece that was burning. As the cloth fell to the ground, Eilean watched in horror as it burned away to nothing, gone before it reached the forest floor.

"The hell was that?" Eilean panted.

Cernunnos sighed. "That is why you must leave. Whatever has trapped me here is far more vicious than I believed."

"What do you mean?" Eilean questioned before remembering what Danu had told her. "You went to investigate something..."

"And I have found an answer, if only a partial one."

"And I'm meant to save you from it?" Eilean looked at the tar and oil that smothered the three beings. "Do I need to get you out of this mess or do I, like, fight a big bad or something?"

Cernunnos shook his head. "There is nothing to fight. Only I can free myself."

"And how well's that going?" Eilean didn't intend the level of snark, but she was getting tired of the God's passive behavior. "Come on, just... tell me what it is and I'll do whatever you need me to." She went for the jugular. "Your wife needs you back."

"My Queen." Cernunnos bowed his head. "She will have to be stronger a little longer. I cannot defeat what's here."

"Why?"

"Because it is not really here."

Eilean fought the urge to pinch her nose in irritation. "Cernunnos, sir, you aren't making sense."

The God offered her a grimace of a smile, the kind of one given to a child. Which, she supposed, given his age, that's what she was to him. "Eilean, my dear child, please do not take offense. I need you to go home." Eilean opened her mouth to argue, but he was faster. "I am not unappreciative. No, it is because of what you must do if I ask you to stay." He sighed. "Things are far worse than I originally thought, and I have led you right into its path."

"If you mean the Leannan Sìth—"

Cernunnos shook his head. "Something far worse. And not something you should be burdened with."

Her jaw tensed. Eilean hated when adults made decisions for her. Whether they thought it was best for her, or because they didn't think she was strong enough to handle it, it didn't matter. She knew what she could do. Not them.

"Tell me."

"Eilean—"

"If I'm not allowed to rescue you, tell me what it is and I can tell Danu, or Brigid, or someone." Eilean's gaze fell over the two animals at his side who, from the slow movement of chest and tongue, she figured they didn't have long. "If Ar Dachaidh is in danger, they should know, right?"

Cernunnos sat silently. She'd got him there.

He sighed. "I do not know what it is that has come to Ar Dachaidh. I have not seen their faces or felt their presence."

"Then how do you know—"

"The seal has cracked," Cernunnos interrupted, a frown forming on his face as he closed his eyes. "It has not been fully broken nor entirely severed, but the crack was enough for… something to slip in." He opened his eyes once more. "It must have been fighting through for some time. It is no simple thing to crack the Henge. But it did. And whatever it is has brought this *sewage* from the mortal world with them.

"I do not know how, but it is why I was not reborn last spring. I am sure of it. And I have been fighting it since it took my creatures. Whatever it is, it wants to consume Ar Dachaidh. Thus far I have been here to stop it but," he wheezed, "I am failing."

"What do I tell Danu to do?"

"Tell her to fortify the seal. Perhaps we can prevent anything further from seeping into our world."

"Okay, I'll take that back to your wife," Eilean promised. "Now, I'm going to cut you free and get you guys out of here."

"You are as stubborn as your grandmother," he muttered. "It is a trait I admire greatly, young one. A trait I needed to survive." He laid his hand on his chest, pressing at the ooze. "But I have already taken too much."

"What does Mamó have to do with this?" Eilean asked. "This giant mentioned her too. She even knew that you were in trouble. How did she know that?"

"Ruth…" Cernunnos said in a tone far more cautious than he had sounded before. "She has seen much in her time."

"But she knew," Eilean countered. "She told me not to come. Was terrified about the idea of me doing it. Why?"

Cernunnos dropped her gaze. "Your family line is a powerful one, dear child."

"What are you on about?" Eilean demanded.

"I did not call for you. You took on what she could not finish."

Eilean opened her mouth to speak, but the words died on her tongue. There, uncovered by the grime that he had swept away, she saw something familiar hanging from his neck.

"Why…" her voice broke. "Why do you have my Mamó's necklace?"

29

A CHOICE IS MADE

"Why do you have her necklace?" Eilean demanded a second time.

Cernunnos' fingers drew around the spiral within the wood. Eilean couldn't tell if he was following the design or just trying to keep the oil off it.

"It is his now," a familiar musical voice sang from amongst the fog.

The God released a breath. "Liana Shade, how have you pierced the barrier where others have failed?"

Liana Shade stepped out into view. Any sign of injury caused by Freya had since gone. No missing hand, no frenzied look in her eyes. She would have appeared just as she had when she'd first approached Eilean, if not for one thing. Her eyes, once fluorescent blue, dulled to a listless gray.

"I answer to a different power," she smiled, her smokey gaze finding Eilean. "And that power has drawn me to you, child."

"What are you on about?" Eilean asked her. "And how did you find me?"

"Why," Liana tilted her head, "you called out to me."

"Eilean?" Cernunnos spoke up, drawing her attention back to the sickly God. "You have dealt with the Leannan Sìth?"

The animals at his side watched her. She could feel their judgment in their gaze as they stared—blankly—in her direction. Just like she'd seen with Freya and Bhradain. They didn't get it. None of them did.

"Yeah," Eilean replied quietly. *No, I have no reason to be ashamed.* She spoke up. "I was going to accept her offer."

"You know of the consequences?" Cernunnos asked.

"If it means I'd fix things for everyone," Eilean said. "Then I don't care what happens to me in the future."

"Ah," the God said, his tone soft. "I understand."

Eilean blinked. "What?"

"I have seen much." Cernunnos tugged lightly at her Mamó's necklace. "I understand why you feel you must make this choice."

She stared at the pendant between his oily grip. "Can you see her memories?"

"Only those strongest."

The strongest. Eilean had to fight to hold back the tears. If Cernunnos knew why she was going to take Liana's offer, that means he saw what she did. And if he only saw the strongest memories, then that meant her Mamó...

She sees me as a monster, too.

"You can change that, Eilean." Liana Shade stepped forward, the smog passing around her just as it did for Eilean. "Everything you now know will be forgotten. Everything you did will be erased."

Eilean closed her eyes and thought of the visions Liana had shown her. Her parents proud of her as she excelled in school. Mamó healthy and happy.

This time, however, she added her own images.

Unlike the rest, this one was different. It was quieter. Peaceful. It was just Eilean and Mamó, together at the loch, sitting on a picnic blanket. Mamó was complaining about the stones digging into her bum and Eilean just laughed as she pulled out a pillow from her bag. She knew what Mamó was like. The two then sat in silence, watching as the wind disturbed the reflective nature of the loch and the trees swung back and forth. They didn't speak again. Content to be beside each other.

That's all Eilean wanted.

She turned to Liana Shade, whose smile grew wider as she held out a hand to Eilean. Eilean went to step toward her, but something still tugged at the back of her mind.

"Why do you have Mamó's necklace?"

Her focus returned to Cernunnos, who still held the spiral in his grip.

"Your Mamó was a brave woman, Eilean," Cernunnos replied gently.

Eilean's heart thudded in her chest. Last year, near the end of the summer holiday, her parents had told her about Mamó. They'd said the dementia had been so rapid and vicious. One morning she had gone for her walk perfectly fine and happy. Then, that evening, she'd been found dazed and confused near the loch. Eilean hadn't thought much of it at the time. She'd never really understood dementia, anyway. But now, it was all starting to make sense.

"She was the one who answered the call first, wasn't she?"

Cernunnos bowed his head.

"What did you do to her?"

"Her necklace held and bound her spiral of life." Cernunnos began, his voice strained. "In passing it to me, it has been wound with mine. Only when my own is restored in my freedom will she be set free."

"Did you know what would happen to her?" Eilean asked quietly.

He didn't respond.

Eilean's voice cracked when she spoke. "And yet you still took her life? Her mind?"

"It takes so much for a mortal to aid a God with their own life force," Cernunnos said wearily. "Your Mamó offered me much, but with her age, she had so little to give."

"So *little* to give?" She brushed a tear from her cheek. "She gave you everything."

"And he intends to take your everything too," Liana Shade spoke up. "Tell her why she is here, Cernunnos. Tell her why the call did not end with her Mamó."

Cernunnos released a sigh. Not a sigh of annoyance but, from how drawn out it was, one of exhaustion. "Your Mamó gave all she could from her spiral. But it was not enough to restore my strength and escape this place."

"Which means…" Eilean trailed off.

"To escape here," Cernunnos started, before coughing so harshly that it shook the oil from his horns onto his companions at his sides. "To escape here, I need more life than your Mamó could give."

"I don't understand."

"He needs a new sacrifice," Liana Shade interjected, sneering. "Your Mamó was too weak for him. He needs one stronger, one he can siphon far more life from."

"Like what you do?"

Liana Shade raised her hands in the air, as if surrendering to her point. "I admit, I partake of the spirals of life. But only from those who take my deal, and they at least have the chance to live a happy life."

"They all die," Eilean argued.

"They may not live their full span of lives, but they are happy for all that. What Cernunnos takes, on the other hand…"

Eilean's attention returned to the God who, once again, was clearing the dirt from his animals' eyes. Her Mamó's pendant dangled around his neck.

"Are you still taking Mamó's life?" she asked him.

Cernunnos closed his eyes and took a deep intake of breath. "Unless I am freed, her spiral will continue to feed into me until there is nothing left." He drew a hand across his mouth, pushing away the muck forming there. "Both she and I will fade when the last thread is spun."

"That's why I'm here, then, right?" Eilean glanced between the two beings. "I free you, you release Mamó, and then I can fix everything through Liana Shade. Right?"

Liana Shade laughed. The once melodious sound, one Eilean was sure was intended to draw her victims in, now sounded hollow. "You are naïve, child. I can understand the appeal of such thoughts. Unfortunately, you cannot have both."

"Why not?" she asked, annoyance in her voice. Why were things never easy?

"Cernunnos and your Mamó can only be freed with an exchange, a life for a life," Liana Shade told her. "Isn't that true, Lord?"

The God stared, not disputing a word.

"To save your Mamó," Liana Shade continued. "You have to surrender your own life to him. Your pendant for hers."

"But that'll save her, right?" Eilean asked Cernunnos. "If I give you my necklace, that'll save her?"

"There is no guarantee," he told her, a weariness to his voice. "I do not know what will happen to her. Only what will happen to you."

"God, why can't you guys get to the point?" Eilean shouted, tired of being talked to like a child. "Tell me what it takes to save her."

Cernunnos met her gaze as well as he could with his clouded eyes. "In exchanging the necklace for yours, I will siphon from your spiral the strength I need to escape." He took a deep breath. "In doing that, you forfeit your future. You will not live to see old age."

"What?"

Cernunnos coughed once more into his fist, his voice cracking. "It is the price. You will feed into my spiral the strength I need to free myself. And I do not know how much that will be."

"I—"

"That is one choice," Liana Shade said. "Cernunnos offers you a limited life to save your Mamó, but I…" She moved toward Eilean, her feet barely brushing the toxic earth beneath them. "I can make it so that you will never have left home. Your Mamó will never have been sick. You can turn it all back if you take my deal."

"You'll take my life too."

"But not as fast, or as much." Liana Shade held out her hand to her, just as she did outside the woods. "You will never have made the mistake. You will get to live the life you wanted without it following you wherever you go."

Eilean's mind ran a hundred miles a second as she tried to process what that would mean. She was guaranteed a shorter life whatever choice she made, unless she turned and left, rejecting both. But she couldn't. Her Mamó had sacrificed everything, she couldn't let her die knowing she could have stopped it.

But she didn't want to die either.

She thought of her parents holding her funeral. She could almost hear their speech about how parents shouldn't be burying their children. She imagined finding the love of her life and never wanting to be without her. She could see the ticking clock that would hang over that relationship. It wouldn't be fair for them to love someone they couldn't share a lifetime with. Could she even have a life if she knew she'd die soon?

There was so much she wanted to do. So much she had to live for. Freya had been right. Eilean didn't want to die. She didn't mean that. She'd only been angry and upset. She was only seventeen. She'd barely lived.

Then she thought of her Mamó back home in that chair. Despondent and empty in her eyes. So different from the woman she'd grown up around. She may be older, but she still had so much life to live. So much love to give. So much love to receive.

Eilean's eyes fell to the necklace around the God's throat.

She thought of what Cernunnos had said. Mamó was old. There had been next to nothing of her spiral to give to him. While her sacrifice was important and incredible, it wasn't much of one in comparison. Mamó had the chance to live her life. Eilean had barely started hers.

Is it selfish of me to want to live?

Her heart pounded in her chest and panic pulsed through her veins. Flashes of her life came to her as the feeling thrummed through her body. Her fist against David's nose. Waving goodbye to Mamó after she and her parents had to leave Balloch because of her. Slamming her hammer hard into the metal at Lawton forge as she cried over what she'd lost. Learning of her Mamó's dementia. Rejecting Freya's friendship and practically threatening her with a sword. Abandoning both Freya and Bhradain because of her own needs.

Then the image of what the Leannan Sìth had shown her came to mind, the one that called out desperately to her. Her walking away from David, and though the guilt and anger would burn in her stomach, she wouldn't make the mistake again. She would continue to decorate the house with Mamó every year, and even learn guitar with her Pa, like he said he would teach her. Her parents would never have left the work they loved and, maybe, one day, Eilean would make friends. Maybe even Freya.

Then there's her career, the life she'd make for herself. She could be a real blacksmith. Maybe start out selling custom items online and then set up a shop. She could even make videos for YouTube. Eilean knew it would be hard, but she could try it. And if she failed, well, at least she tried. She'd have a life to make mistakes and find success. It may not be a whole one, but it'd be enough to find happiness.

Until she hurt someone again and it all came crumbling down. Liana Shade may be able to change what happened with David, but she couldn't change her. As much as Eilean wished she could. Eilean wasn't even sure she could save Mamó in the end.

Cernunnos getting tricked and trapped wouldn't change. Nothing in Eilean's life had caused what had happened to him. Going back and fixing her life wouldn't stop Mamó from, one day, traveling to the loch, answering a call, and being found a different woman.

Eilean stared at the God, wondering what it was about him that had called her Mamó to save him. She wondered what there was about him that she herself should save. Even now, he didn't fight for his life. Nor did he offer the chance to save her Mamó from him. He sat there, silent. As if he knew there was no hope for either of them.

No, if I find a way to keep my memories, Eilean thought desperately, m*aybe I could stop her from going.*

"If you stay with her," Liana Shade continued, "you can protect her."

Eilean could believe that. She could take this deal and, sure, she'd die young, but she'd be with her Mamó in Balloch. She'd never have left, never have caused her family harm, and never have hurt herself. This ache inside wouldn't exist. If she pushed down the anger that she felt and channeled it, she could live a normal life. Eilean could be happy and Mamó would be alive.

But Eilean didn't believe that.

"How do I save my Mamó?"

Liana Shade stepped closer. "By taking my deal—"

"No." Eilean shook her head. "No, your deal won't help her."

"Eilean—"

"I reject your offer."

Liana Shade's eyes solidified into black. Her teeth sharpened, and she hissed like a hungry lioness. Her outstretched hand clenched tightly, drawing blood from her palm. Her voice, once melodic, crackled like the sound of static on a car radio. "*You will one day wish you had accepted.*"

And with that, she vanished into the smoke.

Eilean tried not to think about what the Leannan Sìth said. She had a feeling she would be right, but she couldn't risk her Mamó. She was everything. It had become an easy choice after that.

"I'll do it," Eilean whispered to Cernunnos.

Cernunnos said nothing about her choice. Eilean was grateful for that. She watched as he reached up to the pendant around his neck and tugged at it. The necklace snapped free easily and lay loose in his hands. His wheezing grew heavier as he held out the necklace to her. She took it from him quickly.

The solid wood of the spiral medallion felt heavy in her hand. It was like she was literally holding the weight of her Mamó's life. It felt well-lived. She took the clasp of the chain and, ignoring the slickness of the oil, Eilean attached it around her own neck. It belonged to her family, after all. She wouldn't leave it behind.

She thought of her Mamó's reaction to seeing it again, if what had happened to her was reversed. With how frantic she had been about Eilean not going, Eilean wasn't sure she wanted to see it.

Wiping that thought from her mind, she stepped closer to the God with her own pendant in her hand. She was only half surprised when the sludge on the ground didn't try to swallow her like before. Taking the cord in her hands, Eilean reached forward to Cernunnos. Only briefly did she wonder what would happen to her protection she had received from the pendant, her mind instead slipping back to her Mamó. Her fingers were shaking as she slipped the material behind the God's neck.

A hand touched her shoulder. Just like when she held her pendant, a calm washed over Eilean. The smell of lavender and the warmth of the sun brushed over her skin. Taking in a breath of this fresh air, Eilean clasped the necklace around Cernunnos' neck.

30

THIS IS NOT THE END

Cernunnos closed his eyes and took a deep breath in —a breath that, for the first time since Eilean had arrived here, didn't sound like it hurt.

Then he breathed out.

When his eyes opened, the white of blindness had vanished. In their place was a beautiful green that showed her the image of an untouched wilderness. Trees that grew tall and bountiful, a lake that was alive with all sorts of creatures and flowers of different species and color. It wasn't until a familiar woman appeared in the reflection that Eilean realized what she was seeing.

His eyes showed his home.

The animals beside him stirred. His horned snake's eyes had healed too, and he poked out his forked tongue to taste the air in delight. The deer on the other side clamored to its wobbly legs. He moved like a freshly born fawn; he was stronger now.

The gunk that had once covered the three of them… slunk away—as if it were a chastised puppy. Unlocking from the being's skin, slithering back up the tree and away from their bodies. Even the sludge at Eilean's feet hardened, no long sucking at her feet. Eilean thought she may have struggled among the still floating smog but, near Cernunnos, she was able to breathe easily.

"Thank you, Eilean," Cernunnos said in a whisper. "We can never repay you for what you have done."

Eilean was still a little stunned. She'd expected to feel different; she had given up her life, after all. She'd have thought that would make her feel a certain way. But she felt nothing.

"You will not feel it," the God said solemnly. Eilean turned toward him in surprise. "Not many feel the call of Death until it is too late."

"How…" Eilean swallowed. "How long?"

Cernunnos didn't meet her gaze. "I am… unsure. You may last until your thirtieth year, maybe longer."

Thirty. Thirty-years-old.

"What…" Her throat felt tight. She couldn't tell if she was starting to feel the intensity of the smog around her or if she just wanted to cry. "What do I do now?"

"You do what the young have always done." Cernunnos reached out a hand to touch her cheek. "Live. And know that you are not alone."

Eilean pulled her face away from his touch. She was tired of the cryptic answers. "So, what now? You're fixed, right?"

The God rested his hand against his chest, a frown forming. "I feel… stronger, but I know something is still wrong."

"What more do I have to do, then?" Eilean said, fighting the urge to just run away. "Cut down the poison vines, carry you out of the woods?"

Cernunnos shook his head. "There is nothing else for you. Your family has done more than I should ever have asked of you," he said in a whisper. "I am grateful."

"It's—" she was going to say fine but, in reality, she knew it wasn't. Eilean knew she wasn't.

"I am sorry for what you have sacrificed." He reached a

hand out to her. With only a brief hesitation, Eilean clasped his wrist in return. "And I thank you."

"What... what happens now?" she asked.

The deer at Cernunnos' right stood, and the snake slithered up the God's side and looped himself around the horn. "Now," Cernunnos smiled, "I return home to my wife."

Eilean watched as the hair on his face and the fur on his arms and legs began to fall away from his body. She wanted to pull away but she couldn't, too stunned by what she was seeing. His skin began to peel away, exposing a green underneath that Eilean hadn't expected. A green as dark and light as the grass of Ar Dachaidh.

"Thank you, and farewell."

Cernunnos, and his creatures, dissolved into blossom petals. Lifted by a gentle breeze that brushed against Eilean's face, the blossoms were carried through the woods. As the wind took them, a path through the smog was formed when each petal touched the mist. Eilean guessed that this was Cernunnos' way of guiding her out.

Clasping Mamó's necklace around her neck, Eilean took a breath and started running. Passing through the woods again without the smog in place, Eilean became more aware of the devastation that had infested this world from hers. Bogs of water bubbled with acid. Pools of molten tar and oil formed along the ground, having dripped down from the trees above. Eilean kept running forward, watching her step as she went.

As she leaped the acidic river once more, Eilean glanced down at the ground beneath her feet. The smog was closing in around her and the temporarily clear pathway was fading.

She ran faster. So fast she could hardly breathe. Which was probably a good thing. What breaths she could take were starting to burn in her throat...

At last, Eilean burst through the wall of smog, took a breath of pure fresh air and collapsed.

"Eilean!"

She couldn't look up. She could barely lift her head from how much it swayed. But Eilean would know that voice anywhere. And she wasn't sure if she could face them right now.

Then a pair of brown-skinned arms wrapped around her body, pulling her close. The embrace was warm, tight, and filled with so much care that Eilean didn't deserve but, for once, accepted.

She had no idea how long they sat there before she found herself being pushed away and forced to face a pair of furious brown eyes.

Freya's cheeks were marked with tear tracks that were hard to ignore. Her tight curled Afro had been loosened from the braid and now framed her face, making it hard to look away from her angry glare.

"What the hell were you thinking?"

Eilean went to say, but all that came out of her mouth was a wailing sob. One that she couldn't fight back. It tore at her throat, clawing its way out into a loud whimpering cry that, with the way her chest loosened suddenly, seemed to have been waiting to come out.

To both of their surprise, Eilean pulled Freya into the hug this time. Burying her face into the girl's shirt as hot tears streamed down her cheeks. Freya only hesitated for a moment before wrapping her arms around her and holding onto her as tightly as she seemed to know Eilean needed.

"Never go off alone like that again," Freya said in a gentle but warning tone. Eilean would have been apologizing again if she hadn't still been crying.

"I am glad you are well," another voice said from behind her. "But please stop proving to me mortal foolishness. I do not need that lesson."

Eilean let out a tearful laugh but didn't move herself out of Freya's embrace. Fingers gently moved through the loose pieces of her hair in a soothing manner. A few more tears trickled down her cheeks. She didn't like to be touched and, she knew, she was likely pushing all forms of boundaries right now with how mad and upset Freya must be, but she didn't want to move away. She needed this. Desperately.

Eventually, and reluctantly, Eilean pulled herself out of Freya's embrace and looked at them both. "I am so sorry for what I said before and for..." she gestured to the surrounding forest, "everything."

"We'll talk about that later, okay?" Freya's hand laid atop hers, her thumb drawing a soothing pattern on the skin there as she focused on her. "What happened in there?"

"I found Cernunnos," Eilean said, though she found herself reluctant to say any more. "He was in a bad way, but I managed to set him free."

"You did?" Freya asked, surprised. "How?"

"Uh, you know," Eilean fumbled on an answer she was willing to share. "Chosen one type rubbish. It was somewhat anticlimactic."

Bhradain watched her in silence. When the kelpie came closer, she almost feared she was about to be taken then and there. He was a creature of death after all. What she hadn't expected was for him to bow his head.

"Of course," he said quietly. "And I am sorry."

"What are you sorry about?" Freya asked.

Eilean avoided Freya's question. "That wasn't the main thing, though. I think Cernunnos will probably tell everyone himself, but, in case he's late, he told me to say that the seal is cracked. That something is trying to force its way into Ar Dachaidh and the seal needs to be fortified to stop it."

Bhradain nodded. "I will make sure to take this news to Danu and the others. But this is... troubling. We have never had such a breach. I may need to call for my mistress to return from her journey."

"You're married?" Eilean asked in surprise.

"You are as foolish as ever, mortal," Bhradain rolled his

eyes. "My mistress is the one I serve. Lady Morrigan, mistress of death and battle, among other things."

"Oh… cool, that's cool."

"Will one of you tell me what's going on?" Freya demanded. "I know you've left something out."

Eilean didn't want to talk about it. Didn't even want to *think* about it right now. But she also didn't want to keep Freya in the dark. After everything that had happened, it was the least she could do to tell her. Just not here.

"I'll tell you… later," Eilean said. "I don't really want to be here when I talk about it. This place, I don't know, it makes me feel…"

Eilean didn't know how to end that thought. There was something about the Otherworld that made her feel more raw. More dangerous. The spark that came with Phobia was just one element. She wasn't ready to explore the rest of it yet.

"Can you keep Phobia safe for me?" Eilean asked Bhradain. "I know you're not a packhorse or whatever, but, well, I know you and—"

"It would be an honor."

Bhradain bowed himself down, offering his side saddle for her. Eilean detached Phobia from her side and held the sheath in her hand. She had a feeling that this wouldn't be the last time she would be holding her sword. Shaking off the thought, Eilean attached it to Bhradain's saddle and, without thinking, patted his neck in thanks.

"Can you send us home?" she asked him.

The kelpie nodded his head. "I will have one of my kind take you as gently as they can."

"You aren't coming with us?" Freya spoke up.

"I am afraid there is work for me here." Bhradain stepped toward her. "I will be sure to come and visit, if you wish me too."

With only minor hesitation, Freya stepped toward Bhradain and patted him on the neck. "I… I would like that."

Eilean knew that what had happened between the two of them would not heal overnight, but Freya knew his reasons, even if Bhradain didn't know she did. It may take some more time, but the two would return to their annoying friendship again… one day.

Bhradain stepped back and bowed his head. "Until we meet again."

"Wait, how are we—"

Something grabbed onto the back of Eilean's clothing—and Freya's too, if the yelp meant anything. Glancing over her shoulder, she saw a skeletal horse-like figure gripping onto her and Freya from within a recently unfrozen puddle.

"Oh, craaap!—," both she and Freya screamed as they were yanked backward and vanished into the water.

31

THE FRIENDS WE MADE ALONG THE WAY

DROWNING AGAIN WAS SOMEHOW THE LEAST TRAUMATIC thing Eilean had experienced within these last few days. Thankfully for Freya, Bhradain's friend had dumped them close to the shore, so they didn't have to swim back to the beach. Only stand.

Squinting against the blinding sun, a headache forming already after being in the darkness for so long, Eilean moved to stay as close to Freya as possible. Despite not needing to swim, she was hyperventilating again, all the way up to the shore. Eilean made sure to keep a hand hovering around her back for support.

The moment they hit the shore, Freya clamored up the bank and as far away from the water as possible. With enough space between her and the loch, she took a deep, shaky breath.

"Will never be okay with that..." she said with a shake of her head.

With only a second of hesitation, Eilean came to sit next to her. They still wore the same outfits Brigid had given them, which, Eilean realized, meant her borrowed overalls had been left in another world. She'd have to see if Bhradain would bring them back to her so she could return them to

Walter. But that wasn't the priority right now. All she could focus on were the curls drooping into Freya's eyes. Eilean considered reaching out and brushing them out of the way, but with Freya still trying to calm down, it didn't feel right to.

"Talk to me," Freya said, her eyes still closed, body shaking from either the cold or the fear. Eilean wasn't sure. "Distract me, okay?"

"What do you want me to talk about?"

"Well," her voice gained a slight edge to it. "You could start with what happened in the woods."

If there was one thing she liked about Freya, it was that she didn't hold back what she was thinking and feeling. Freya laid things out straight. So Eilean did the same.

Eilean told her of how she'd found the God and his creatures. Describing how bad they had looked, "zombie-like" she said. Then she told her about what happened with Cernunnos before she saw her Mamó's necklace around his neck.

She had to fight to not let the shame take over her as she told Freya about Liana Shade's reappearance and how she nearly took her deal again. Eilean had been so close to doing it. Until she found out what had happened to Mamó and why.

Freya, who seemingly knew when she was in crisis, reached out a hand to her. Eilean flinched away. Without question, Freya withdrew her hand and dropped it back into her lap.

"What happened after you found that out?" Freya asked quietly. It seemed like she'd finally calmed down from her water-induced panic.

"I rejected Liana Shade and offered Cernunnos a trade."

Eilean could feel Freya's eyes on her, but she couldn't meet them. She was afraid of what that would do to her resolve if she did—afraid of what she would see in them after she told her what that meant.

Her mind was still a conflict of emotions about it all. She

didn't know whether she was angry, sad, heartbroken, or just plain empty.

"I gave him my life spiral in place of Mamó's." Freya was silent. "I know she's older and all that but, I couldn't… I don't know. This was the least I could do for her after everything she's done for me."

As scared as she was thinking about what her future—or lack of one—may hold, Eilean couldn't help but feel some kind of relief. Her Mamó would hopefully be better, and Eilean had, for once, done something right in her life. She may still feel afraid, but at least she knew she'd made the right decision.

"How… how much?" Freya's voice was barely audible above the sound of the loch.

"Well, I won't have to worry about getting a mortgage," Eilean said with a choked laugh. "Or about having kids, or…"

Freya pulled her in for a hug. She was soaking wet, but her body felt warm somehow as she held Eilean. She didn't cry, forced herself not to. Nor did she hug Freya back. Eilean just let herself breathe in the moment.

"You aren't alone with this, okay?" Freya murmured into her ear, her breath warm on Eilean's cheek. "Whatever happens next, I'm with you. Even if I'm still pissed at you." Freya pulled back from the hug and looked at her. "You have to swear you won't be that much of an idiot again."

"I wasn't an idiot, I was—"

Freya's dead stare silenced her.

Eilean swallowed a lump in her throat and dropped Freya's gaze. "I can't say I won't do something stupid again." She rubbed at the back of her neck as she met Freya's eyes. "But I promise I'll try."

Freya stared at her silently for what felt like hours. Eventually, Freya offered her a small smile. "I'll accept it for now… just know that I mean it when I say you aren't alone. I mean, you stood up to a literal giant for me. No matter what happens, I'm here. Swords and angst aren't going to chase me away."

"If that's the case, I hope you know of some local forges. Think I may have to convince my parents to move back here."

"Really?" Freya asked with a raised eyebrow. "Why's that?"

"Cernunnos told me that I was done, that he didn't need my help, that he'd asked too much of me already."

"I mean, he's not wrong," Freya said.

"But, everything that we saw in the Otherworld, plants losing color, animals and insects missing, and what he told me about something cracking the seal." Eilean shook her head. "I don't know. It feels like there's something more going on."

Eilean stared at her hands and pictured the blue sparks she'd seen there. She'd always felt an electric feeling whenever intense negative emotions took over her, but in Ar Dachaidh it had been real. Eilean had too many questions about that to agree with Cernunnos about never returning. There was something about that world that was connected to her anger and strength, and she needed to find out why.

"Guess we'll have to find out together, yeah?" Freya knocked her shoulder with hers.

Eilean laughed. She had no idea about what would be coming next. Had no idea about what kind of life she would be living from here on out. All she knew was that she was happy to have someone like Freya at her side.

"Girls! You're back already?"

The two jumped in surprise at the sudden voice. They turned to find Freya's grandfather lightly jogging down the beach toward them.

"Granda?" Freya stood in surprise. "What are you doing here?"

Walter made it to their side and smiled.

"I wasn't sure how long you would be. I was just coming to lay out these bags of towels and fresh clothes for when you did, but… You're back sooner than I thought."

Eilean frowned. "How long have we been gone?"

Raising his wrist to his face, reading his watch, Walter hummed before answering. "Around two hours."

"What?" both of them said, stunned.

"Wait, it can't be that little time," Freya said, turning to Eilean in her confusion. "I mean, even if time here moved slower, surely it'd be more than that..."

"Yeah." Eilean nodded. "We were there for like a week or something. This is so weird."

"What happened there?" He then seemed to immediately think better of his question as he shook his head. "No, an answer for later." He pulled out a pair of towels from the bags in his hands and handed one to each of them. They wrapped them over their shoulders instantly. "Let's get you both dry and—Ah, I forgot the spare clothes. I'll go get them and—"

"It's okay Granda, we'll be alright," Freya said kindly. "You can head back. I'll catch up with you in a bit. I just want to talk to Eilean for a second."

"You do?" Eilean asked, surprised.

"Yeah, just a quick thing, then you can get back home, too."

"Right then." Walter clapped his hands together. "I'll see you at home soon for hot chocolate." He turned to Eilean and smiled. "Get home safe and tell Ruth hello from me."

"I will, sir—er—Walter."

Walter then disappeared back over the hill as quickly as he'd appeared.

"When do you want to meet up to discuss what comes next?" Freya tugged at one of her now-drying curls.

"Next?"

"Like you said, it seems like there's more going on in the Otherworld. I don't know about you but if some Gods are going to pull us back into their business, I think maybe we should be prepared somehow." Freya smiled. "Or at least ready to tell 'em where to go."

Eilean laughed, "you're probably right."

"We've got magic too, or at least, I think what you have is magic as well. It'll be worth learning more, right?"

"Yeah." Eilean thought of the spark at her fingertips. "Yeah, it'd be worth doing that."

"And, well, even if it wasn't, I'd still want to hang out with you and, you know, do… friend stuff."

Eilean tilted her head. "We're friends?"

Freya smiled. "Of course."

"Cool." Eilean smiled right back at her… friend. It felt different to know she had one now. It felt nice.

She wanted to step forward and hug Freya. Something to solidify the friendship title that she was sure she didn't fully deserve yet but accepted either way. Eilean just wasn't ready for something like that. Instead, the two of them stood there smiling at each other for what could only be described as an abnormal amount of time. Eilean wasn't sure if she was blinking or not.

"I—" Freya pointed behind her. "I should probably catch up with Granda. Will you be all right getting home?" She tugged at a curl. "I could walk you back if you want?"

"I'll be okay," Eilean said a bit too quickly. "But I could walk you back, if you want?"

"Don't worry, it's not far, but um," Freya's cheeks darkened slightly as she dropped her eyes from Eilean's gaze. "We should probably grab a coffee or something tomorrow? I mean, we still have a lot to talk about."

Even though Eilean dreaded the words of needing to talk more, she still found herself saying, "Tomorrow sounds good."

"Cool, um, I'll get going then," Freya gestured behind herself again. "I'll see you tomorrow?"

"See you tomorrow."

Eilean smiled as Freya rushed away with an awkward wet-jean waddle, the towel her Granda brought wrapped over her shoulders. When she reached the top of the beach, she turned and waved to Eilean before disappearing from sight.

The smile never left Eilean's face.

32

PROUD

EILEAN FOUND HERSELF DAWDLING AT THE EDGE OF THE water. To her surprise, she half hoped that Bhradain would appear beside her with his sarcastic words and give her a reason to linger rather than rush home. When no such distraction came, Eilean sighed and started walking.

The wind whipped against her still-wet clothes and skin. If Eilean's head hadn't been elsewhere, she probably would have been complaining about the cold as she headed up the hill in squelching shoes. But her head *was* elsewhere.

All she could think about was what would happen when she got home. She'd been out of the house, without her parents knowing, for at least two hours now. They may have been watching the Celtic game when she left, but it had probably finished by now. Would they be wondering where she was? Would she be walking right into a fight the moment she got back?

Then there was Mamó. She could still be sitting in her room with no knowledge of who Eilean was or even what she had done.

More than once, Eilean wondered if she could double back and head to Freya's. She had offered to walk her home...

Maybe if she went back to her and asked, it could delay her finding out for a little longer.

Eilean was almost about to turn back to take Freya up on her offer, but she had reached the familiar brick walls that lined her Mamó's garden. She stopped, hardly daring to move. One more step, and she might be able to see through her Mamó's window. Would she still be there, staring blankly out at her?

Eilean ran her fingers along the brick wall, tracing the lines between the cracks, as she stared at the house. She didn't want to go in. Couldn't go in. What if she was the same; what if she was *worse?*

She came up to the wrought-iron gate that led up to the house. It was worn and in need of deep repairs. She'd promised Mamó that, when she was good enough, she would make them a new one. One filled with spirals and other symbols her Mamó and Pa had around the house.

Eilean couldn't help but pray to whatever Gods were out there that, once she stepped past this gate, and headed up the path and saw her Mamó again that she would remember that. That she would be okay.

With a deep breath, she opened the gate and headed to the door. The golden sunlight washed over the house and gave it an ethereal look. Eilean reached the entrance and laid a hand on the doorknob. One thought ran through her mind as she turned it.

Please, remember me.

When Eilean slipped through the door, she half expected her mum or dad to come running toward her, worried or annoyed at her for disappearing without telling them where she was going.

As she walked toward the living room, ready to announce

her presence, she overheard her parents and Pa doing their usual post-match discussion. Eilean found herself smiling at the sound of them discussing Kyogo Furuhashi's amazing score and Callum McGregor's passing skills for the win. That's when her dad caught sight of her.

"Lean, you missed it!" her dad called out as he came to meet her at the door. "Celtic won four to one. Where were—why are you wet?" He narrowed his eyes. "And when were you wearing this? Have I seen these clothes before?"

"I, um—" She blinked back the tears she could feel rising. "Yeah, it's new. I–I got Mamó some sweets and then I just needed a walk, you know?"

"Into water?"

"Dad, please, not now."

"Lean?" he said, stepping closer to her, concern in his gaze. "What's wrong?"

"Nothing, it's…" she sighed. "It's fine."

"I understand. It's hard to see her like that." He rubbed the back of his neck. "Do you want to talk about it?"

"No, no, it's okay, thank you, though," she glanced toward the end of the hall. "I want to see her again. Maybe she'll know me this time."

Her dad nodded, and she saw his hand move toward her, as if he wanted to reach out and pat her on the shoulder like he used to do, but his hand dropped back down. "Shout us if you need anything, okay?"

Before her dad had the chance to head back into the living room, Eilean pulled him into an unexpected hug. She'd never been a hugger, especially with her dad, but she really needed one right now. After a pause, Eilean felt a hesitant pat on her back. Eilean had to pull herself away. If she started crying now, she'd not be able to explain why.

"Um, I'm going to check on Mamó. I'll come to you guys about the game soon, okay?"

"All right."

She didn't give her dad the chance to ask questions before she headed down the hallway. Thankfully, her dad wasn't one to keep pushing, so he returned to the living room and was immediately back to game discussion. When Eilean reached the end of the hall, she glanced back and found herself half wishing her dad or even her mum would come out and make her talk about her feelings so she wouldn't have to go inside. She didn't want to find out that everything she'd done was for nothing.

As she stood in front of the white-painted door, her hand hovering just above the handle, Eilean couldn't help but notice how much she was shaking. With a breath, she gripped onto the doorknob and opened the door.

Mamó was sitting in the same place as before: head turned to look out the window and chin resting on her hand. Her chest moved in a simple rhythm, showing that she was breathing. That sign alone was enough for Eilean to push the door wider and move closer to her Mamó.

She didn't move. Seeming to barely register her presence. Eilean held back the sob that clawed at her throat as she knelt at Mamó's feet.

"Mamó, it's me," Eilean whispered. "I came home." Nothing. "I brought your necklace back."

Eilean raised her arms to the back of her neck, unclipping the pendant from around hers, and, with careful movements, reached out to Mamó. A sigh was all she received as she slid her hands behind her neck, clasping the ends together. Lowering herself back to the floor, Eilean watched, desperately praying to whatever deities existed out there that she wasn't too late.

Mamó closed her eyes and took a deep, deep breath. When she released it, it was as if all the tension that had built within her shoulders, neck, and life faded away.

And then those green eyes opened to her. Her gaze was so bright, so awake, and so in awe as they stared at Eilean. She scanned her from head to toe in desperation. It was as if she were searching for any sign that she wasn't okay. Just as she always had.

"Mamó?" Eilean's voice wobbled.

She reached her arms out toward her. "Eilean…"

A sob tore from her throat as she threw herself into Mamó's arms. Tucking her head into her shoulder, she wept.

Mamó rocked the two of them back and forth in her chair in a gentle rhythm that reminded Eilean of when she was young. And then she began to sing the song Eilean knew so well.

Coisich, a rùin, hù il oro
Cum do ghealdadh rium, o hi ibh o
Beir soraidh bhuam, hù il oro
Dha na Hearadh, hoch orainn o

Eventually, Eilean calmed down. Her heartbeat slowed enough that she no longer felt the thumps in her throat. Removing herself from Mamó's arms in embarrassment, she sat herself down on the floor and rested her head on Mamó's lap instead. A fresh new wave of tears began to trickle down her cheeks as Mamó's fingers ran through her hair. Just like she used to do when she was younger.

"Eilean, my dear, what's wrong?"

She didn't have the chance to answer. Mamó figured it out all on her own. A weight she'd lost around her neck had finally returned. Mamó raised her fingers up to touch the pendant, tracing the familiar lines. Eilean couldn't say anything.

"Oh… Oh my love…" her fingers reaching out to Eilean's own missing necklace. Her green eyes watered in disbelief. "What have you done?"

Eilean rested her own hand on top of Mamó's, pulling her attention away from the absent pendant and back to Eilean. Eilean squeezed her hand tightly. "It was worth it."

Mamó closed her eyes and took a breath. "You shouldn't have gone, my love," she said in a gentle voice. When she opened her eyes to look at Eilean, she offered her a heartbroken smile. "You have so much more to give in this world than I."

Eilean swallowed hard and stared down at their clasped hands. Though she had never been happier than seeing her Mamó back to herself, she felt the ache in her own heart over what she had lost. Eilean didn't even realize she was hyperventilating until Mamó was slowly patting her back and letting her rest her head on her lap once again.

Only when her breathing slowed did Mamó speak. "You aren't sure you made the right choice, are you?"

Shame built within her.

A finger pressed beneath her chin and tipped her head upward. Facing her Mamó, who stared at her with so much love in her gaze that Eilean had to stop herself from crying again. Mamó leaned forward and pressed her forehead to Eilean's, her graying hair tickling Eilean's cheeks.

"It's okay to be scared, my love," Mamó whispered. "You have given up something so precious and that will always be frightening. No matter what you would have chosen, I would have been proud of you. I have *always* been proud of you."

"You… you have been?"

"*Always*."

EPILOGUE

THE PAST CATCHES UP

Mamó had to hide her recovery for a few days. There was no way to explain why she suddenly didn't have dementia anymore. It's not like Eilean explaining that she sacrificed her thirties and beyond to a God with horns in trade for Mamó's health would get her anywhere. It was near the end of the first week that she made it clear that she was herself again. The doctors were surprised, of course, but chalked it up to an extended virus of some kind that had been misdiagnosed. Eilean and her Mamó shared a somber smile, knowing the truth.

It was her Mamó's recovery that led to Eilean sitting down with her parents ahead of their final week back home to tell them what she wanted.

Her dad raised his eyebrows in surprise. "Come back? But you've grown so much in Carlisle—"

"No, I haven't," Eilean said, being honest for the first time. "Sure, therapy and the smiths have been going good but, being here, it's helped way more than I thought it would."

"It won't be easy," her dad told her.

Eilean knew it. But that didn't change her mind. "I know

being back is going to be tough, but this… this is home. This is where I need to be if I'm going to… get fixed."

Her mum reached out to her. "Oh, honey—"

"And I've made a friend too, so it'll be easier."

Her parents shared a look, clearly filing away that information for later. That wasn't the priority for them right now.

"What about your studies?" her mum asked.

"There's a smith that I can come to here." Eilean rubbed at her neck sheepishly. "I kinda already reached out to them to see if I could transfer."

"Your mother and I have our jobs—"

"They never filled your positions," she glanced at her mum, "you say that all the time. And I know you don't like the surgery in Carlisle. It's too… quiet."

Her parents didn't respond straight away, seemingly speaking in silence as they locked eyes on the sofa. They asked Eilean to give them some time to think about it. When she'd left the living room, she heard her dad on the phone speaking to a Dr. MacIntosh at the Glasgow Infirmary and she knew she was finally coming home.

A few days had passed since that conversation. Her parents planned their return and Eilean made her own calls to Mr. Lawton who, in his words, was "bloody thrilled" that she was making her own way. Eilean had never felt happier. While what happened with Cernunnos still hung over her, Eilean did what she did best: put it in a box to deal with later.

That's what led her to head into town the Friday before her parents would go back to Carlisle. They needed to deal with the house and finish up their time at the surgery before they could move back officially. That meant Eilean would be alone with her grandparents for a few weeks, and she couldn't wait. Eilean would also start her new blacksmithing classes at the same time. It would be weird starting at a new forge with new people, but Donald Cox seemed to be a brilliant teacher. They just needed to get a new therapy group for her and she'd be sorted.

Eilean was home, and she was ready to embrace it. Those in town still gave her some stares, but Eilean ignored them. She was back. Her Mamó was back. Nothing would knock her off her high today. Even better, Freya was meeting her at the library. She wanted to study more about Druid magic and wanted Eilean for moral support, or a test subject. Eilean would find out.

Before heading for the library, another ten-minute walk, Eilean decided to stop by a corner shop and grab some snacks. Beyond the Fox's boiled sweets, which she picked from the shelf instantly, she wasn't too sure what Freya liked. They were still getting to know each other at the moment. She grabbed a bit of everything, some sweet and some savory. Eilean tried not to go too overboard. She only had so much money to spend, but it was worth it for the brain food.

With an assortment of chocolate bars, fizzy sweets, and a bag of cheese savories and pretzels, she was ready. Holding the items awkwardly in her grip, she took them up to the counter and dumped them on the side.

"Hey, uh—"

There wasn't anyone manning the till. Eilean leaned forward, wondering if they were crouched down getting something, but nothing. She noticed the open door behind the till, and cringing as she did, she spoke up.

"Hey, uh, anyone here?" Eilean called out. "I'd like to pay, please."

"Comin'!" a deep voice replied from the open door behind the till.

Eilean put her hands in her pockets and waited, glancing briefly at the few display sweets next to the till. She knew they were there to tempt her...

She grabbed the lollipop and only slightly judged herself for it.

"Sorry, one sec," the cashier shouted, still in the storeroom, "my manager stepped out and I'm new."

"No worries, I've got time," she said, glancing around the shop with a smile, wondering if she should grab something else.

Eilean heard more shuffling from the room and saw someone with two boxes in their grasp walking toward the till.

"Do you need a hand?" she asked, worried about how precarious the boxes were placed.

"Nah, I'm all right." He placed the boxes down and came up to the cash register and started scanning without looking up. "Do you need a bag?"

Eilean couldn't answer him. She just stared in stunned silence as he casually scanned her items. Eilean hadn't recognized his voice. Though, she supposed, it had been five years.

"We have a bag for life for a pound—"

His brown eyes met hers, and he stopped talking. A glaze of fear flickered in his gaze. Eilean tried not to let the shame fill her at the sight, but as her stomach churned with the need to be sick, she knew it was too late to stop it.

She had put him in the hospital, after all.

"David?"

THE STORY CONTINUES

The second lesson Eilean learned in blacksmithing: Nothing is unfixable, unless you've polished.

Only then are you screwed.

Then you must start from scratch.

A few months ago, Eilean gave up her lifeline to save her Mamó and a God. She'd hoped that would be the end of it, until a Goddess gave Eilean vague hints of her future. Because Gods never make things simple.

Now with Ar Dachaidh's color still fading, Cernunnos' strength yet to return, and a dead Goddess, Eilean must find an Order who will help her save the Celtic Gods from their impending doom. Totally easy, right?

Enter The Order of Albion, an ancient Druid society who have centuries of knowledge and magical skill to pass on. And they've been waiting for Eilean and Freya's arrival. With their guidance, Eilean discovers new abilities, gains lessons in restraint, and, for once, is finally feeling normal. But with time running out, if Eilean doesn't temper her skills, they risk losing the Otherworld entirely.

Will Eilean be able to master her powers fast enough to save Ar Dachaidh? Or will the pressure crack her poorly forged façade? This Summer, things are only getting more complicated.

Find out why in *The Breaking of Worlds*, the second story in the Eilean in the Otherworld series, a young-adult fantasy inspired by Celtic mythology.

ACKNOWLEDGMENTS

A huge thank you to my incredible beta readers, Laurel Fredericks, Luna Gerrits, Michael Griswold, Seth Hansen, Chloe H-C, Shay Hammad, Rufina Kaloyanova, Andy Lara, Brian Letang, Poppy Love, Katie Mack, Ken Pham, Marie Reed, Andrea Septién, Darien Smartt, Madeline Thomas. Your directness and guidance helped me find what this story needed.

To my editors Emily Dragon, Callan Brown, and Antoine Bandele. Thank you for all your help in guiding this novel to its final stage.

Special acknowledgements to my fellow Old Gods Story authors. Specifically, Seth, Andrea, and Emily who joined me for late night rambles.

You all rock!

ALSO BY FRANCESCA MCMAHON

EILEAN IN THE OTHERWORLD

The Spiral of Life

INTO THE WILD

Home to the Wild

Way of the Wild

INTO THE WILD SHORTS

Echoes of the Past

Before I Go

Finding Home

TALES OF TUATH DÉ

The Green Man Falls

ANTHOLOGIES

Tales of Cthulu Invictus

Terror of Octobernomicom

Tales from the Otherworlds

ABOUT THE AUTHOR

Francesca McMahon was born in Oxford, England, to a Scottish father and an Essex mother. They gained a B.A. in Creative Writing at Edge Hill University and was shortlisted for the university's Dame Janet Suzman Playwriting Award in 2019. Since graduating, Francesca has worked consistently in publishing while working on their writing of fantasy, horror and romance fiction, as well as various tabletop RPGs and screenplays. As a queer person, their work is dedicated to the LGBTQIA+ community, and they hope that anyone who needs it will find a home in their imaginary worlds.

You can learn more over at www.francescamcmahon.com or follow Francesca on social media, via Instagram, and TikTok (@adoseoffran).

GLOSSARY

- **Ailm:** a symbol in the Ogham alphabet, associated with the silver fir tree and representing strength, resilience, and healing in Celtic tradition.
- **Annwfn**: the name of the Celtic Otherworld in Welsh mythology.
- **Apollo**: the Greek God of the sun, music, prophecy, archery, and many more things.
- **Ar Dachaidh:** a Scottish Gaelic phrase meaning "Our Home."
- **Avalon**: the name of a mythical island featured in the Arthurian legend.
- **Balloch**: a village in Scotland that resides at the foot of Loch Lomond.
- **Balor**: in Irish Mythology Balor was the leader of the Fomorians, a group of malevolent supernatural beings. One story has him locking his daughter away due to a prophecy saying he would be killed by his grandson.
- **Banshee**: a wailing creature of death. If you hear her screams three times you are destined to die.

- **BBC:** British Broadcast Channel, a network for television in the UK.
- **Bear Grylls:** a British survival expert who hosts a show in which he tells an audience how to survive in certain terrain and environments.
- **Brigid**: a member of the Tuatha Dé Danann. She is associated with wisdom, poetry, healing, protection, smithing and domesticated animals.
- **Benandonner:** a giant from Scottish and Irish mythology, known as the antagonist in the legend of the Giant's Causeway, where he is outwitted by the Irish giant Fionn mac Cumhaill.
- **Caledfwlch**: the Welsh name for King Arthur's sword, Excalibur.
- **Celtic F.C.:** is the professional football team for Glasgow, Scotland. Pronounced as SELL-tick instead of KELL-tick for the other uses of the word.
- **Celtic Mythology**: a body of myths and folklore of the Celtic peoples. Includes Ireland, Scotland, Wales, Breton, and Cornish.
- **Celtic Otherworld**: an island paradise and supernatural realm of everlasting youth, beauty, health, and joy.
- **Cernunnos:** a Celtic god associated with nature, fertility, animals, and the underworld, often depicted with antlers and sometimes referred to as the "Horned God."
- **Cthulhu**: a Lovecraftian horror monster of God-like power.
- **Coisich, a rùin:** a Scottish Gaelic song, titled Come On, My Love in English, performed by the group Capercaillie and others.
- **Coke:** a coal-like form used in forges.
- **Cúchulainn**: a warrior hero and demigod of the Ulster cycle, hailed in both Irish, Scottish, and

Manx mythology/folklore. He was prophesied to gain everlasting fame but that his life would be short.

- **Danu:** an ancient Celtic goddess associated with rivers, fertility, and the earth, considered the mother of the Tuatha Dé Danann in Irish mythology.
- **D&D:** Dungeons and Dragons, a Table-Top Role Playing Game from Wizards of the Coast where people play as fantasy creatures and beings going on adventures.
- **Dian Cecht**: in Irish Mythology he is the God of healing. He specifically heals the Tuathe Dé.
- **Druid:** often seen as religious leaders as well as legal authorities, lorekeepers, medical professionals and political advisors. They were known for leaving no written accounts of their practices.
- **Excalibur:** the magical sword owned and wielded by King Arthur.
- **Fox's Sweets:** a hard-boiled sweat of various fruity flavors.
- **Fionn Mac Cumhaill**: a hero in Irish Mythology and Scottish folklore. He is the leader of a group of young hunter-warriors, as well as being a seer and poet.
- **Giants Causeway**: a row of 40,000 interlocking columns that form stepping stones that can be found on the coast of County Antrim in Northern Ireland. The story is that the giant Fionn Mac Cumhaill created this pathway to meet and fight the Scottish giant Benandonner.
- **Henge:** a type of New Stone Age Earthwork. The essential characteristics are that they feature a ring-shaped bank and ditch, with the ditch inside the bank. Stonehenge is one example.

- **Hercules**: a divine hero in Greek mythology, a son of Zeus.
- **Herbology:** the study of plants and plant lore.
- **Katie McGrath:** an Irish actress most known for her roles as Morgana in BBC's Merlin and Lena Luther in The CW's Supergirl.
- **Kelpie**: a monstrous water horse creature of the rivers and lochs that would lure in its victims and drown them. Can also take the form of a dog.
- **King Arthur**: the mythological, sometimes believed to be real, King of Britain.
- **LARPing:** Live-Action-Role Playing, an event where people dress up as characters, often fantasy, and act out story scenes.
- **Leannan Sìth**: a creature from Irish folklore that takes human lovers who live inspired lives before dying young because of their connection to the creature. Spelt in the Scottish Gaelic way.
- **Loch Lomond**: a loch in southern scotland. The term Loch is specific to Ireland and Scotland, unlike Lake which is used in most other places.
- **Loch Ness Monster:** Loch Ness is a specific body of water near Glasgow in Scotland. There is a folk story that there is a water monster, often nicknamed Nessy, that lives within the loch.
- **Lyre:** a stringed musical instrument that has two arms and a crossbar. The strings run from a tailpiece on the bottom or front of the instrument to the crossbar
- **Mamó:** an Irish term of endearment used to refer to a grandmother.
- **Merlin:** the sorcerer/druid to King Arthur, also the name of the British television series telling the story of how Merlin came to be the all powerful sorcerer.

- **Merthur:** a popular ship name combining "Merlin" and "Arthur," often used by fans of the BBC TV series *Merlin* to represent a romantic or close bond between the two characters.
- **Normalized:** a blacksmithing technique which is used to heat the steel to just above critical and letting it air cool to a black heat. This relieves stress and refines the grain structure of the steel.
- **Olokun:** an orisha spirit in Yoruba religion. Olokun is seen as the ruler of all bodies of water and is the authority over other water deities.
- **Orisha:** divine spirits that play a key role in the Yoruba religion of West Africa.
- **Quenching:** a mix of oil or water used to rapidly cool a blade to harden. Used after heat treatment.
- **Scottish Gaelic**: one of the Celtic Gaelic dialects, an indigenous language of Scotland. Also found to be spoken in Nova Scotia.
- **Spiral of Life:** can represent the cycle of life, death, and rebirth. The single spiral is what is represented in this story.
- **Stonehenge:** one of the most famous English landmarks.
- **Tempering:** involves reheating a previously hardened or quenched material to a specific temperature and then cooling it in a controlled manner.
- **The Fae**: a term used for unearthly spiritual beings in the Otherworld.
- **The Morrigan**: Morrigan, occasionally known as The Morrigan, Morrigu, and Mor-Rioghain, is a figure from Irish mythology who is mainly associated with war and fate, especially with foretelling doom, death, or victory in battle.

- **The Otherworld**: In Celtic mythology, the Otherworld is the realm of the deities and possibly also the dead.
- **Tha beatha ro ghoirid**: Scottish Gaelic for "Life is Too Short".
- **Tír nan Óg**: one of the names for the Celtic Otherworld. It is specifically the Scottish Gaelic spelling version of the name.
- **Triskelion:** a three-legged spiral image that is often used to represent the dead or the dying. Can sometimes be seen in modern hospitals used as this symbol.
- **Tuatha Dé Danann:** a mythical race of god-like beings in Irish mythology, known as the "People of the Goddess Danu," who were skilled in magic and warfare and ruled Ireland before the arrival of the Milesians.

www.ingramcontent.com/pod-product-compliance
Lightning Source LLC
Chambersburg PA
CBHW020335310726
48979CB00015B/2378/J

* 9 7 8 1 9 5 1 9 0 5 4 3 9 *